"Jeremy, I'd best go—"

"No. Not yet." His hand loosened, but instead of releasing her it slid up her arm ever so slowly, until it reached her shoulder. Thea swallowed hard, as with his other hand Jeremy traced a line softly along her jaw. "Do you know, when I saw you at the ball, Thea, I felt I'd never seen you before," he said softly.

"Maybe you hadn't," she answered just as softly, fighting the treacherous urge to lean against the fingers that now stroked her cheek.

"Maybe. But now . . ."

"Now?" she prompted.

"I've been blind. So blind." His thumb brushed across her lips, and then his hand slipped down to hold her other shoulder. "And every kind of a fool."

Thea watched, standing quite still, as his face came closer. She should leave. She should, but something held her. It was the magic of the night, of this room. Her eyes closed as his arm slipped around her waist, his fingers tilted up her face. This was real, this was right. She raised her lips to his and felt his kiss upon her lips . . .

An Intriguing Affair

Mary Kingsley

ZEBRA BOOKS
KENSINGTON PUBLISHING CORP.

To Rona S. Zable, for all the conversation, critiques, and chocolate. Thanks, writing buddy. I couldn't have done it without you.

Chapter 1

"But it is a perfectly unexceptionable match, my love," the dowager Lady Stanton said in some surprise, looking up from her reclining position on the chaise longue. "Why do you object to it so?"

The man standing at the window in the fashionable Grosvenor Square drawing room turned, his hands restlessly twitching at the drapes. Jeremy Vernon, Viscount Stanton for little over a year, was finding the responsibility of being head of the family very heavy. "A sister of mine wed to Denby? What is there in that to make me happy?"

Lady Stanton's eyes opened wide. "He is so handsome!"

"He is a fool."

"But he has money," a soft voice said, and Jeremy turned in its direction. His sister Margaret was so quiet one could forget her presence, but the eyes she lifted to him were candid and intelligent. "We need that."

"Yes I know, but good lord, Margaret! Denby?" He dropped onto a chair facing her, his hands clasped between his knees. "You can do better than him."

"Can I? Without a dowry?" Margaret gazed at him. "He's offered to settle Papa's debts."

"It's not his job to do so," Jeremy retorted, rising and pacing again to the windows. "Denby. Good God."

"It's not so bad, Jeremy—"

"When he came to me to offer for you I was never so shocked in my life." He turned back to face her. "I refused him, of course."

Lady Stanton gasped in dismay. "Jeremy! You didn't."

"Of course I did."

"Oh dear, oh dear! Please sit down, you are making me nervous pacing like that. You never used to be so restless. That terrible war!"

"Mother," Jeremy said, exasperated.

"I do wish you hadn't done it," Margaret said.

Jeremy studied his sister. "Do you love him, Meg?"

"No. But I am persuaded I could be comfortable with him."

"You're but ten and eight. This is your first season!"

"And how are we to afford a second one? Jeremy, someone has to repair the family fortunes."

Jeremy returned her gaze. He knew that look well. Meg was being brave and stubborn. He couldn't let her sacrifice herself. "I'll consider it, little one," he said softly, taking her chin in his hand.

She jerked her head away. "I am not your little one, Jeremy, and if I want to marry Denby then I will!"

"Oh dear, children, please don't argue," Lady Stanton pleaded.

"We'll see." Jeremy smiled down at his sister. "Who knows what might happen?"

"Jeremy?" Margaret stared up at him questioningly. "Are you thinking of marrying again?"

"Perhaps." He bent to kiss his mother. "If you'll excuse me, ma'am, I've another appointment. Meg, I'll speak to you later."

"Jeremy, don't do anything foolish!" Margaret called, but her brother was already gone, out the drawing room door.

Denby. Good God! he thought as he strode down the street. Not for Jeremy the sedate pace dictated by polite society; he ran through life, meeting every challenge headlong. This, however, was altogether different. He had nothing against Denby personally. He came of good family and had a considerable fortune. But he was also balding, running to fat, and remarkably foolish. Not the sort of man one wanted to see one's sister marry. Margaret, however, had a very potent argument. The family's finances were in a dreadful state. Someone had to do something to mend them.

It should be me. Scowling so fiercely that a young lady walking with her maid down Brook Street skittered away to avoid encountering him, Jeremy considered the idea. He was head of the family now. It was his duty to make certain there was enough money, so that his sisters had dowries and his brothers an education. Father hadn't meant to leave his family penniless, but speculating on wild ventures while ignoring his various estates had nearly ruined him. Jeremy had been struggling with the resultant mess since acceding to the title, and had reached, reluctantly, the same conclusion as his sister. Someone in the family would have to marry for money.

Jeremy tugged at his neckcloth. It would have to be him. He needed to talk to someone about this. He needed to talk to Thea.

Looking up, he was somewhat startled to find that he was nearly at her house. Althea Jameson was, surprisingly, a very good friend. Very surprisingly. He'd met her several months before, at the first ball he'd attended since selling out of the army. He had been in between *affaires,* looking for a new attachment, bored, restless, glad to be home and yet incurably distracted, nearly ready to bolt from the crowded, overheated ballroom. Somehow, Thea had calmed him. Thea, with her chestnut hair and fine gray eyes and slender, graceful hands. A widow with as little desire to remarry as he, she didn't expect things of him the way other women did, didn't flirt, didn't desire their relationship to be more than it was. She didn't smother him, didn't make him feel trapped. He could talk to her about anything, and any advice she gave him was invariably sound. Odd that he'd thought of her in connection with marriage. She was certainly young enough and pretty enough to marry again, but she wasn't his type; she was far too levelheaded and independent. But if anyone could help him with his latest troubles, she could.

Taking the stairs two at a time, he reached the landing of the narrow brick house and rapped on the door with the knob of his walking stick. Hanson, Thea's butler, promptly admitted him. He knew this wasn't Thea's normal at-home day, but he wasn't surprised when Hanson returned to the hall to lead him to the drawing room. Already he was feeling better; Thea's house, like the woman herself, always had that effect on him. Though small, it was immaculately kept. A turkish carpet in exquisite colors was laid on the polished parquet floor of the hall, and spring flowers bloomed in a china bowl on the small mahogany table that stood under a gilt-framed mirror. A feeling of peace, almost of homecoming, stole over him. He was suddenly very glad he had come.

Thea smiled up at him as he entered the drawing room, her hands outstretched. "Jeremy! This *is* a surprise."

"Yes, well, I was passing by." He took her hands in his and stood smiling down at her, grateful she didn't expect him to do the pretty. She was, as usual, a picture of serenity, in her afternoon gown of dove gray with white ruching at the throat, her glossy hair caught into a chignon. On another woman the color might have been unflattering, but it suited her, making her eyes seem even larger and her cheeks glow pink. "You don't mind if I visit awhile?"

Thea smiled warmly. "No, of course not." She picked up an embroidery frame and after studying him for several moments, frowned down at it. "Is there a problem, Jeremy?"

"Problem?" Jeremy turned from the window where he had been pacing restlessly. "Why should I have a problem?"

"You're rather mangling my new curtains," she pointed out gently.

Jeremy looked down at his hands, crushing folds of oyster-white brocade, and let the draperies drop. "I'm sorry, Thea. I didn't mean—"

"If there's a problem, you might as well tell me."

"Oh, the devil!" He wheeled from the window and walked to the unlit fireplace, his shoulders slightly

11

hunched. "The deuce of it is, Thea, I have to get married."

"What!" Thea's eyes widened and she began to laugh. "Jeremy, have you sunk so low in iniquity, then—"

"No, the deuce take it, Thea, nothing like that!" He threw himself into a cream-colored satin chair, his legs flung out, his fingers drumming on the arm of the chair. "You don't have to look at me like that. I'm not that much of a rake."

"Oh, no," Thea murmured, looking down at her embroidery to hide her smile, and something else, a feeling she didn't quite want to acknowledge. Heavens, she surely didn't wish to remarry, especially not someone with Jeremy's reputation with the ladies. She prized his friendship; nothing more did she want from him. She wished, though, that he had found someone else to discuss his marriage with. "Far be it from me to think such a thing. But why, then?"

"Money."

"Money?"

"Precisely. Money. Do you know, that is an abominable piece you are working on."

Thea looked ruefully at the crewel, neat enough on the front but hopelessly tangled on the back. "Yes, I know. I detest needlework. I only do it to keep Aunt Lydia company. Money, Jeremy? I thought things were settled."

"So did I," he said gloomily. "But my man of affairs has turned up more debts of my father's."

"More?"

"Yes. A canal scheme gone wrong."

"At least he didn't gamble his money away."

"It comes to the same thing. I don't know what happened to him before he died. He used to be the most rational of men. But now there's not enough for my sisters' portions."

"Oh dear."

"Precisely. Deuce take it, Thea, but I've an expensive family. The worst of it is, my sister Meg has got it into her head that she has to do something about it. She claims she wants to marry Denby."

"Good heavens!" Thea stared at him. "But he is much too old for her. Surely she hasn't a *tendre* for him?"

"No. But he has money, Thea, there's no denying that. Meg has a point. Someone has to do something."

"So instead you'll sacrifice *yourself* on the altar of matrimony?"

"You needn't laugh."

"Oh, I'm not laughing," Thea said, staring fixedly at the embroidery. Jeremy married, and to someone other than herself. Why should that bother her so?

"And then there's my mother. How do you tell a lady who has never needed to skimp in her life that now she has to practice economy? I tried to explain matters to her the other day and do you know what she said? That she would do her shopping at the Pantheon Bazaar, it is so much cheaper."

"Oh dear. I know it's not funny, Jeremy, but—"

"But you see the tangle I am in. I haven't the heart to cut her allowance." He glanced at the fireplace, which was filled on this warm spring day with an arrangement of fresh flowers. Upset though he had been when he left his mother's house, he was beginning to feel calmer. "I may have to sell one of my estates."

"As bad as that?" Thea exclaimed. If he were thinking of selling property then he must be rolled up indeed. No gentleman would do so unless it was absolutely necessary.

"As bad as that. Unless I marry an heiress with a good deal of money."

I have money, Thea thought, and bit her lips to keep from blurting the words out. Yes, and hadn't she paid dearly for what she had? She'd never marry again. Not even Jeremy.

Her eyes flickering up from her embroidery, Thea studied the man as he paced back and forth across the room. He surely didn't lack for willing females; it seemed he only had to smile at one and she became his slave. It wasn't that he was so extraordinarily handsome, not with that strong Roman nose, and yet there was something about him that attracted every woman she knew. He did have marvelous eyes, a heavenly shade of blue, and his dark, straight hair insisted on falling onto his forehead, tempting a woman's fingers to brush it back. Undeniably he was well built, too, trim and lean, but with broad shoulders that usually made Thea, tall though she was, feel small and feminine. Until today, though, she had been immune to his charm. Or so she'd thought.

"So, who is the lucky girl?" she asked, keeping her eyes on the crewel.

"I don't know." Jeremy turned from the window. "You?"

A curious pain went through her. "If I thought for one moment you were serious—"

"Well—"

"It would serve you right if I said yes."

"Why? We rub along tolerably well together."

"Come, Jeremy, I'm not at all your type. You like small, delicate girls who bow to your every wish. I could never do that, you know."

Jeremy smiled, the charming smile that was another of the tools he used to unfair advantage. "No, you're much too independent and sensible."

Thea stabbed at the canvas. "How odious of you!"

He took the chair across from her and leaned forward. "I meant it as a compliment."

"Well then, I'm too sensible to marry you. How many flirts have you had this season?"

"That doesn't signify."

"It does to me. No, Jeremy. I've no desire to marry again. You know that."

Jeremy sighed and sat back, stretching his legs. "I was afraid of that. You'll consign me to my fate, then?"

"It's what you deserve."

"So harsh, Thea. Will you at least be my mistress?"

Thea's head jerked up. "What!"

"You wouldn't regret it." His voice, his smile, were caressing. "I would make certain of that. In fact, I daresay you would enjoy it."

"Enjoy—of all the nerve!" She snatched up a pillow and threw it at him. "I am *not* one of your flirts, Jeremy!"

"No, worse luck," he said ruefully, hastily raising his arms as Thea took up another pillow. "Hold your fire, Thea! I'm only funning you."

"You had best be," she said, lowering the pillow. A reluctant smile touched her lips as she saw the glint in his eye. "Why cannot I ever stay angry with you when you are such a detestable man?"

15

"Perhaps because you like me."

"Lord knows why."

"Admit it, Thea. You like me." He smiled at her. "Pax?"

She glared at him, then shook her head and smiled. "Pax."

"Then we'll go on as we are."

"Of course." She bent her head to her needlework again. Oh, would he never leave? She had been glad when he had come to visit, but now she wished only that he go. He would marry another. How could they possibly go on as they had? "The season's nearly over. If you're going to marry, you'd best find someone soon."

"I know. Yet I haven't the slightest idea who."

"You haven't a *tendre* for anyone?"

"What, Thea, so romantic? Love doesn't last. You know that."

She avoided his gaze. "I suppose you are right. There must be someone you fancy, though. Some very pretty girls made their come-out this spring."

"They all look alike to me," he said cheerfully. "They all sound alike too. I've never been much for young girls just out of the schoolroom."

"Are your flirts any more suitable?" she asked, giving him a level look.

Jeremy returned her look, though his eyes glinted. "Thea, for shame. A lady shouldn't refer to such things."

"Well, if you would not make yourself such an *on-dit*—"

Jeremy suddenly rose and paced to the window. "I can't help what people say."

"Can you not?"

"No."

"Jeremy, why do you—"

"Leave it, Thea," he said, his voice hard. Thea stared at him in surprise and then shrugged. The ways of men always had been a mystery to her. "I have to go into Berkshire to look over my estate there. When I return I shall start looking about for a suitable bride."

Pain stabbed through her again. "What does your daughter think of this?" she asked.

He turned, his shoulders relaxing at last. "Gillian doesn't know. But I would like to give her a mother."

"Of course." Thea secured her needle in the crewel and rose. "Not to be rude, Jeremy, but I must start getting dressed or I won't be ready for Lady Alwich's dinner party tonight. Will you be there?"

Jeremy made a face as he rose. "Deuced dull affair, that sounds. No, I'm going to Vauxhall with my sister and a party of friends. Wouldn't you like to come along?"

"I cannot cancel so late, Jeremy."

"I suppose not. Well then, I shall probably see you tomorrow." He raised her hand to his lips and pressed a lingering kiss on her palm, his eyes holding hers. "You won't change your mind?"

"About Vauxhall? No."

His face was impish. "About being my mistress."

"Oh, get out!" Thea exclaimed, pulling back.

"Your wish is my command, madam." Bowing, he took his leave.

Thea stood holding the hand he had kissed as if it were a precious jewel. Good heavens, what had happened to her?

* * *

Jeremy strode along Brook Street, feeling better already. He had a plan, a purpose, something he hadn't had since he left the army. He would remarry. Of course. He didn't know why he hadn't done it sooner. He'd then have money enough to secure the family's finances, and he would be giving his daughter a mother. And himself someone to warm his bed. Not that that mattered very much; there was no lack of willing, available females for an unmarried man with a title. If only Thea—but then, he'd always liked her precisely because she never had been on the catch for him. Nor would she be a comfortable wife. There was no reason their friendship would have to change. No reason, perhaps, except the look that had appeared briefly in Thea's eyes when he had talked about his plans. And that, for some reason, bothered him out of all proportion. Nothing had changed. Nothing needed to change, and yet it evidently would. As he swung up the stairs to his own house in Grosvenor Street, he had the strangest feeling that nothing would ever be the same again.

Thea turned away from the window, where she had drifted almost against her will. Jeremy was gone, striding down the street away from her. He was like no one else she knew, her Jeremy. No fashionable ennui for him; he embraced life, and when a thing entered his mind, he acted on it. That was why he had proposed to her, of course. Impetuousness. She couldn't take it seriously. After all, he didn't love her.

But love doesn't last, she reminded herself, turning

18

away from the window. At least, he believed so. She wouldn't know; she had married for many reasons, but love wasn't one of them. Until today, she hadn't cared about remarrying, or about love. Until Jeremy had announced he would marry someone else.

"Thea, dear," a breathless voice said at the door. "Is he gone, then?"

Thea turned and smiled at the small, fragile-looking woman. "Yes, Aunt. It really was too bad of you, leaving me alone with a gentleman. Think of my reputation!"

"Now you are funning me, dear. You'll come to no harm with Stanton," Lydia said, crossing the room and picking up Thea's discarded needlework. Her face under her lacy cap puckered into a frown. "Oh my, this will never do, Thea."

"Dear Aunt, you know I am not a needlewoman." Thea sat across from her, smiling. "I thought you didn't like Stanton."

"No, dear, I never said that."

"You said he was like the silver thread you were using that was giving you so much trouble."

"Well, yes, he is rather quicksilver, isn't he? But only, I think, on the outside. Underneath I think he's far more like the tent stitch. Very steady and dependable."

Thea laughed. Aunt Lydia's habit of viewing the world, and people, in terms of the needlework she so loved had always amused her. "And what am I, Aunt?"

Lydia tilted her head to the side. "You, dear? Why, you are like the stitch I used on that footstool."

Thea glanced down at the stool at her feet. "Which is?"

19

"For shame, dear, haven't I taught you? The flame stitch. There's fire in you, Thea."

"Oh, nonsense!" Thea got abruptly to her feet and walked over to the window again. "I am only a quiet widow."

"Nevertheless, I think I understand why Stanton is attracted to you."

"He's marrying someone else."

Lydia looked up, her eyes bright and sharp. "Is he? What an extraordinary thing."

"It is what he said."

"Ah. I expect he wishes an heir."

Thea went very still. "Of course."

Lydia looked up at her again, her eyes unexpectedly shrewd behind her spectacles. "Come to that, Thea dear, I've often wondered why you don't marry him yourself."

"Because I wasn't asked," Thea snapped, and then, seeing the look on her aunt's face, was filled with remorse. It wasn't Aunt Lydia's fault that Jeremy hadn't really meant the proposal. "We don't have that kind of relationship, Aunt." Thea sank into a chair again. "We are merely friends."

"Oh?"

"You needn't look at me like that. You know I've no desire to marry again. Five years with Hugh was quite enough for me."

"Far be it from me to say anything against Hugh, but—"

"And why shouldn't you? He treated you ill, for all that you were his aunt."

"No, no, I am persuaded that he didn't mean to. He just didn't think."

"And I fear that is how Stanton is, with all his flirts."

Lydia's lips pursed as she laid down Thea's needle-work and picked up her own. "Of course," she replied absently, and Thea frowned. Lydia was a dear, sweet-natured and even-tempered, and eternally grateful to Thea for giving her a home. Sometimes Thea found her reasonableness and eagerness to please annoying. Sometimes she would have relished a good argument.

"Well." Thea straightened, her hands resting lightly on the rosewood arms of the chair. "In any event, it was not me he asked. I expect I won't see much of him in the future."

"But of course you will, dear." Lydia held up two strands of wool. "Oh, I can't tell. Do these colors match? No, this one is darker." She set down the rejected strand and threaded her needle. "You'll be bound to see him everywhere."

"Perhaps." Thea's hands twisted in her skirt. "But our friendship is over. I won't put another woman in the position I was in." *Too many times,* she added to herself. Too often she had seen her husband go off to the arms of another woman. That was not something she would put Jeremy's bride through. And never would she let herself remember that, for one mad moment, she had been tempted to accept his proposal. "I do hope he chooses someone suitable."

"If he doesn't, dear, then you'll have to do something about it, won't you?"

Thea looked up startled, but her aunt was concentrating on her needlework. "Why what a thing to say, Aunt! As if I would interfere in Jeremy's life like that."

"Well, Thea dear, perhaps someone should."

Thea laughed and rose. "Not I, Aunt. I hope he finds someone very nice. He deserves it."

Lydia frowned down at her needlework. "Oh, this color won't do at all. As you say, dear. Though I don't think he'll find anyone nicer than you."

Unable to resist, Thea bent down and hugged Lydia around the neck. "You are kind, but I'm not quite in his usual style."

"As you say," Lydia said, her concentration already elsewhere, and Thea rose with a smile. She did hope Jeremy would find someone nice. She did, she told herself firmly, and left the room.

Some weeks later Thea sat at breakfast alone, as was her custom. Years of rising early to ride or to work at the stud farm left to her by her husband had had their effect; it was only rarely, and then after a late night, that she slept in. There were advantages to starting the day so early, of course, for she had the breakfast room to herself. She dearly loved Lydia. She also, sometimes, craved peace.

Hanson had already stacked the morning's post by her plate. As she ate, Thea sorted through it, putting aside the small square envelopes that held invitations for further consideration, and searching for those missives that demanded immediate attention. The one that caught her eye was addressed in a bold, black slanting hand and carelessly franked by a signature she knew well. In spite of herself, her breath caught in her throat. Jeremy. Not bothering with the knife she usually used to slit open her mail, she tore the envelope open, eagerly scanning the pages within. She missed Jeremy. He'd been gone for barely more than a fortnight, and she missed him already.

Her bright smile faded as she read the letter more closely, and then disappeared altogether. A few moments later, the pages fluttered down onto the snowy linen tablecloth unheeded, as Thea sat staring blankly into space. The letter brought news she should have been expecting, yet jolted her as she never would have expected. Jeremy was engaged. She had lost him.

Chapter 2

Jeremy pulled up his horse, a big bay gelding, in the middle of the field that had gone to seed, and surveyed the grounds, frowning. The Stanton estate in Berkshire had been in particularly bad shape, although he was working on it with the estate agent he had hired to replace the one who had been in his father's employ, and he thought they were making progress. Crops had been planted and his father's blooded and expensive horseflesh sold, which had brought in some needed money. Now there was evidence of recovery, though it had been a wet spring so far and the crops had suffered. But the land, more than anything else in his life, was solid and real. To part with any of it would nearly kill him.

His horse shifted under him; exerting a subtle pressure with his knees, Jeremy rode on. He was at peace here, content. He could breathe in the country. In town he felt smothered, hemmed in. Lately everything seemed to bore him. He was restless; he constantly needed to be on the move, seeking out new sights, new experiences. New women. Jeremy had never considered himself a rake, but since selling out of the army he had

had more than his fair share of women, never staying with one very long. It wasn't that he lacked morals, or even purpose. Every time he began an *affaire* it was with a sense of excitement, that perhaps this one would bring him the peace and contentment he found so elusive. As each liaison progressed, however, the excitement wore off, and he found himself in another entanglement. The woman he had thought beautiful, perfect, became vain, silly, or grasping. The prettiest was marred by hitherto unnoticed flaws; her conversation was meaningless, or centered only on marriage. Jeremy ended up feeling trapped. Only with Thea could he breathe freely.

He was between *affaires* now; oddly enough, no one had caught his eye. Nor had he found anyone suitable to wed. Nearly two weeks had passed since he had decided to marry, and still he was no closer to solving his problems. This late in the season most of the eligible young ladies already had offers. Those who didn't, Jeremy had found, were too insipid and silly to be borne, even for a fortune. If Thea had agreed to his impulsive proposal, everything would be settled by now. Odd he'd proposed to her, when it had been the furthest thing from his mind; odder still that, for one mad moment, he'd hoped she would accept. That she hadn't had come as both a disappointment and a relief. He didn't want to lose Thea's friendship. But that did nothing to solve his other problems. What he was going to do, he didn't know. But he'd have to decide something soon.

Riding back to the manor house, he swung off his mount and went inside. It was late. He would have to change quickly if he were to dine with his neighbors, the Powells, whose lands marched with his. A good family, that, Jeremy thought, changing, with the help of his valet, into well-tailored black pantaloons and evening coat, and carefully tying his neckcloth. Not aristocracy, but their pedigree was long, and the estate large. Mrs. Powell was something of a trial, true; her family had been in trade, and sometimes her origin showed. It didn't hurt, however, to keep on good terms with one's neighbors. Looking at his reflection, Jeremy sighed. What would he do if he had to sell his estates?

A little while later he walked into the Powells' drawing room. "My lord, how wonderful to see you again," Agatha Powell gushed, bustling forward to greet him and holding her hand out to be kissed. She was a stout woman, dressed rather unfortunately in purple satin that strained at the seams, and smelling of entirely too much scent. Yet there was nothing else to be done; hesitating briefly, Jeremy bent his head. Mrs. Powell simpered, an odd reaction for a woman her age. "I told Mr. Powell that life would be quite exciting with you here again."

Jeremy shook hands with Mr. Powell and then, smiling, sat on the sofa beside her, flipping the tails of his coat back. "Oh?" he said, rather at a loss for words. Mrs. Powell usually had that effect on him.

"Oh yes, my lord, we have been very dull lately," she said, running her eyes over him rather conspicuously. "That is a very fine coat. You didn't have it made in the country, I'll wager."

"No, I had it from Weston."

"Of course. He charged a pretty penny, I'll be bound. Really, my lord, the price of things nowadays, and the way our tenants complain—"

"My love, I'm sure his lordship doesn't want to hear about our tenants," Mr. Powell said.

Mrs. Powell fixed Jeremy with a basilisk stare. "Ungrateful wretches, if they only knew what their upkeep costs us! But there, my lord, I'll wager Mr. Powell is in the right of it. We'll talk no more of tenants. But I do resent their lack of gratitude, that I do. I'm sure you've had the same problem."

Jeremy shifted restlessly, crossing his legs. "I understand your daughter will be making her come-out next year," he said, attempting to change the subject.

"Yes, we thought to keep her to ourselves for one more year. I cannot imagine where she is. She knew you were coming, my lord."

"Here I am, Mama," a soft voice said from the doorway, a vision in golden ringlets and white muslin curtsied. "My lord, I am sorry for being late."

"Ah, child, there you are," Mrs. Powell said as Jeremy rose. "My lord, may I present my daughter, Evadne."

Evadne curtsied again, and Jeremy, for once in his life, stood absolutely still. Good lord, she had grown! The last time he'd seen her she had been running around in pinafores and pigtails. Now she was a beauty, pretty, petite, an heiress, and, to all appearances, docile. All, in fact, that he claimed he wanted in a bride. "Miss Powell," he said finally, taking her hand as she rose. Here was the answer to his problems. He wondered why he didn't feel happier.

It was late. Most people in the quiet Berkshire countryside were abed, their houses in darkness. Tomorrow would be another day of work and people needed their sleep. Not everyone could rest, however. In her room,

Miss Evadne Powell, just recently turned ten and eight and impatient to begin her life, sat up in bed, hugging her knees.

"Just think, Fluffy!" she said to the brindled cat stretched out on the eiderdown. "I am getting married! And to a viscount. I shall be a lady!" The light of the single taper glinted off her pale golden curls and made her blue eyes glisten. "Lady Stanton," she murmured. "The Viscountess Stanton. I shall wear a coronet and be presented at court. Oh my!" She hugged herself with joy, and the cat raised its head to look at her through slitted eyes. With a sigh, it lowered its head down again.

Evadne, lost in dreams of the future, sighed too. Just last week she had had no idea of what was to come, and yet now it all seemed inevitable. She'd always known she would marry well. To marry a viscount, though, was special. The day she had learned that Lord Stanton was in Berkshire and had been invited to dinner, she'd gone downstairs wearing her best frock, the sprigged muslin that was rather daringly cut. That had won her a sharp look from Mama, but Stanton, bowing over her hand, had looked at her with warm approval. Well, of course he would, she was the prettiest girl in the country, and every boy was in love with her. Stanton, however, was a man, not a boy, and thus more of a challenge. Then and there, she had determined she would have him.

From that moment, events took on a momentum of their own. She had met Stanton again at church, and when she was in the village shopping he had stopped to talk with her. She was not really surprised when, several days later, Stanton met her in the rose garden and said that her father had given him permission to pay his addresses to her. Sensing that something of the sort was

28

coming, she had worn her most charming chip straw bonnet, and she made certain to look up at him through her long eyelashes as he spoke. She had also widened her eyes when he at last proposed, and made her voice breathless in reply, having learned that men found both actions appealing. He had smiled at her and bent his head toward her, so that she had thought he was going to kiss her, but at that moment Mama had come into the rose garden. Evadne was still cross with her for the interruption.

"Lady Stanton, Fluffy," she said. "I shall be the leading lady of the country! Of course, he's old." She frowned. "And so dark, almost like a gypsy. But I shan't mind that, because he is so much more sophisticated than any of the boys in Berkshire. We shall look quite well together, I think." She smiled smugly, knowing quite well that Stanton's darkness would set off her own golden looks. "I shall go to London and wear satin and diamonds, Fluffy. Oh, I am going to be a fine lady!"

With that she jumped out of bed and waltzed about the room in the arms of an imaginary partner. "And I shall have all London at my feet, and lots of admirers, and I won't have to listen to Mama anymore!"

"Evadne!" At the sound of the voice, stern and imperious, just beyond the bedroom door, Evadne scrambled back into bed.

"Yes, Mama?"

Mrs. Powell, her hair in curling papers, squinted into the room. "Whatever are you doing?"

"Nothing, Mama."

"I should hope not. Go to sleep, now. We've a busy day tomorrow if we're to get you outfitted in time for London. You don't want the viscount to be ashamed of you because of your clothes! And a pretty penny they'll cost, too."

"Yes, Mama," Evadne called back, lying stiffly until the door closed and the footsteps faded away. At last she blew out the candle and in the darkness stared up toward the ceiling. "No, Fluffy," she said, her voice soft and determined. "I won't listen to Mama anymore." And with that she at last fell asleep, with visions of the future shining in her mind.

It was late evening. Save for the slap of pasteboard onto green baize as the cards were dealt, a hush lay over the card room in Watier's, the exclusive gentlemen's club where the gambling stakes were always high. The candles illuminated a group of men seated around a table, intent on their game of macao. For the most part they were older men, dedicated gamesters all, for whom the turn of the card could mean a fortune won or lost.

Leaning back comfortably in his chair, Roger DeVilliers held his cards negligently, his expression almost bored. A bottle of burgundy stood on the stand next to his left elbow, and though occasionally he lifted it, the hand that held his cards was rock steady. His eyes were heavy-lidded, but an astute observer would notice the brightness that appeared in them from time to time as he surveyed his opponents. DeVilliers was neither sleepy nor any the worse for drink. He could not afford to be; it was his fortune riding on the cards tonight.

"Mine, I believe," the gentleman opposite him said quietly, and laid down his hand. DeVilliers stared at it for a moment without expression and then tossed his cards down. From a pocket he withdrew a notebook and carelessly scribbled on a piece of paper his name and the amount he had lost: three thousand pounds.

"I shall pay a call on you tomorrow." He pushed the paper toward the victor and rose. "A good thing I was not playing deep," he added, and walked out.

Once in the hall his expression hardened. *Damn!* He had been certain the cards would go his way. He could ill afford to lose three pounds, let alone three thousand, but he was a gentleman. No matter what else was said of him, he always paid his debts of honor. His other creditors would simply have to whistle for their money.

Shrugging into the greatcoat the cloakroom attendant held out for him, he headed for the door. There was nothing the least bit poverty-stricken about his appearance; his coat was flawlessly cut, his neckcloth meticulously tied, his luxuriant dark hair lay in carefully styled waves, one lock curling carelessly over his forehead. Only he knew how desperate his situation was, the mounting debts, the estate that, nearly drained dry, no longer supported him. He needed a great deal of money to restore his fortunes. He had almost had it once, he thought, clenching his jaw at the memory.

"I say, DeVilliers," a man entering the establishment addressed him. "Not leaving so early?"

DeVilliers stopped and looked down at the other man's hand, clutching at his sleeve. He was short and rotund, with a bulbous nose that attested to a great deal of wine already consumed that evening. "Truth be told, Kinsdale," he said, smiling, though his eyes remained watchful, "I find the play here rather boring this evening."

"Pity. I had hoped to engage you in a hand of piquet. Next time, I hope?"

DeVilliers nodded and turned to leave.

"Oh, by the way, have you heard about Stanton?"

DeVilliers stopped abruptly on the threshold and turned, ignoring the porter who held the door open. "No. What of him?"

"He's said to be engaged, old man." Baron Kinsdale smiled. "Not to anyone you know this time?"

DeVilliers' lips set in a hard straight line. "No. Nobody I know, old man." He stressed the last two words, all the while holding Kinsdale's eyes with his own. "If you will excuse me?"

"Of course," Kinsdale muttered, and turned away hastily.

It was a mistake to bait DeVilliers in such a way; the thin scar running down his lean cheek attested to his danger. Kinsdale was distinctly lucky to have escaped with his skin whole.

Outside, DeVilliers stood at the bottom of the steps, breathing deeply of the soot-scented air and composing himself. Finally he set off down the street, his eye constantly alert for shadows in the fog, his ears straining for any sound. Should anyone be foolhardy enough to tangle with him, he would soon learn that the walking stick DeVilliers carried concealed a sword operated by a hidden spring, and that he was a very good swordsman, indeed. It was something he wished he could teach bloody Jeremy Vernon, Viscount Stanton. Were it not for Stanton, DeVilliers would not be in such straits now.

His grip on the walking stick tightened, as if he indeed faced his enemy on the dueling ground. He nearly had, all those years ago, and the thought of what had happened instead still made him shake with anger. Long had he wanted revenge for the wrong done him, and now he just might be able to have it. News of Stanton's engagement had given DeVilliers an idea. How satisfying it would be to serve Stanton the same trick that had once been served him.

Grinning, DeVilliers used his stick to cock his hat at a jaunty angle and walked on, contemplating sweet vengeance.

Jeremy swung up the stairs to his mother's house after a session of boxing at Gentleman Jackson's saloon the following afternoon. Life was rather pleasant for a change. With his decision made, his future was set. He didn't love Evadne; and he doubted he ever would. She was, however, all he could wish for in a bride. While his friends were amazed by his decision and the *ton* gossiped, he went on his way, able, at last, to pay off his father's creditors, able, at last, to relax. He had yet to see Thea since his return from the country; somehow their paths hadn't crossed, nor had he visited her. He wasn't certain why. Doubtless, though, he'd see her soon enough. He would tell her about Evadne's mannerisms, the way she batted her eyes and lisped, and would at last be able to laugh about them. Thea would probably be the only one who would see the humor of it all. Deuce take it, but he missed her. He would have to make an effort to see her soon.

"Good afternoon, Saunders," he said to his mother's butler as he opened the door. "Is all well?"

"Oh, my lord, such a day we have had," Saunders

said agitatedly. "Her ladyship said as you were to go right up."

"Thank you." Jeremy turned to the stairs, taking them two at a time. So. Just as he had suspected when he had received his mother's note, written in her spidery handwriting and filled with incoherent ramblings, there were problems ahead. Lady Stanton, sweet and gentle though she was, looked to her son to rescue her from the scrapes, usually of a financial nature, that she often fell into. Thank God, he thought devoutly, that he didn't have to face her scenes every day.

Simon, Lady Stanton's dresser, opened the door to her sitting room, and he went in, finding his mother prostrate on the chaise longue, one arm flung dramatically across her eyes and the other dangling down. Such a posture was so unusual for his ebullient mother that he crossed the room to her swiftly. "Mother? What is amiss?"

Lady Stanton's hand flew up and caught his in a strong grip. "Jeremy! Why did you not warn me?" she demanded, staring up at him.

"What is it, Mother?" he asked, pulling over a chair and sitting beside her. "Another scrape?"

"No, it is not another scrape!" She subsided onto the chaise with a groan.

"Mother?" Seriously concerned, he spoke gently. "Won't you tell me what is wrong? What has upset you so?"

Lady Stanton lowered her arm and looked up at him with her blue eyes, so like his. "Such dreadful people, Jeremy. You might have warned me."

"Yes, Mother." He made his voice patient. "Who?"

"Your fiancée, of course. And her mama."

"The devil you say!" he exclaimed before he could stop himself. "They are in town?"

"Yes, didn't I say so?" She looked up at him, her eyes wide, and he wondered vaguely why that expression was so familiar. "They arrived this morning, and nothing would do but that they must pay a call on me! Oh, Jeremy. Must you marry her?"

"But Mother, you were happy about my engagement. Come, you are tired and upset. Rest, and you will feel better—"

"Do not patronize me!" she said with the sudden clear-eyed sharpness he always found so disconcerting. "You have made a dreadful mistake, Jeremy. You must get out of it."

"I can't in all honor cry off, Mother. Besides, I don't want to." He clasped his hands loosely between his knees. "I grant you Mrs. Powell is a little hard to take—"

"A little!" Lady Stanton sat up, sputtering with outrage. "She had the nerve, Jeremy, to ask me what I pay in rent for this house! As if I couldn't afford to own it! And when I wouldn't answer, she went on to tell me how much they are paying, and how much Miss Powell's gown cost—and a perfect fright that was, I must say—and even how much they had to tip the postilions who brought them here!"

Jeremy bit his lower lip to keep from laughing. "I am sorry, Mother. Mrs. Powell does tend to be overly concerned with money."

"I should say so! But then, what can you expect of someone connected with trade? Oh, Jeremy." She subsided again with a groan. "I wish to see you married, but not like this."

"Come, Mother," he coaxed. "Mrs. Powell might be difficult, but you must agree that Miss Powell is very sweet."

"Yes, for now. Someday, however, she'll be just like her mother—"

"God forbid," Jeremy said fervently.

"And she'll lead you a merry dance." Her lips pursed. "She *flirted,* Jeremy. First with her own coachman, and with a footman, and even with Saunders."

"No!" Jeremy feigned amazement, trying hard to keep his lips straight at the picture that conjured up. "Not Saunders!"

"Laugh if you will, but it isn't funny. She batted her eyelashes at him. The poor man didn't know where to look! Believe me, Jeremy, I know flirting when I see it."

"I believe you, Mother." His mother had been a notorious flirt in her day, and she had lost none of her wiles. "She'll outgrow it, I'm sure. She's very young."

"Yes. She'll always be too young for you." She looked at him directly. "You'd do better with an older woman, Jeremy, someone calm enough to settle you down."

"Mother—"

"I've worried about you since you came back from the war. You don't seem to be able to settle down to anything."

Abruptly Jeremy rose and strode to a window, his hands shoved into his pockets. "I'm all right, Mother."

"Break the engagement," she urged. "Miss Powell is wrong for you. I'm sure you could give her reason to cry off."

Jeremy turned, smiling. "Are you suggesting I should allow her to jilt me, Mother?"

"Yes. You'd survive it, better than she would. And then you could find someone else."

"Such as?"

"Such as Althea Jameson."

Chapter 3

"Thea!" Jeremy let out a bark of laughter. "Come, Mother, you can't be serious! I admit I'm fond of Mrs. Jameson, but we are merely friends."

"Then more fool you," Lady Stanton retorted. "She would be the perfect wife for you. Especially after your unfortunate experiences in the war."

"Mother—"

"Yes I know, you don't wish me to speak of them. Do you think I don't know why you cannot settle down?" Lady Stanton's eyes were sympathetic. "Mrs. Jameson is good for you. She calms you."

"She is sharp-tongued, managing, and independent. You said yourself you think it's scandalous that she manages her own stables."

"Nonsense! I quite admire her for it. You really should consider her, Jeremy."

"Mother." Jeremy tugged at his neckcloth. "I am going to marry Miss Powell. I hope you will help make her welcome."

Lady Stanton gave in with bad grace. "Oh, very well, I'll do what I must. But don't expect me to get her vouchers for Almack's, Jeremy, for I fear it can't be done!"

"If anyone can do it, you can, Mother." Jeremy bent and kissed her forehead. "I must go. The Powells will likely be expecting me to call and see how they are settling in. They gave you their direction?"

"Yes, they are in Curzon Street. Jeremy?" She caught at his hands and looked up at him anxiously. "You know I only wish you to be happy?"

"Yes, Mother." Jeremy gently freed his hands. "I do know that." He smiled at her and turned to go. His mother meant well, but she was wrong. Thea as his wife? Ridiculous.

A few minute's brisk walk brought him to Curzon Street. Surprised though he was by the Powells' quick appearance in town, he approved of their choice of houses. If they wished to make an assault on the *ton,* they had at least chosen a good location, and that he credited to his future father-in-law. Mrs. Powell might be connected with trade, but Mr. Powell's family was old and their heritage long. It was not such a mismatch as his mother feared.

"My lord!" Agatha Powell exclaimed as he was shown into the drawing room. "Why, we didn't expect you today. As you can see, we're at sixes and sevens."

Jeremy held out his hand, forcing a smile to his lips. Lord, it was hard to believe that this woman was Evadne's mother. Where Evadne was angelically fair, Mrs. Powell's hair was steel gray and her skin was coarse. Evadne was slender; her mother was, to put it kindly, plump, as attested to by the creaking of her stays when she walked. And Mrs. Powell's voice was hardly a pleasure to hear with its loud and penetrating tone. Thank God Evadne did not resemble her. "You've chosen a good location," he commented after returning her greeting. He cleared his throat and stifled a sneeze.

"Well I should hope so, it cost enough! But there, you won't want to hear about that, I'll be bound. Evadne! Where are you, girl?"

"Here, Mama." Evadne appeared beneath an archway, her head demurely lowered. "Good afternoon, sir," she said, peeping up at him through her lashes. Jeremy smiled at her, suddenly realizing why his mother's wide-eyed look had been so familiar. Evadne looked at him the same way, he thought with amusement.

Unable to contain himself this time, Jeremy sneezed. Something in the room was bothering him, unless he was coming down with a cold. Come to think of it, he had had a cold when he was in Berkshire. Odd. He was never ill. "Good afternoon, Evadne. You are settling in, I hope?"

"Oh, yes." Evadne's voice was breathless. "It's all so exciting. I've never been to London before."

"I'll show you about," he promised rashly as they sat down, Evadne and her mother on a sofa, he in an uncomfortably spindly arm chair of gilt and blue velvet. The drawing room was furnished entirely with such chairs. Jeremy reminded himself that since the house was leased, the decor was not the Powells' fault. However, Evadne's gown, trimmed with several rouleaux about the hem and too many ruffles, was. Her mother's taste, he supposed. He would have to do something about her clothes once they were married.

Over tea, they talked easily about the Powells' journey and their visit to his mother, and discussed activities for the weeks to come. Mrs. Powell dominated the conversation, talking about the cost of Evadne's new clothes and the vails one was expected to give to footmen as a tip, as well as asking about the cost of attending the theater and the opera. Through it all Evadne sat quietly beside her mother, her hands folded in her lap. Only occasionally did she glance up at Jeremy, the brightness of her eyes belying her meekness. She seemed not the least embarrassed by her mother's obsession with money, which Jeremy was beginning to find rather funny. Thea would be amused by it also, he thought, and rose abruptly.

"I hope you will excuse me, ma'am, Evadne," he said, taking Mrs. Powell's hand. "I fear I have another appointment. However, I shall be happy to escort you to the opera tomorrow evening, if you wish."

"That's very gracious of you, my lord," Mrs. Powell said. "Do you not agree, Evadne?"

"Oh, yes," Evadne said, smiling brightly. Life in the country must be vastly dull for her, he thought. Suddenly Evadne, with a little cry, dropped down on one knees. "Fluffy!" she exclaimed. Jeremy turned, startled, to see a large, brindled cat stroll into the room. It was an ugly cat, looking, with its notched ears, as if it belonged out on the streets rather than in a Mayfair drawing room. Yet it paused and surveyed the room's occupants quite as coolly as any dowager. In no way did it resemble the name by which Evadne had called it. Jeremy stepped back, dismayed. He could feel another sneeze coming on.

"Fluffy," Evadne called again, beckoning with her hand. "Come to Mummy, precious." The cat looked at her again and then, with unerring instinct, headed for the one person in the room who detested cats. With a powerful leap, it jumped into Jeremy's arms. Jeremy sneezed so explosively that the cat, startled, jumped down again, its sharp claws snagging Jeremy's fine buff pantaloons.

"Fluffy!" Evadne flew across the room to the cat, who crouched near the door, unconcernedly grooming itself. "Oh dear. Do you not like cats, Stanton?"

"They make me sneeze," Jeremy said, brushing his sleeve and blinking hard. "I must be on my way. I shall see you tomorrow evening, then?"

"Yes of course, Stanton. We're looking forward to it," Agatha Powell said. Both ladies rose, and as Jeremy left the room he took with him the picture of them standing, Mrs. Powell with her bosom jutting like the prow of a ship, and Evadne, the wretched cat struggling in her arms. He felt briefly as if he had just escaped from Bedlam.

Agatha remained standing for a few moments. "That coat cost a pretty penny, I'll warrant," she murmured. "And boxes at the opera do not come cheap. And you, girl!" She rounded on Evadne, who was kneeling on the floor stroking the cat. "When that cat jumped on Stanton I was like to swoon with embarrassment!"

"Fluffy was just being friendly, Mama," Evadne said, hugging the cat again.

"Friendly! We are lucky Stanton didn't cry off right then. I don't know why you must needs drag that mangy thing to town with us."

"He would have been lonely. Wouldn't you, my pretty little kitty?" she crooned. "Mummy's little love."

"He should get used to it. You may be certain that Stanton will not let you keep him when you marry."

Evadne raised stricken eyes, and her lips set in a stubborn pout. "I won't give up Fluffy! I won't!"

"You'll have no choice. Put him down now, and come sit with me. Come." Mrs. Powell patted the sofa imperiously; reluctantly, Evadne joined her. "Now. We have much to discuss. You've done well, girl, attaching Stanton. But now that you are in London, you may be able to do better."

"But Mama! I want to marry Stanton."

"Now really, girl, you're not in love with him, nor he with you. It's his title that's important." *And Evadne's dowry.* Mrs. Powell was nothing if not realistic. She knew that her background, connected as it was with trade, was a handicap in the *ton.* She also knew, however, that there were other noblemen besides Stanton who were in dun territory. That, along with Evadne's prettiness, should make a potent combination. "But you may be able to find someone higher."

"I hadn't thought of that." Evadne's eyes looked dreamy. "Just think, Mama. I shall have the highest rank in the county."

Mrs. Powell looked aghast at that thought, which had not occurred to her. She must be careful that, rank or not, Evadne knew where the true power lay. "Of course, you shall have your mama to guide you," she said, and it was Evadne's turn to look alarmed. "I think it would be remiss of me not to tell you that the *ton* is very different from us. They care a great deal about manners, so I expect you to behave, miss."

"Yes, Mama."

"You must also realize, though, that they may not behave well. Particularly the gentlemen."

Evadne looked up at that, and the dreamy look left her eyes. "I expect you mean that Stanton has a mistress."

"I expect he does." Agatha sat back, relieved. She had not raised her daughter to be ignorant of the facts of life, and she had no desire to send her unprepared into the world, advantageous marriage or not.

"I wonder what she is like."

"That is neither here nor there," her mother said sharply. "It is just something you will have to accustom yourself to."

"Yes, Mama." Evadne looked down at her clasped hands. Her mother was wrong. It mattered very much what Stanton's mistress was like. She would have to do something about it.

Jeremy brushed again at the sleeve of his coat as he walked along, frowning slightly. His visit to his intended had not gone quite as anticipated. Oh, she was as sweet as ever, but he had to admit that his mother had a point. Mrs. Powell was something of a dragon. Thank God his principal estate was in Kent, far from his future mother-in-law's influence.

Preoccupied with such thoughts, he gave little notice to the direction in which he was walking, but upon looking up he realized that he was near Thea's house. Instantly his jangled nerves were soothed, and he took a deep breath. He could talk to Thea. She would understand and sympathize. He also wanted to tell her that the Powells were in town before she heard it elsewhere, though why that was so important to him, he wasn't sure.

It wasn't until he had been led upstairs by Thea's butler and heard voices coming from the drawing room that he realized he'd made a mistake. Devil take it, he'd forgotten this was Thea's at-home day, and that she'd have guests. Now he wouldn't be able to sit and talk with her as he had planned, to tell her about Evadne and to laugh with her. He was annoyed out of all reason at the thought.

His name was announced and he strolled in, aware of people staring at him but not caring. There was Lord Jerrold, a dandy who lived for gossip; several matrons, watching avidly; and, to his immense surprise, his sister Margaret. He was used to being the subject of gossip; it was something he'd accustomed himself to in his past months of wild living. Let people talk. What he didn't like was the way all eyes seemed to follow him as he crossed the room to where Thea sat behind the tea tray. He took the hand she offered him. He and Thea were friends, nothing more. Why should there be this avid interest in their meeting?

"Stanton," Thea said, smiling, though he noticed that her eyes were just a little wary. That surprised him, too. "This is a pleasant surprise. Would you care for a cup of tea?"

"Yes, thank you." He bent over her slender hand. She looked quite well today. She was wearing green, a color that complimented her delicate complexion and brought out the copper highlights of her hair. The high neck of her chemisette of white muslin emphasized the graceful curve of her throat. In contrast with Evadne's fussy gown Thea's was simplicity indeed, far more pleasing to the eye. A pity Thea couldn't advise Evadne on fashion, but then, one didn't ask one's flirt to give advice to one's fiancée. Thea his flirt? Where had that come from?

"Jeremy!" A small, slender figure hurtled itself at him before he could contemplate that question, and he found himself hugging his sister. "Oh, 'tis so good to have you back!"

"Meggie." He hugged his sister briefly before releasing her. "Quite improper behavior, you know."

Meg tossed her curls, looking almost pretty. "As if you care what people say! You're acquainted with Lord Danbury, are you not?"

"Of course." Jeremy held out his hand to the very young, very callow man who hovered behind his sister. Viscount Danbury wasn't known for his sense, but he was a far more suitable companion for Meg than Denby ever would have been. Thank God he'd scotched that match. No matter what his own circumstances would be, saving his Meg would be worth it. "I am surprised to see you here."

Meg's eyes danced with something that looked suspiciously like mischief. "I like Mrs. Jameson. One forgets that she is older." She went quickly on before her brother could remonstrate. "What is that on your coat, Jeremy?"

Jeremy made a face and brushed at his sleeve again. He had no doubt whom to blame for the awkward position he was in. His mother, evidently, had been talking. "Cat hair."

"What? But cats make you sneeze. How on earth—"

"Never mind," he said hastily, not wishing to mention Evadne in this group.

"Someone you don't wish us to know about? Honestly, Jeremy!" Margaret's eyes sparkled. "Don't tell me you've found someone else, with Miss Powell in town?"

"How the deuce did you know that?" he exclaimed, glancing quickly at Thea. She was staring at them, a cup held halfway to her lips and an arrested expression in her eyes. Lord, he was in for it now.

"I had it from our mother." Margaret leaned forward. "I am so looking forward to seeing her, Jeremy. 'Tis been so long since we've met. Has she changed?"

"Yes, just as you have, Meggie." He smiled at her. "That's a pretty gown you're wearing."

"I collect you are trying to change the subject. Well, it won't fadge. Come, Jeremy, I am dying of curiosity."

"There's not much to tell, Meg. Not here," he added under his breath. Margaret stared at him for a moment, and then looked past him to Thea. Jeremy groaned inwardly. His sister would never learn discretion.

Thea looked at Jeremy's averted head and set down her cup. "I must admit to being curious as well, Jeremy," she said, her voice matter-of-fact. "There's no help for it, you know."

Jeremy smiled at her, grateful to her for rescuing him from an uncomfortable situation. She deserved better than this. He'd hurt her. He could see it in her eyes, and he cursed himself for a clumsy fool. For all Thea's serenity, there was sometimes a vulnerability to her that made him want to protect her. With a jolt, he realized

47

that his friendship with her might very well be in danger, all because of his sister's indiscretion and his own tardiness in speaking with her. That hurt more than he would have thought.

"They are in Curzon Street," he said, turning to his sister. "Likely they'll have a ball, once Evadne has been presented, and Mama will try to get her vouchers for Almack's."

"That's not what Mama said," Margaret murmured, just loudly enough for him to hear. He had to resist the impulse to strangle her. What was the matter with the females of his family? "She told me she was feeling fatigued."

"I see," Jeremy said, his eyes meeting hers briefly. Both knew well that Lady Stanton pleaded fatigue only when there was something she didn't wish to do.

"Nothing serious I hope, Stanton?" Thea said, and Jeremy looked at her. She was smiling, with just a hint of concern in her eyes, and for some reason he felt chagrined. Did she not feel the slightest bit jealous at hearing about his fiancée? Did she not care that he was marrying another? And here he'd been so concerned about her feelings.

"No, nothing. I expect she'll recover in time for the wedding," he said abruptly, and rose. "I must leave. I've an appointment with my man of business."

"Of course." Thea smiled so warmly that he felt annoyed all over again. Barely returning the smile, he bowed over her hand, and then, with a nod to the others, strode out.

* * *

Thea watched him go, her brow smooth in spite of her inner turmoil. Well! This would make another tidbit for the gossips to discuss, the way Jeremy had come to her and told her about his fiancée. *Men!* she fumed silently as she poured another cup of tea for a guest. They had no idea how difficult they could make life, with their careless disregard for others' feelings. He had come in, made his startling announcement, and then left, leaving her to bear the brunt of everyone's sly glances and excited chatter. She and Jeremy were friends, merely. She knew that, and so did the rest of their fashionable world. That didn't mean, however, that their friendship was immune from gossip. As she sat politely listening to Lord Jerrold, seated beside her and speculating about Miss Powell, Thea smiled, hiding her anger and another, deeper feeling. Jeremy was marrying another. She had never felt quite so lonely in her life.

Hanson entered the breakfast room the next morning as Thea was finishing her chocolate. "Excuse me, ma'am. Mr. Thorne is here."

Thea looked up, the circles under her eyes testimony to the hours she had lain awake the night before. "My brother?" She set down her coffee cup. "Did he say what he wants?"

"No, ma'am. I've put him in the morning room." He hesitated. "I have the impression that it is a delicate matter."

Thea's lips tucked back with annoyance. Of course it was a delicate matter. With Francis it usually was. "Very well, Hanson. I'll see him." Rising, she tossed her napkin onto the table, next to her plate which was still half-full. Hanson clucked in concern as he cleared the table. Things weren't going well for Mrs. Jameson lately and that was a shame. She deserved better from the gentlemen in her life.

"Francis?" Thea said, walking into the morning room.

The young man standing by the window turned and smiled. He looked much more like their father than she did; he had the same lean, rangy height, the same fine, fair hair, the same patrician, chiseled profile. And, Thea noted with dismay, the same air of seedy dissipation, the circles under his eyes and the barely discernible softening of his jaw, though he was only three and twenty. "What brings you here this morning?"

"Hullo, Thea." He crossed the room to kiss her cheek. "Can't a man visit his sister without facing an inquisition?"

"You usually don't," she pointed out as she sat down. "Are you in another scrape?"

"Do I have to be in a scrape to visit you?" he responded hotly, and Thea's eyebrows rose.

"Usually. Out with it, Francis."

"Oh, the devil—you're right, Thea. I'm in trouble this time. I've lost money gambling." He took the chair opposite her.

Thea's face grew stony. "How much?"

"I didn't mean, to, you know." Francis's voice was coaxing. "Luck was running with me and I thought I'd make a recover—"

"Stop trying to cut a wheedle! How much?"

"Dash it, but you're awfully unsympathetic, Thea! You might understand that sometimes a man can't help these things."

Thea leaned her head back, closing her eyes tiredly. "You sound so like our father."

"Thea!"

"You do." She gazed at him steadily. "Well?"

"Oh, the devil," he muttered. "A thousand pounds."

Thea drew in her breath. "What! Whatever were you thinking of, Francis?"

"I told you. I kept thinking I'd recover."

"And if you didn't, you'd come to me." She stared at him and he, sprawled in an armchair, could not meet her eyes. "I'm tempted, Francis, not to pay this time."

"You can't do that!" he said, alarmed. "It must be paid."

"You should have thought of that before you started playing so deep. Where was it, at White's?" Francis muttered something in reply. "Excuse me?"

"I said it was at a gaming hell, Thea," he said defiantly, staring straight back at her.

Thea gripped the arms of her chair. "I suppose you were with those rackety friends of yours?" Her voice was dangerously soft. "Pelham and Monkford and—who else?"

"It doesn't signify," he muttered. "Thea, please. This is a debt of honor."

"Oh, yes. Men and their precious honor," she said bitterly. "It must needs be satisfied, no matter the price."

"All right then, dash it, I'll go to a moneylender—"

"You most certainly will not! Though I should let you. Maybe it would teach you a lesson." She sighed. "I am getting very tired of towing you out of the river Tick, Francis. I haven't worked as hard as I have simply to support your gambling."

"I know, Thea. I wouldn't ask if there were anyone else." He smiled again, and dispassionately she noticed how charming a smile it was. The same as their father's, and look how he had ended up, in debt till the day he died. "Please?"

Thea let out her breath. "Oh, very well. But this is absolutely the last time, Francis."

He beamed at her. "It will be, oh best of sisters. I promise it won't happen again."

Thea looked at him for a moment and then nodded decisively. "That I can guarantee." She crossed to her desk and quickly scratched a few words on a piece of paper. "Take this to my man of affairs. He'll give you a cheque. But"—she pulled the note back as he reached for it—"you'll have to earn this."

"Yes, Thea, I'll do anything. Maybe I could work it off at that farm of yours."

Thea's eyebrows rose. "You'd want to?"

"Well, no," he said frankly. "But it would be something to do."

He sounded so world-weary that Thea's brow furrowed as she handed him the note. "Are you bored, Fran? Tired of all the drinking and gambling you've done since leaving Oxford?"

"Everyone does it. Even your friend Stanton."

"My friend Stanton, as you put it, can afford it." *Now that he has a wealthy fiancée.* "There must be something you want to do with your life."

"What?" Francis rose, pacing restlessly back and forth. "Father left me without an estate, which is probably just as well, considering the shape he left it in. The war's over, so the army's no good. And I can't go into trade."

"Why not?" Thea asked, and Francis stared at her. "There are some perfectly decent people in trade."

"Bad *ton*, Thea," he said, shocked. "I can't believe you'd even suggest such a thing."

"Is it so terrible to think of working for a living? I'd be willing to stake you to something, if it were what you wished to do." Her lips curved. "I'd suggest a gaming hell of your own, but you seem to be particularly inept at that."

Francis returned her rueful smile. "Damn, I'm sorry, Thea. I've put us both in the devil of a coil."

"No, it's not that. I worry about you, Francis. If you keep on this way you'll end up worse than Father."

Francis shuddered. "God knows I don't want that. But is there anything wrong with a fellow enjoying himself?"

Thea bit back a smile at the plaintive note in his voice. Sometimes he seemed so young. "No, Francis. Just don't carry it to such extremes." She rose, tucking her arm through his as they walked toward the door. "I won't be going down to Linwood just yet, so you have a reprieve. In the meantime, will you promise to escort me when I need you?"

"Of course."

"Good. Then please be here at nine tonight to escort me to Almack's."

"Almack's!" Francis looked horrified. "That dull place? I'm sorry, Thea, I've plans for tonight."

"Have you?" Thea said, her voice deceptively pleasant, and Francis cast her a look.

"Oh, the devil. I know better than to argue with you when you've that look in your eyes. Very well, oh best of sisters." He bent to kiss her. "I'll be here."

"Good," Thea said again, and smiled as he left.

The smile faded, though, as she turned back into the room. Truth to tell, she wasn't looking forward to the evening anymore than Francis was. For Jeremy was certain to be there with his fiancée. And what she would do when she saw them together, God only knew.

It was nearly time to leave, and still Thea hadn't decided which gown to wear. Ordinarily her choice of frock mattered little, since she wasn't on the catch for a husband and she cared not what the gossips said about her. Tonight, though, was different. Tonight Jeremy and his fiancée would be present. She could still remember the way he had looked when he had said Miss Powell was beautiful. He'd never looked at her like that. Not that she wanted to, of course, they were merely friends, but still, it was quite annoying. And so, tonight it mattered how she dressed. Certainly she had enough from which to choose. Since putting off her blacks Thea had indulged herself, buying gowns with the new, longer skirts in the bright, vibrant colors she loved. There were gowns of gold tissue and emerald silk, crimson gauze and azure muslin, all beautiful, all appealing. The only problem was, she had yet to find the courage to wear any of them. As a young girl she had longed for more flamboyant styles, but the years of her marriage had changed her. She knew she was not beautiful; Hugh had taught her that. Much as she loved her new gowns, she knew deep inside that she would never wear any of them. They required a woman certain of her attractiveness.

On impulse she pulled out a gown of sapphire blue

satin and stared at it, shaking her head. What in the world had possessed her to buy it? Besides being such a bright color, its cut was positively indecent, so low at the neck that it bared her shoulders, styled in such a way that it draped over her curves, leaving little to the imagination. She would only make herself a figure of fun, an old woman trying to look young. The burgundy silk was a much better choice. Much safer.

Thea felt confident as she entered Almack's that evening. As usual the fashionable assembly rooms were crowded; she concluded that many who mattered in the *ton* were in attendance, along with young ladies still hopeful of catching a husband. She smiled at the patronesses, who returned the greeting with great condescension, and greeted various acquaintances. Her gaze circled the room, settling unerringly on Viscount Stanton.

Her breath caught. It shouldn't have surprised her that he was so handsome, but it did, every time. He was, again, in faultless black and white, a sapphire stickpin thrust into the folds of his neckcloth shining almost as brilliantly as his eyes. He was so alive, so vital, that he made every man in the room pale in comparison. And he wasn't alone. Hanging on his arm was a vision in pink and gold, garbed in a frilly white muslin gown and dimpling up at a dazed-looking Lord Ware. Jeremy's fiancée. It had to be, she thought, feeling the world crumble beneath her feet. Never before had she felt so lost, or so alone.

The girl took Jeremy's arm, looking up at him with the same sweet smile with which she had favored Lord Ware, and Jeremy smiled back. It broke Thea out of her trance. Anger, more familiar and so much safer than the odd sensations she'd had a moment before, began to fill her. Miss Evadne Powell, if such she was, was a fool. Imagine flirting with another man, any other man, with Jeremy standing next to her! Jeremy deserved better. Jeremy, she thought with a little shock that went all the way to her toes, deserved *her*.

Chapter 4

Thea stood as if turned to stone. Jeremy deserved her? Goodness, no one deserved that fate, she told herself in a pitiful attempt at humor. Whatever had come over her, to think such a thing? She had no desire to marry again, none. And if Jeremy deserved her, she didn't deserve him. He was too vibrant, too handsome, too alive. He certainly deserved better than the little vixen hanging on his arm, pretty though she was.

Francis tugged at her arm again. "I said, Thea, everyone's watching us," he muttered, his voice low and urgent.

"What? Oh. Oh yes, of course, Fran." At last she moved, though her eyes never left Jeremy. If people were watching, she didn't care, though normally she avoided making herself a figure of gossip. The girl was beautiful. Of course. Since his return from the army Jeremy had seldom been seen with any girl that wasn't. Trust him to go into Berkshire and find a beauty lurking there too. They looked so well together, she thought, her heart twisting painfully, she so fair, he so dark, bending over her protectively. Except that *she* didn't seem to notice; she was smiling again at Lord Ware, the silly moonling, and batting her eyes at him. Thea was seized by an emotion so fierce, so primal in its intensity that it shook her. What it was, she couldn't for the life of her say, except, in that moment, she knew she'd taken Miss Evadne Powell in extreme dislike.

"I say," Francis said beside her. "Who is that with Stanton?"

"His fiancée, I believe," Thea said, shaking herself slightly. This wouldn't do. She could not let herself go to pieces at Almack's, of all places, in full view of the *ton*.

"She's beautiful." There was a note in Francis's voice she'd never heard there before, but she paid it little heed.

"Well enough, I suppose." But she was lovely, Thea thought, seeing even at this distance the cornflower blue of Evadne's eyes, enormous and fringed with dark lashes, and the sheen of her golden ringlets. And young, so young. Though she was only six and twenty and certainly still attractive, Thea knew she was past her first youth. On the whole, she was glad. There was little to be said for the fresh, dewy ignorance of youth, and she had a poise now that she'd lacked as a young girl. There was no denying, however, that someone so innocent and fresh could be enormously appealing. Thea only hoped that Evadne was as sweet as she looked.

She allowed herself one more look at Jeremy and then turned away. "He'll have his hands full with her, I fear."

"Lucky dog," Francis muttered. Thea glanced quickly up at him. Men could be such fools. Anyone could see that all Miss Powell had to recommend her was her beauty. Thank heavens Francis was safe.

"I suppose I should meet her," she said. "It will only give the gossips more to talk about if I snub her."

Francis's gaze was curious. "I say, Thea, if you don't mind my asking, what is there between you and Stanton?"

"Nothing," Thea said quickly. "We are friends, nothing more."

"If I thought he'd hurt you—"

Thea glanced up sharply, alarmed at the note she heard in his voice. "Fran, this is none of your affair."

"You're my sister. Up to me to defend you."

"I don't need defending. Jeremy hasn't done anything to hurt me."

"Except betroth himself to someone else."

"He asked me first," she blurted, her face going red. That was a secret she'd intended to take with her to the grave. "I refused, of course."

Her brother's gaze was searching. "Did you, Thea?"

"Yes." She held his eyes. "You know I've no desire to marry again."

"After the way Jameson treated you, I'm not surprised," he said grimly, startling her again. She'd had no idea he knew anything about her marriage to Hugh.

"It's past," she said briefly. "I like my life now."

Francis's eyes followed Jeremy and his fiancée as they stepped out on the floor to join a country dance. "But you don't like it that he's engaged."

"For heaven's sake, Fran, Stanton and I are simply friends! And I don't wish to see him hurt."

"Let's dance." With all the impetuousness of a younger brother and none of the grace of a suitor, Francis

59

pulled her out onto the floor. "But if he hurts you, Thea, he'll answer to me."

"He's said to be an excellent shot," she teased.

"It doesn't matter." Francis's face was grim.

"Fran, don't be silly," she began, just as the steps in the dance took them away from each other. Men! They had such silly notions of honor. If Jeremy chose to marry someone else, what was that to her? Nothing. Raising her chin defiantly, she turned, hands outstretched for the next movement in the dance, and found herself face to face with Jeremy.

For just a moment, her breath stopped. Then she recovered. She was, after all, no green girl. She could handle this. "Stanton," she said, smiling. "This is a pleasant surprise."

"Thea." He smiled back. "You look beautiful tonight."

Thea's laugh sounded brittle, artificial even to her own ears. "You can say that when you have such a lovely fiancée? You are lucky, Jeremy."

"I am," he agreed, smiling down at her with that special warmth that was his alone, the warmth that he should not be using on other women now that he was engaged. "We'll talk later?"

"Oh, assuredly," she said, and let the dance whirl her away again. Her breath was unsteady, her legs shaky. Jeremy. If she'd been prepared—but then, she never could have been prepared for tonight. Never.

"Althea. And Thorne," a voice spoke behind her when the dance ended and she had laid her hand on Francis's arm. In spite of herself, Thea jerked her head around only to see Jeremy with his future bride on his arm. All the chaotic feelings she thought she'd soothed suddenly rose up within her again, stronger for having been suppressed. At the moment, she immensely disliked both Jeremy and his betrothed.

"Stanton." She smiled. "A fine dance, was it not?"

"Yes. We were about to take some refreshment. Would you care to join us?"

Francis made a face. "Lemonade and stale cakes? No offense, Stanton, but I should say not."

Thea's hand tightened on her brother's arm. "Actually, I am a trifle warm after that dance, Fran. Shall we join them?"

"Of course." Francis stood, unbudging. "Haven't introduced us to your partner, Stanton."

"Haven't I? My apologies." Jeremy smiled down at the girl on his arm. "Mrs. Jameson, Mr. Thorne, may I introduce you to Miss Powell. My fiancée."

Thea smiled at the girl. "A pleasure to meet you."

After a quick, frankly appraising glance, Evadne smiled back. "Thank you, ma'am." She lowered her eyelids. "You are most kind."

"Are you enjoying your stay in London?"

"Oh, yeth," Evadne said breathlessly, suddenly batting her eyelashes at Francis. Thea felt her brother's arm jerk in surprise. "Everyone has been so kind. And I've been so enjoying meeting Stanton's friends, though of course they are all so much older than I."

"Evadne, shall we see about that lemonade?" Jeremy said hastily, but not before Thea saw what she could swear was a gleam in his eye. He was enjoying this, the wretch! She could quite cheerfully kill him. "Thea?"

At that moment, the orchestra began to play again. "Oh, a waltz," Thea said, looking at her dance card. "I wonder if I am promised for this—"

"A waltth, Stanton!" Evadne exclaimed at the same time. "Oh, please, letth danth. Pleath?"

"Not this time." Jeremy patted her hand. "The patronesses haven't approved you yet."

Evadne pouted. "But Stanton, you promithed."

Jeremy smiled. "Next time. Thea? Are you promised?"

Oh, the wretch! How *could* he ask tonight with his lovely, young, lisping fiancée with him? Lisping! Good lord, what had Jeremy got himself into? "Of course, Stanton," she said graciously. "I'd like that."

"I'll escort Miss Powell to her mother, shall I?" Francis said. "If you don't mind, Stanton."

"No, of course not," Jeremy said, and swept Thea out onto the floor.

It was just a waltz. Nothing more. She'd danced it with Jeremy many times before; doubtless she would again. Just a waltz. Just his hand at her waist, hers at his shoulder. Not an embrace. Just a dance.

"Out with it, Thea," Jeremy said, and she looked up to see him regarding her with a smile.

"She lisps," Thea said, the first thing she could think of to say.

Jeremy grinned. "Only in polite company. It's funny, is it not?"

"Does she always flirt so, Jeremy?"

"Always," he said cheerfully. "She's young. She'll grow out of it." He swung her in a turn that left her quite breathless. Only a dance, she reminded herself. "I think, too, that she's nervous."

"Nervous!" Thea glanced across the room. Evadne and her mother had been joined by Sally Jersey and a man she couldn't, at the moment, identify, and Evadne was, as usual, smiling and flirting. "I don't think she has a nervous bone in her body, Jeremy."

"Now, Thea. Don't you remember your first season?"

"I didn't have one, Jeremy, I was already married."

"And you've faced the gossips ever since, nevertheless. Lord, I've missed you, Thea!" he said suddenly, turning her again.

She must have been out of breath from dancing. That was why she was suddenly so dizzy. "Oh, what a plumper!" she managed to reply. "With your fiancée by your side?" She glanced away. "She is lovely, Jeremy."

"Yes, that she is. I think I've made a good choice."

"Do you—love her?" She had to ask. She had to know.

Jeremy gave her a puzzled look. "No, of course not. I told you before, Thea. I don't believe in love."

"Yes, I remember."

"I do, however, believe in friendship. You and I are still friends?"

Thea forced her eyes to meet his. "Yes, Jeremy."

"Good. And I hope you'll be a friend to Evadne, as well. She'll need one."

It was too much. Thea nearly stopped dancing right then and there. How dare he ask her to befriend his little bride! Had he no sense? She and Evadne had disliked each other on sight. Well, no. She didn't really dislike the girl, she didn't know her well enough for that. Thea just didn't think she was right for Jeremy. "I think she'll manage quite well for herself. She seems to be able to get what she wants," she said, and Jeremy followed her gaze across the room. Evadne was being led out onto the floor by a tall man garbed, like Jeremy, in faultless black and white.

"Oh, the devil!" Jeremy exclaimed, his hold on Thea tightening.

"Who is it, Jeremy?"

"Roger DeVilliers, deuce take it. I'd best stop them—"

"She appears to be enjoying herself," Thea said, looking up at him in surprise. Jeremy's face had gone grim.

"Mm." Jeremy pulled back. "Thea, do you mind—"

"Yes, Jeremy, I do mind! If we stop dancing now the gossips will be talking about it for the rest of the night."

"I don't care—"

"I do. And I'm willing to wager Miss Powell's mother does, too."

"Deuce take it," Jeremy muttered, but he resumed the dance as if nothing untoward had occurred.

"You said yourself she's a flirt," Thea pointed out, glad to have just a bit of revenge.

"That's not what I object to."

Thea glanced over his shoulders. "Mr. DeVilliers, then? But he's always seemed perfectly pleasant."

"Mm." He looked down at her, his eyes serious. "Evadne's never been in town. She thinks she knows how to go on, but she doesn't. I'll do my best to guide her, of course, but she needs more than me. She needs someone like you."

Thea returned his gaze straightly. "I will be pleasant to her, Jeremy, of course. But don't expect any more of me."

"No?"

"No."

Jeremy looked at her in silence for a few moments, his eyes intent. "Very well. Friends, Thea?"

Thea swallowed hard. "Yes," she said, forcing herself to smile. "Friends."

The waltz between Jeremy and Thea had not gone unnoticed. As Thea had feared, the gossips were indeed wagging their tongues about the events taking place. One person, however, watched with more than passing interest. Standing near the wall, holding a glass of punch, Roger DeVilliers looked here and there, seeing first the expression on Thea's face, and then the look of youthful rapture on Evadne's. So that was the girl who had at last captured Stanton's heart. There was something he could do about that.

Leisurely he made his way across the room to the patronesses. His reputation was that of a rogue. Well earned, he admitted, even as he knew it had closed more than a few doors for him. Sally Jersey, however, one of Almack's powerful patronesses, was known to harbor a soft spot for a charming rogue, and charming he could be. Within a few moments he had managed to persuade her to accompany him across the room to the Powells, and to introduce him to Miss Powell as a suitable partner for the waltz. There, he thought, leading her out onto the floor. Let's see what Stanton had to say to this.

He looked down to see Evadne regarding him, her huge blue eyes wide and unexpectedly shrewd. "How did you come by your scar?" she asked without preamble.

Just in time, DeVilliers remembered to let his eyelids droop, giving them a heavy, mysterious appearance. "It's not something I care to discuss in polite company, child."

"Oh. A duel. I am not a child, thir."

Roger raised an eyebrow. *Thir?* God help him, she was flirting with him. He could almost bring himself to feel pity for Stanton. Almost. "Are you enjoying your stay in London, Miss Powell?"

"Oh, yes!" Evadne said, and went on to tell him, at great length and with ample enthusiasm, all that she had seen and done since arriving in town. Roger listened to her prattle with only half an ear. Seducing this young miss away from Stanton, should he choose to do so, would be ridiculously easy. What did Stanton see in her, apart from her undeniable prettiness and her exuberant youth?

"And everybody has been so kind," Evadne went on. "Though they're so much older than I expected."

DeVilliers hadn't much of a sense of humor, but even he was tempted to laugh at that. "But one can't help being kind to someone as lovely as you," he said, and Evadne turned pink with pleasure. "Tell me. Does Stanton treat you well?"

Evadne's eyes widened. "Why, sir, what a question! Of course he does."

"Peace, child, I ask only because I would not wish to see you hurt. You must know that your engagement came as a surprise to everyone."

"I don't know why. It must have been expected he'd marry."

"Yes, but, you see, his name has been linked with others."

"Is it linked with someone's now?" she asked, with such swift curiosity that Roger was taken aback.

"Well, as it happens," he murmured, turning his head a bit until his gaze rested on Jeremy and Thea. Deep in conversation, they might as well have been alone in the room for all the attention they paid to anyone else.

Evadne followed his look. "Mrs. Jameson?" she said in surprise.

"Ah. You've met her, I see."

"Yes, just now. Stanton said she is a friend."

"Very much so," DeVilliers agreed, and Evadne looked up at him, her eyes shrewd again.

"His special friend, sir?"

"Now, Miss Powell," he chided. "You know I can't tell you such a thing."

"She is, then." Evadne watched Jeremy and Thea as she whirled, her brow furrowing. "But she's so old."

"Not so very," Roger said wryly.

"I must talk to her." Evadne thrust her chin out and pulled back from his hand. It was only by luck, and strength, that Roger kept her with him, swinging her around in the dance.

"Bad *ton,* child, to go charging up to her in such a way. You don't want to give the gossips such a tit-bit."

Evadne sent him a look withering with scorn. "I wouldn't. But will you escort me to them when the dance is over, sir?"

Roger made a little face. "I cannot, child. Stanton does not like me much."

"Why?" She studied his face. "Does it have something to do with your scar?"

"I fear so. We quarreled some years back." He let the silence lengthen, while Evadne's mouth shaped itself into an O. Good. Let her think what she would. "We have not been friends since."

"But that's not fair! If he did that to you—"

"Peace, child. It's past. But you must see I cannot go

67

over there. May I bring you back to your mother? The waltz is nearly over."

"Oh, very well," Evadne said, pouting. As he led her across the room Roger glanced at her. What *did* Stanton see in the girl? He himself would be bored silly before the honeymoon was over, no matter how wealthy she was. He was rather glad to leave her with her mother, a veritable dragon of a woman, and walked away, well satisfied with the evening's work. A wedge had been driven between Stanton and his fiancée.

With every appearance of docility, Evadne allowed herself to be escorted to her mother, and with every appearance of pleasure she greeted the young man who came to lead her out for the next dance. Underneath, however, she was calculating her next move, and she kept a sharp eye on Mrs. Jameson. No matter what it took, Evadne intended to speak with her.

Evadne had thought long and hard about her marriage since Stanton's romantic proposal in the rose garden, determining its disadvantages as well as its advantages. She was not at all surprised to learn that Stanton had a mistress. What did surprise her was her own reaction, for she wasn't the least bit jealous. One couldn't be jealous of someone so old, she thought, with the sublime arrogance of youth. Still, she would have to do something.

Her chance came some time later, when during a cotillion she noticed that Mrs. Jameson was, for the moment, alone. A winsome smile and a glance through her eyelashes were all it took to persuade Lord Ware, who had quite gratifyingly begged her for another dance, to procure something for her to drink. Left alone at last, she purposefully made her way to the window where

Mrs. Jameson stood. What did Stanton see in her? Why, she was tall and thin, almost skinny, and her gown of burgundy silk didn't have even one ruffle. Her hair was a common brown, though shiny, Evadne conceded reluctantly. And she was well past her prime, Evadne thought pityingly. Really, no competition at all.

"My, it's warm in here, isn't it?" she said when she reached the window, snapping open her fan.

Thea glanced down with surprise and instantly stiffened. It was one thing meeting Evadne with Jeremy, quite another to converse with her in private. Irrational jealousy stabbed her. Did the girl have to be so pretty, with such petal soft skin and so sweet a smile? It was unfair. Next to her Thea felt old, plain, and much too tall.

Quickly she glanced about the room to see if they had been noticed, but the window embrasure afforded them a measure of privacy. "Quite warm," she admitted. "Of course, when you have been dancing, it can be uncomfortable."

"Oh yes, I've hardly sat down all evening!"

Thea's smile was rueful. Had she ever been so young that such a boast would have thrilled her, too? "You are enjoying your stay in London, Miss Powell?"

"Oh yes." The woman was certainly no rival, Evadne reminded herself, but somehow she felt more uncertain than she had just moments before. She'd have expected Mrs. Jameson to be cross, at the least, and instead she was smiling at Evadne, if not with pleasure, at least out of politeness. For the first time since accepting Stanton's proposal, Evadne began to wonder just what she had done. "Stanton is very kind to me," she said aggressively.

"Of course he is. Jeremy is a very nice man. You've done well, capturing him."

Perhaps it was Mrs. Jameson's self-possession that rattled her; perhaps the hint of condescension in her smile. "You know him well?"

"We are friends," Thea said lightly, shoving aside her jealousy. Poor child, she must have heard the gossip and had decided to confront her. Hurt though she still was over Jeremy's engagement, Thea had no intention of ruining things for his bride. "Miss Powell, let me assure you—"

"Oh, I realize you are friends," Evadne chattered. "And I don't mind. I know men must have their *chere amies.*"

"Miss Powell, I am not—"

"But I don't mind, really I don't. At first I was concerned, you know, but now that I see you, I'm not. In fact, I don't mind at all if you continue as his mistress."

Chapter 5

For a moment Thea was so stunned she could hardly speak. "But I'm not—" she began.

"I think he's wonderfully handsome, even if he is dark," Evadne chattered, "and so charming. I can understand why you'd want him. Mama told me it's the way of the world."

"Not *my* world," Thea said.

Evadne ignored her. "He's marrying me for my money, you know."

Thea impulsively reached out her hand. "Oh my dear!"

"But that's all right, because I'm marrying him for his title. Mama is so pleased," she added naively. "So you see, nothing has to change."

Thea stared at her as if she couldn't quite believe her eyes. "Miss Powell, I think I must tell you—"

"Oh there you are, Miss Powell," said Lord Ware, approaching from behind. His eyes grew wide as he saw who Evadne was speaking with. "Your lemonade."

"Thank you, my lord." Evadne gave him a ravishing smile that made him blink. "It was so nice talking with you, Mrs. Jameson. Perhaps we can talk again some day."

Thea had recovered some of her poise. To deny Evadne's mistaken idea before Ware would only make matters worse. "Perhaps," she said, and watched them walk away.

There, Evadne thought, grasping Lord Ware's arm. She'd handled that confrontation in quite a grown-up way, she thought, and she'd been so nervous about it beforehand. Mama was right; the world of the *ton* was strange. Better to reach an understanding with Stanton's mistress now, before the wedding, so that the woman wouldn't try to compete with her. Not that she could. Mrs. Jameson seemed nice enough, but she was so old! And Evadne had no doubt she could bring Stanton to heel anytime she wished. Why, just look how Lord Ware, heir to a dukedom, doted upon her. That thought made her glance up quickly at the young man. Stanton wasn't the only available man. This new world might suit her fine.

Lord Ware cleared his throat. He was tall and just a bit gangly, with large hands that he didn't seem to know how to control, but his eyes were kind. "I say. Miss Powell?"

Evadne turned the full force of her smile upon him again, and he blinked. "Yes, sir?"

"Ahem. Feel I should warn you. Mrs. Jameson. Nice lady and all that, but her name's been linked with Stanton's."

"Has it?" Evadne batted her eyelashes, pleased with

72

herself at her newly acquired air of nonchalance and maturity. "But she's accepted here."

"Ahem. Of course. Ahem. Miss Powell?"

"Yes?" she said encouragingly when he hesitated.

"We're to have a house party at Rochester Castle. M'father and stepmother, you know," he said in a rush. "Be honored if you would come. Stanton, too, of course."

"Why, thir, I'd like that ever tho much." She smiled up at him. "How sweet of you to think of me."

"Ahem. Well." Lord Ware looked down at his feet. "I'll speak to my stepmother about it."

"Thank you, thir." Evadne beamed as he led her back to her mother. A house party with a duke and duchess! This was beyond her wildest dreams. She'd been accepted, and now the world was hers.

Thea stood in the window embrasure, still with shock. "Wasn't that Miss Powell?" a voice intruded upon her thoughts. She looked up to see Lady Hartford, one of the worst gossips in the *ton*.

Inwardly, Thea groaned, though she managed a smile. "Yes. If you'll excuse me—"

"A pretty thing, isn't she? Very sweet, too."

"Oh yes," Thea said, aware of Lady Hartford's interested gaze. "Excuse me, ma'am, I see my brother, he's probably looking for me."

"She must be, if she approached you," Lady Hartford went on. "Either that, or terribly naive."

Thea stopped, turning slowly to face her. "What do you mean?"

"Why, Mrs. Jameson, all the world knows about your friendship with Stanton." The woman paused, smiling. "Your *special* friendship."

Thea's temper started to rise. "I am not, and I have never been, Stanton's mistress."

"Why, dear, of course not. Did I say so?" Lady Hartford's eyes were bright with malice. "But no one would blame you if you were."

Several retorts rose to Thea's lips, but she bit them back, habit and training preventing her from making a spectacle of herself. She didn't know when she had ever been so angry in her life. "Excuse me, ma'am," she said, her smile tight. "I really must join my brother." With that she swept away, the swish of burgundy silk the only sign of her agitation. Lady Hartford thought she was Jeremy's mistress! If she thought so, then so must everyone in the *ton*. Thea's fingers clenched on her dance card, mangling it beyond redemption. She had lived a blameless life. Because she had chanced to fall prey to a man's easy charm, because she had befriended him, her reputation was in tatters. She didn't know whether to cry or rage.

No wonder Miss Powell had spoken to her as she had. Thea's ire abruptly dissolved in a wave of pity. Poor girl, trying to act sophisticated, and all the time looking young, so young. Thea well recalled her own bitter disillusionment when she had learned that her husband had been unfaithful. Would she herself have had the courage to speak to Hugh's paramour in such a way? Not likely. She had, in spite of everything, been fond of Hugh at first and had wanted her marriage to succeed. What, Thea wondered, did Miss Powell want?

By the time Thea took her leave that evening, her head was aching in earnest. Several people had quizzed her about Evadne, and with each encounter she barely managed to restrain her temper. She was grateful to reach the sanctuary of her carriage, away from prying eyes and gabbling tongues. Wise to the ways of society, Thea knew this sensation would not soon die down. At least though, she had a respite, however temporary.

The carriage stopped in front of her house, and wearily Thea went in, alone, Francis having gone on to some other entertainment. And that was another worry. At the moment, the world seemed very heavy on her shoulders.

To her surprise, the lamps in the drawing room were lit. She paused in the doorway to see Lydia frowning over her latest piece of needlework. "Why are you not asleep, Aunt?" she asked.

"Hm?" Lydia looked up, her expression vague, and then her eyes focused. "Thea, dear. You are home. Is it that late?"

Thea smiled as she walked into the room and dropped into a chair, pressing her fingers for a moment to her aching temples. "Have you been stitching all night?"

"I fear so." Lydia looked like nothing so much as a guilty child, caught at some forbidden activity. The thought made Thea smile. "Did you have a nice evening, dear?"

"Yes. I'll tell you about it in the morning, Aunt."

"And was Stanton there with his fiancée?"

Thea paused in the act of rising. "How did you know that?" she asked, sitting down again. Lydia could sometimes be amazingly well-informed.

"What is she like, Thea dear?"

"Very pretty, very sweet, and very young."

"Oh, dear. Too young for him, I'll wager."

"No, on that I have my doubts. She's no fool, Aunt." Thea did rise then, pacing restlessly to the fireplace.

"You've the headache, I collect," Lydia said, looking up at her with eyes unexpectedly sharp and bright. "I'll have one of my possets sent to you."

"Thank you, Aunt. If you'll excuse me, I think I'll go to bed."

"What did she say to upset you, Thea dear?"

Thea stopped near the doorway and then turned, walking back again to the chair. "Not just her. Everyone. Did you know, people have been assuming I'm Jeremy's mistress."

Lydia clucked. "Oh dear."

"You don't sound shocked."

"Well, Thea dear, I've always thought you deserved some happiness after Hugh."

Thea laughed, surprised and just a little bitter. "Not this way. Not when I've tried so hard to live a blameless life. And then for that girl to say—"

"What?" Lydia prompted when Thea didn't continue.

"Oh, Aunt." Thea sank her head into her hands. "She made me the most incredible proposition." She then proceeded to tell Lydia of her conversation with Evadne.

"She didn't really say that," Lydia exclaimed, shocked at last.

"Oh yes, Aunt, she did. I still cannot believe it." Thea paced back and forth. "Young girls aren't supposed to know of such things. I didn't, at her age."

"Yes, Thea dear, but I've often thought, you know, that girls should be told."

"Yes, I agree with you. But how could she say such a thing? I'd never want to share my husband with anyone."

"She doesn't love him, I fear. And what is worse, she doesn't care about him."

Thea sank into a chair. "No she doesn't, does she? Poor Jeremy." He had been unhappily married once, and now it would happen again. "He doesn't deserve this."

"No, he doesn't. You must do something, Thea dear."

"What?" Thea spread her hands out. "What can I do? I'm only his friend."

"Yes, dear, but everyone believes otherwise."

"Everyone is wrong," she replied in clipped tones, angry again at what was believed of her. She had never been tempted to have an affair, never, not when she was married, not since.

"Oh yes of course, dear, but you must see there is some truth in it. Haven't you ever noticed how Stanton looks at you?"

"No. How does he look at me?"

"Not as he would look at a friend."

"That's silly." Thea rose and began to pace again. "He is a rake. He looks at all women that way."

"Oh no." Lydia shook her head. "Only you, dear. I noticed it most particularly. Perhaps he would like the rumors to be true?"

Unbidden to Thea's mind came the memory of what had transpired in this very room, when he had suggested just such a thing to her. "Gammon!"

Lydia looked faintly reproving. "No, dear. You could

77

stop him from making a dreadful mistake. You do agree it would be a mistake for him to marry Miss Powell?"

"Yes."

"Then you must stop him." Thea stared at her. "If he feels that way about you, you have more power than you think."

"You mean—Aunt, you're surely not suggesting I take him away from her!"

"Why, yes, Thea dear. Someone has to."

Thea went very still. That odd mixture of emotions she had felt when she had first seen Jeremy with his fiancée went through her again, powerful and shattering. Then, as before, anger set in. "Not I," she snapped, and strode out of the room, angry at Lydia, at Jeremy, and most of all at herself, for caring. Jeremy was lost to her. It would be best simply to forget him. She doubted, though, as she blew out her candle and climbed into bed, that she ever would.

Miss Evadne Powell took London, and the *ton,* by storm, charming the younger men with her smile and her huge eyes, the older ones with her fresh youthfulness. She wasn't so well liked among the women, but that seemed not to bother her. Thea watched as, at each ball or soiree or assembly she attended, Evadne was surrounded by a court of admiring young men, and gradually she felt her frustration and anger deepen. It was proving impossible to avoid seeing Jeremy with his fiancée, just as Lydia had foretold. They moved in the same circles, and so were bound to see each other nearly every day. Evadne seemed not to notice the awkwardness of it, but Thea did.

At breakfast one morning Thea poked at her food and mulled over the situation. On the one hand, she didn't want to believe that anyone so young and innocent could have understood the enormity of the suggestion she had made to Thea. On the other, Thea had watched her flirt with every available male while Jeremy was left to his own devices, and was indignant on his behalf. It didn't matter that he didn't appear to mind, that Evadne's antics seemed even to amuse him. He was certainly heading for sorrow and unhappiness.

Part of her wanted to do something about the matter. She considered and discarded various strategies to make Jeremy aware of the truth about his betrothed. Part of her urged that a friend would not let another friend go blindly into a situation that could only bring him pain; another, more cowardly, selfish part, told her that he would not thank her for such news, and that she might lose even his friendship. That, she couldn't bear. Odd, but she thought more about him now than she had before he had become engaged. She was more aware of him; she watched him closely, studying his moods and wondering if he was really as content as he appeared. *As a friend would do,* she reminded herself hastily. Attracted though she was to him, she knew there could be no future in an affair between them. Jeremy was engaged, and she would not encourage him. It would do neither of them any good. And yet she didn't want to see him enter into a marriage that would only bring him pain. What could she do to help him?

Hanson murmured something as he laid the post beside her plate, and Thea started. What good was moping going to do her? She attacked the mail with sudden vigor, quite cross with herself. She had gone through hard times before and had survived them. Difficult though it was for her to admit, Jeremy's problems weren't hers. If he chose to marry a pretty little ninny-hammer, he deserved what he got. She would not repine, she told herself firmly, pulling a heavy card from a creamy, square envelope. She would go on with her life.

A moment later she laid down the invitation she had pulled from the envelope and stared into space. She had been invited to a house party at Rochester Castle, of all places. Why, she didn't know; she was not particularly friendly with either the duke or his new duchess. Nor did she think she'd enjoy herself, honored though she was. In the act of placing the invitation with those she planned to refuse, however, she stopped. Had she not heard that Jeremy was to be invited to the house party, as well? With the lovely Miss Powell, of course. Lord Ware, being the duke's son, would be there, too, and Miss Powell would likely flirt with him. It would not do.

Thea sat straighter. She couldn't allow it. No matter her inner battles, she could not allow Jeremy to plunge headlong into disaster. It might be foolish beyond permission, but she was going to accept the invitation. She was going to go to Rochester Castle. She was going to try to win Jeremy back.

Moira, the Duchess of Rochester, adored making mischief. The widow of one duke and now the wife of another, Moira sometimes found life dull, though she had everything she could want. Thus she had to find ways to add spice to her days. Arranging house parties with the most unlikely combination of guests was one such way. An avid lover of gossip, Moira knew well who was conducting *affaires* with whom, or who might have a quarrel with another, and would send out her invitations accordingly. That this usually led to situations that could best be described as awkward bothered her not in the least, nor did her doting, foolish husband appear even to notice. Her house parties were the talk of the *ton*, and she always had delicious stories to tell. What more could she ask?

Her current house party hadn't been planned with quite such an object in mind, however. The duke's daughter, Lady Catherine, had at last settled on a suitor, the young Earl of Pelham. It would be a deadly dull affair, of course, entertaining the earl and his very proper mother, but worth it, to have Catherine off her hands. She had been quite vexed when Lord Ware, the silly moonling, had, without consulting her, invited that vulgar Miss Powell and her mother. Of course she had confirmed the invitation; it was the only polite thing to do. Thank heavens they would be accompanied by Stanton; that alone would make their presence bearable.

It wasn't until the day her guests were due to arrive, however, that she thought of another way to make her house party interesting. Before leaving London she had, of course, heard the talk about Stanton and his friendship with Mrs. Jameson. Being observant, she doubted that any of the rumors were true; Mrs. Jameson certainly didn't look like a woman who was happily having an *affaire*. That she was displeased about Stanton's engagement, however, was evident. Bored already with the thought of the week ahead, Moira succumbed to impulse. An invitation was sent, by special messenger, to Mrs. Jameson.

So far, matters had fallen out quite as Moira had expected. Lady Catherine had sulked in Evadne's presence, especially when that girl had flirted so outrageously, not only with Ware, but with Pelham. Jeremy was charming; Pelham's mother was a pillar of rectitude; and the Earl and Countess of Chatleigh, originally invited so that Moira could flirt with the earl, were proving to be agreeable guests, forming friendships with everyone. Even Roger DeVilliers had been pleasant. Last night he had read some of his poetry; the ladies had loved it, while the gentlemen had found convenient excuses to leave. Today, however, there was a distinct feeling of boredom in the castle. It was the third day of the house party. It was also the third day it had rained, and everyone was growing restless.

Late on this damp morning, the guests had assembled in the blue drawing room to await the announcement of luncheon, for lack of better things to do. Jeremy, not used to being so inactive, sat hunched forward in his chair, his fingers restlessly tapping out a tattoo on his leg, and smothered another yawn. Why he had been invited to this gathering was quite beyond him. He had little in common with his host and the other guests, with the exception of the Earl of Chatleigh, who, like him, had served on the Peninsula. Nor was he interested in setting up a flirtation with the duchess, though more than once over the past days she had signaled her availability to him. Even now, with her husband in the same room, Moira occasionally blinked her sleepy cat's eyes at him. Wearing a gown of crimson muslin that was rather inappropriate for morning wear, she lounged back in her chair, carrying on a conversation with Roger DeVilliers, who hung over her, his eyes hooded in their usual fashion and a lock of dark, glossy hair falling onto his forehead. Undoubtedly he was spouting some bit of poetry, in that world-weary way he had. Apparently no one had told him that the Byronic mode was somewhat out of favor, with Byron himself in disgrace. Nor did Moira seem to mind. Women could be fools about men, Jeremy thought. Why in the world had he and DeVilliers been invited to the same house party? Everyone knew of the enmity between them. He suspected, as Moira sent him another slantwise look, that the duchess was up to mischief.

His restless gaze passed from Moira to the spinet, where Evadne was cheerfully mangling a Bach sonata while Lord Ware turned the pages of the music for her. If Jeremy had no idea why he had been invited, he had no doubt as to why Evadne had been. Lord Ware was gazing down at her with as fatuous an expression as Jeremy had ever seen, and she was preening herself beneath it. Lord Pelham, a close friend of Ware, was leaning on the other side of the spinet, much to Lady Catherine's displeasure. Jeremy frowned. After three days of watching his fiancée practice her wiles on another man, he was becoming annoyed. Not that he was jealous, but he wished she'd show a bit more discretion. She would have to learn, he thought grimly. He would not have her acting in such a way once they were married.

"Evadne? Play that little tune you do so well," Agatha Powell said, and Jeremy's annoyance abruptly changed to amusement at the arch way Mrs. Powell smiled at Lord Ware. Jeremy would not have rated

Evadne's chances of a match with Ware very highly even had she not been engaged, but Agatha clearly thought otherwise. Nothing too good for her Evadne, he thought, wondering if she had already calculated the cost of everything in the room. Jeremy doubted the duke would allow his son to marry the daughter of such an avaricious woman.

And that brought Jeremy's attention back to his host, whom he had been trying to avoid for the past few days. Rochester was a pleasant enough man, but his interests were narrow. He cared only for riding and hunting and shooting, and he tended to recreate in words every course he had run, every covert he had flushed. At the moment he was talking, in great detail, about a deer he had bagged the previous fall. Next to Jeremy, Chatleigh and his young countess contrived to look interested. Jeremy suspected they were as bored as he.

Jeremy grunted with annoyance, and the duke looked up. "Say something, Stanton?" he said, his face genial.

"No, no, just something caught in my throat," Jeremy said quickly, leaning back and crossing his legs. Good lord, whatever had compelled him to come, he wondered, as the duke went on with his tale. Life had been much more interesting in town. Where, he wondered, was Thea now?

Just then, the door to the drawing room opened and the butler entered. "Your Grace," he announced "the rest of the guests have arrived."

"More?" DeVilliers drawled. "I thought us quite content as we are."

Moira gave him her secret cat's smile, and again looked slantwise at Jeremy. "Why of course we are, but we have been rather dull of late, sir. I do expect things to be livelier presently." And turning to the door she exclaimed, "Mrs. Jameson, welcome to Rochester."

Chapter 6

Thea! Without realizing it, Jeremy jumped to his feet, his heart pounding. Good God, Thea, here! He felt strange, disoriented, as if his own thoughts had somehow conjured her up. She was no great beauty, not compared to Evadne, yet there was something about her, about her smile. . . . Jeremy swallowed hard, forcing his hands, by his sides, to be still.

"Mrs. Jameson." Moira crossed the room, her hands held out, as Thea entered the room. With her were Francis and Lydia. "How good of you to come."

"How nice of you to invite us," Thea said, touching cheeks with the other woman and quickly scanning those assembled. Her eyebrows rose a little when she saw Jeremy, and, oddly enough, he felt himself relaxing. It was only Thea, after all. Only his—friend. There was no need for him to feel as if he had been struck by lightning.

"Do come in." Moira took Thea's arm, guiding her into the room. "You must be tired after your journey."

"Quite brave of you to come out in this weather, ma'am," DeVilliers drawled. "Are the roads very bad?"

Thea looked up from tugging off her gloves and smiled. "Tolerably so. We only got bogged down twice. Have you ever seen such a spring?"

"No, ma'am, but I believe things will be brighter now." Devilliers looked down at her, his one-sided smile highlighting his scar. Jeremy had the sudden, irrational desire to give him a matching scar on the other side of his face.

"Perhaps." Thea smiled brilliantly at him. "If you'll excuse me, Your Grace, I'd like to change out of all this dirt."

"Of course." Moira smiled. "Rathbun will show you to your rooms."

"Thank you." Thea nodded and smiled at the assembly and exited with Lydia and Francis, leaving Jeremy standing stiff and still, his hands clenched at his side.

"Why, look, Stanton, I do believe it's stopped raining," a soft voice said beside him. A hand stole out to touch his arm, and blue, dark-fringed eyes gazed up at him. "Do you think we might walk outside?"

Jeremy glanced out and saw that the rain had indeed ceased. "It's still rather damp," he said, smiling down at Evadne. "Perhaps this afternoon."

Evadne pouted. "But what shall we do until then, sir?"

"Why don't you play for us some more?" he suggested, and she gave him a brilliant smile.

His own smile faded, though, as he found his seat. Good lord, what had just happened to him? For a moment, all he'd seen was Thea, all he'd been aware of was Thea. It didn't matter that Evadne was in the same room, or Moira, seductive though she was. Thea, in her simple dove-gray traveling gown, looked almost plain in

87

comparison, and yet he hadn't been able to look away. For a moment, as his eyes had met hers, he'd felt the world tilt, shift. For a moment, he'd seen something in her eyes he'd never imagined she possessed. There was fire within her. He'd never realized it before. Thea, here. What did he do now?

Thea sank down at the dressing table in her room, pressing her fingers to her aching temples. She'd brushed through that tolerably well, she thought, trying to ignore the maid who fussed behind her, hanging her gowns in the wardrobe and pouring out water for her to wash in. It had been difficult, though. At the moment she stood in the doorway to the drawing room, her courage had faltered. She couldn't do it. She couldn't. She had, though, and had been rewarded by the look of utter shock on Jeremy's face. He didn't want her here, that much was plain. Her own emotions were much different. At her first glimpse of him, she had felt a rush of pure happiness, and a feeling similar to what she felt when she returned to Linwood. A feeling of homecoming, a sense of belonging. And then she had seen Evadne.

A knock on the door made her look up. "Come in."

Francis ambled in, his hands in his pockets. "I say, Thea, have you ever seen such a pile as this?" he said, gesturing with his hand as he sank into a chair.

Thea smiled at him in the reflection of the dressing table mirror. "It is a castle, Francis, even if a new one. And thank God for that! At least, it's comfortable." She leaned forward, frowning a bit, and tucked a loose strand of hair back into place. "How is your room?"

"Well enough. Thea, did you know Stanton was going to be here?"

Thea didn't look at him. "I'd heard it, yes."

"I see." Francis studied her for a moment, and then, when she didn't go on, shifted, unable to get his long legs comfortable in the velvet-upholstered lady's chair. "Miss Powell is dashed pretty."

Thea looked at him in the mirror again. "Yes, she is."

"Are you sure you want to stay, Thea? We could leave. Say there's trouble at Linwood, or something—"

"Don't be silly, Fran!" Thea forced herself to laugh. "There's nothing between Stanton and me."

"I don't want you to be hurt," he said quietly.

"I won't be." She patted Francis's cheek as he rose. "Was that the bell for luncheon I heard a few minutes ago?"

"Yes, I think so. Shall we go?"

"Let me just wash my face, and I shall be with you directly."

A few moments later, having changed her gown, Thea emerged into the hall where Francis waited for her. The corridor was long, lined with carpets and lighted by cast-iron sconces. "It's like a maze," she said.

"I remember the way." Francis took her arm and conducted her down the corridors to the wide marble staircase. "Thea, what do you suppose she sees in him?"

"Who?"

"Miss Powell. What does she see in Stanton? There's no denying his reputation, and he's too old for her by far."

Thea's lips thinned. She'd thought they were done discussing Jeremy's engagement. "Miss Powell knows what she's doing, Fran. You can depend on that."

Francis stared at her. "Thea, are you jealous?"

"Don't be silly!" Again, she forced a laugh. "But I am not as blinded by a pretty face as you gentlemen are."

"No, only by a handsome one," Francis muttered.

"There's no call for that," she said sharply.

"Sorry." His voice was sulky. "But you make her sound calculating."

"I think she is. Or, rather, her mother is. Francis—" Thea stopped, her hand on his arm—"It doesn't do to ignore a person's faults, no matter how attractive she might be. I learned that the hard way."

"Dash it, Thea, you don't have to lecture me! I know she's not perfect."

"Do you?" Thea's look held both amusement and concern. "She is betrothed, Fran. Even if she weren't, she's a terrible flirt."

"I know," he said gloomily. "I saw the way Ware was hanging all over her."

"Well, there's no danger of anything there, though I'm sure Mrs. Powell would like there to be. I wonder," she began, and then stopped.

"What?"

"Nothing." Thea shook her head. "Come, we must hurry. They've waited luncheon long enough for us." She hurried Francis into the dining room before he could enquire again what it was she had thought of. If Evadne thought she had a chance at a higher title, she might just take it, especially if someone encouraged her. Thea had no reason to believe that Evadne would listen to her, but she might be able to convince her that Lord Ware was interested in her. It was appalling that she would even consider doing such a thing, but the idea

90

had taken possession of her mind and would not let go. For, if Evadne set off after bigger game, Jeremy would be free.

The sun came out while the party was at luncheon, and afterward the weather was considered dry enough for a walk through the estate's extensive gardens. Everyone seized on a plan that most would have considered dull several days earlier with pleasure.

"My dear, you have no idea how dreary it's been here, with all the rain!" Moira said to Thea as they walked down still-damp gravel paths in the rose garden, not yet in bloom. Overhead the sky was a watery blue, and the sun peeped fitfully from behind the clouds. "Rochester had such plans, and he was unhappy at having them upset, poor dear. But I expect things will change now."

"Yes," Thea murmured, adjusting the cashmere shawl she had tossed over her shoulders. At luncheon she had noticed that the guests were an odd assortment. She wasn't pleased to see Lord Pelham, who had been Francis's boon companion in town, and she had been surprised to see Jeremy and Mr. DeVilliers at the same gathering. And Thea sensed Evadne's dismay at seeing her. Surely Moira knew of the gossip concerning her and Jeremy, Thea thought, and wondered just what the duchess was up to.

"But you planned it that way, did you not, ma'am?" DeVilliers suddenly appeared beside them, bowing briefly over Moira's hand, looking up at her from under hooded eyes.

"Why would I do such a thing, sir?" Moira smiled up at him. "I merely wished to bring my friends together."

"Mm-hm." Roger brushed carelessly at the curl on his forehead as he fell into pace with the two women.

"You sound as if you don't believe me, Roger."

"Do I?" He feigned innocence. "Forgive me. Rochester appears to be enjoying himself."

"Yes, he does like having guests here. He's quite proud of the castle, the dear."

"And it appears he is about to show it off to Lady Chatleigh," DeVilliers mused.

Moira followed his gaze, and her eyes narrowed. Thea only saw Lady Chatleigh smiling politely at the duke, but Moira must have seen something else. "Pray excuse me," she murmured, and went off in pursuit of her husband.

"Moira protects what is hers," DeVilliers commented, and turned to Thea, who was gazing at him steadily. "Ma'am?" He held out his arm.

"Thank you." Thea rested her hand on his as they began walking again. She had the oddest feeling that he had engineered this meeting, though she couldn't for the life of her imagine why. Though she didn't know DeVilliers well, she had noticed that, for all his seeming languor, he usually managed to get his way. "Are you enjoying your stay here, sir?"

DeVilliers shrugged. "Well enough. I expect matters will improve now."

"Yes, so you said before. I'm not sure what you mean."

"Why, the weather, ma'am," he said, smiling.

"Oh, of course. The weather."

"Mind you, I'm not sure I trust our hostess. I've been wondering for the past few days what she is up to."

"You think she plans mischief, sir?"

"I wouldn't put it past her."

Thea stopped to admire an early bloom. "I did wonder about the choice of guests."

"Let us be honest, shall we, ma'am? You're referring to Stanton and myself, are you not?"

"Yes."

He sighed, the droop of his shoulders denoting supreme dejection. "It is a trial, but I will bear up."

Thea couldn't help it; she burst out laughing. "Oh, gammon, sir! You sound like a much put-upon young girl!"

Roger's eyes, no longer hooded, gleamed with unexpected brightness, and he let out a laugh. "See through me, do you?"

"Yes. I must tell you, sir, that I never was much of an admirer of Byron."

"The ladies seem to like the prose." Roger studied her. "Do you know, I think Stanton's a fool."

Thea's eyes flew to his. "Why, what a thing to say, sir!"

"Really? When he has treated you as he has?"

"I've no complaints."

"I don't know, myself, what he sees in that ninny when he has you."

"Gammon!" she said roundly. "To compare me with Miss Powell!"

"Of course. My apologies. There is no comparison."

"Of course not. She is young and lovely and—"

"Silly, which is one thing you are not. And you have your own beauty, ma'am."

Thea stared at him and then laughed. "You deal in Spanish coin, sir."

"Not in this matter." DeVilliers tucked her arm

through his as they resumed their walk. "You are much to be preferred to her."

"Most would not agree with you."

DeVilliers's gaze was peculiarly intent as it traveled over her face. "Ah, but I like to believe I am more discriminating than most. Stanton is a bigger fool than I thought."

"I beg your pardon?" a voice inquired frostily, and they turned to see Jeremy standing behind them. Thea started and pulled away.

"Good afternoon, Stanton," DeVilliers said urbanely. "Good to be out of doors at last, is it not?"

Jeremy looked at him hard, but his voice when he spoke was civil enough. "Good afternoon," he said, his eyes cool. "The duchess is looking for you, sir."

"Is she, indeed. I must not keep her waiting, then. You will excuse me, my dear?" He turned to Thea, bowing over her hand. "You are becoming most popular."

"Thank you," Thea stammered, her cheeks pink as he sketched a bow and then strolled away. It was a most novel sensation, to have two men competing for her attention. And this, in company with the lovely Miss Powell! Very odd, she thought. And most pleasant.

"Damned man-milliner," Jeremy growled beside her, and she looked up.

"Did you wish to see me about something, sir?"

"Yes. What the devil do you think you're doing with him?"

"With whom?" Thea asked in surprise.

"DeVilliers, of course."

"Jeremy, what in the world—"

"I don't wish to see you with him again, Thea."

"Who are you to order me about?" she demanded.

"As we are both very fond of telling the world, Jeremy, we are merely friends!"

Jeremy's eyes narrowed. "What is that supposed to mean?"

Thea's anger left her as quickly as it had come, and her shoulders slumped. "Jeremy, don't you know what people say about us?"

"Idle gossip." Jeremy dismissed all the talk, all the speculation, with a wave of his hand. "We know better. But you are right, of course. I have no right to tell you what to do. Except as a friend, of course."

"Of course." Thea linked her arm through his and they continued down the path. "Where is Miss Powell?"

"With her mama and the duke." He snorted with laughter. "Learning about the prices of the duke's more exotic flowers."

Thea smiled. "Mrs. Powell is in alt over being here, is she not? What an odd collection of guests we are."

"Yes. Some odder than others."

"Jeremy, what is between you two?"

"DeVilliers, you mean?" Jeremy shrugged. "Old history."

"Then, why—"

"The man's a blackguard. I would not see you hurt."

"I'm sorry, Jeremy, but I find him charming. I do!" she exclaimed when he turned toward her. "I am more than twenty, you know, and I can take care of myself."

Jeremy's eyes searched hers. "Perhaps. In some ways."

"Why, what does that mean?"

"It means you may not be aware of a person's true nature. You do tend to hold people at a distance, Thea."

"Nonsense, I don't do that!"

"I think you do. You hold me off."

"Just because I wouldn't become your mistress, sir?"

"No, Thea, of course not!" He looked down at her, exasperated. "Very well, have it your way. But be careful of DeVilliers."

Thea freed herself from his grasp. "I shall see whom I wish, sir. I am not your fiancée," she called over her shoulder as she walked away.

Jeremy hastened to catch up with her. "You're taking everything I say the wrong way, Thea."

"Then stop telling me what to do! That may work with Miss Powell, but it does not with me."

"I'm aware of that," he muttered. "You're too damned independent. Come." He held out his arm. "I believe we've seen enough of gardens for one day."

"Oh, very well." Thea took his arm. "Perhaps we'll find that the duke has thought of something for our entertainment."

"Spare us from that, at least," Jeremy said.

A silvery laugh caught their attention as they neared the castle, and they looked toward the source. Evadne, clad in sunny yellow muslin, much beruffled about the hem, with a parasol to match, was walking with Lord Ware and Lord Pelham, apparently laughing at something the latter had said. The muscles of Jeremy's arm tightened under her hand, and he muttered something under his breath.

Thea glanced up at him in surprise, and then back at Evadne, who was now smiling up at Lord Ware. The idea that had flitted into her mind earlier surfaced once again. It just might be possible to shift Evadne's affection from Jeremy to someone else, especially if the match were more advantageous. It would be meddling, she admitted, but it would be worth it, to ensure Jeremy's happiness.

In her room later, dressing for dinner, Thea stopped in the midst of fastening her pearls and leaned forward to study her reflection. Two different men had told her two vastly different things about herself that afternoon. Perhaps she did hold people at a distance, as Jeremy had accused, but she had her reasons. As for being a beauty ... She frowned, studying her reflection. Try though she might, she could see only the same collection of features that had looked back at her all her life, the high forehead with its widow's peak, the large, too-intelligent gray eyes, the short, snub nose, the firm chin, and a mouth that was considered too wide for beauty. "Oh, nonsense, Thea!" she snapped, and whirled toward the door, the silk of her severely cut dark blue gown swirling around her. She opened the door and came face to face with Evadne.

For a moment they stared at each other, and then Thea smiled her most gracious smile. "Good evening, Miss Powell."

"Good evening, ma'am." Evadne, wearing a gown of white muslin, cut low at the neck, with short, puffed sleeves, fell into step beside Thea, eyeing her warily. "I had no idea you were to be a guest here."

"A late invitation," Thea said. Evadne looked young, and more than a little defenseless. In spite of herself, pity mingled with Thea's annoyance. "You are enjoying your stay?"

"Yes, I was."

So much for defenseless, Thea thought. "I am not surprised. Lord Ware seems quite taken with you. Not to mention Lord Pelham."

"Oh, do you think so?" Evadne brightened. "Ma'am, is that your brother who came with you?"

"Yes, my brother Francis. Why?"

"Oh, no reason." Evadne's fingers toyed with the blue satin ribbons that streamed down the front of her gown. "Do you think Lord Pelham is really taken with me?"

Thea glanced down at her again and her heart contracted. Young, so young, and so lovely. No wonder Jeremy preferred her. And Mr. DeVilliers thought that she was a beauty? *Hah!* "Why, yes, I do. He seemed most impressed by the Bach you were playing this afternoon, you know. And so did Lord Ware."

"Yes, that is my best piece," she said naively. "Do you know Lord Pelham well, ma'am?"

"Why, no, he's somewhat younger than I." But just the right age for Evadne. Thea's brain raced. Here was the opportunity she had sought. "But the *on-dit* has been that he is looking for a wife."

"Really? I mean, that is most interesting, ma'am. Of course, that means nothing to me. I am engaged to Stanton, as you know."

Thea glanced quickly at her, but Evadne's face appeared guileless. "Of course, but pardon me for thinking that you haven't much in common with him."

"Oh, that doesn't matter." Evadne waved her hand in dismissal of Thea's words as they reached the bottom of the stairs. "I shall be a viscountess, Mrs. Jameson," she said, laying the slightest bit of stress on the word "Mrs.", and glided into the drawing room. Thea followed, fuming with sudden anger. She had to rescue Jeremy from the clutches of that vain, silly girl! She had to.

Dinner, consisting of rare roast beef and a baked ham,

poached trout and a ragout of veal, and, to finish, a wheel of cheddar and a trifle, was long and uneventful. Afterward the ladies retired to the blue drawing room, where Lady Catherine played on the pianoforte and Lydia sat on a sofa with Lady Pelham, discussing, of all things, needlework patterns. When the gentlemen came in the talk turned to the sights that might be visited in the neighborhood, and an expedition to view the nearby ruins of the original castle was proposed for the next day. All welcomed the plan as a release from the tedium that had gripped them for the past few days. When someone suggested setting up tables for cards, the idea was met with much enthusiasm. "Come, Mrs. Jameson," the duke said, holding out his hand. "I'll exercise a host's privilege and ask you to partner me."

"I'd be honored, sir," Thea said, taking the duke's hand. The guests stood, talking idly, as servants began to set up the tables.

"Pity the weather is what it is," he went on. "Hoped we could get in some shooting. Hear you're a crack shot, what?"

Thea didn't look at him as she sat at a table. "My father taught me, yes."

"Then it is settled. Must come back in the fall for the hunting."

"Rochester loves to shoot," Moira volunteered, leaning for a moment on her husband's shoulder. "Pray do not let him bore you, Althea. He'll go on for hours if he can."

Thea concentrated on shuffling the cards. "Actually, Your Grace, I dislike shooting."

The duke looked scandalized. "What? And you taught by one of the best—"

"I am sorry, sir," she said firmly. "I hate guns."

"Nonsense, girl, just because of what happened with your husband—"

"Was Mr. Jameson shot?" Evadne asked in seeming innocence.

Moira shot her a look, and then, seeing that Thea, riffling her cards, pretended not to have heard, answered. "Mr. Jameson was killed in a duel."

"But how romantic!" Evadne exclaimed. "What did you do to provoke him, ma'am?"

Francis cut across her words. "Do you think Parliament will do anything about reform this session, duke?"

The duke blinked at him. "Reform? Reform, sir?"

"Yes." Francis's gaze was steady, in spite of the duke's glare. "Parliamentary reform."

"Really, Fran," Thea protested.

"Reform isn't needed," Lord Ware said, for once aligning himself with his father.

"Of course it is." Francis leaned forward, a lock of hair falling untidily over his forehead. "It's not fair, power being held in the hands of the few—"

"As it should be," the duke growled. "We're bred to it, boy. What, you'd have us ruled by a rabble, like in France?"

"No, sir, but times are changing, and people want some say in their destiny. Good God, sir, we asked the common man to fight our wars, and what have we given him in return? Most can't even find work."

"So you'd give power to an ill-educated mob?" DeVilliers said, sounding amused.

"No, of course not," Francis said impatiently. "I don't want to see mob rule any more than anyone else, but if something's not done, that's what might happen. People are starving and can't feed their children. Why, the Corn Laws—"

A low growl interrupted him. "The Corn Laws," the duke began, his voice rising to a roar, and quickly Jeremy broke in.

"Why don't we discuss this after dinner tomorrow, when the ladies aren't present? I'm sure there are more suitable topics to discuss over cards. Evadne?" He smiled at her, holding out his arm.

Evadne tossed her curls. "Speak for yourself. I don't want to play boring old cards. I'd rather try the spinet in the music room." She turned to Francis, her smile ravishing. "Will you escort me there, sir?"

Chapter 7

Stunned silence at Evadne's rudeness filled the room, and all eyes turned to Jeremy to see how he would react. "Sir?" Francis said. "Do you mind?"

"We don't need to ask his permission." Evadne tugged at Francis's arm. "Come, I want to see the spinet."

Lord Pelham jumped to his feet. "Er, perhaps I could join you. That is," he went on, as he caught his mother's eye, "perhaps Lady Catherine and I could accompany you."

"If you wish," Evadne said, sounding supremely bored, and turned toward the door. With her hand still on Francis's arm, she all but dragged him away, leaving him little choice but to follow.

Thea's first impulse was to run to Jeremy, an idea she rejected after seeing his face. He was, for once, absolutely still; she didn't need to touch him to know that his arms would be stiff with anger. Had Evadne no sense of decorum, treating him so in front of others? She was young, yes, but youth did not excuse such poor manners. And to choose Francis, of all people, to attend her!

Someone snickered, and Jeremy's head swiveled toward DeVilliers. For a long moment they stared at each other, their gazes cool and measuring. "Can't say I blame her," DeVilliers drawled, and something sparked to life in Jeremy's eyes.

"I daresay she'll be safe enough," he said mildly. "Even if she'd gone with you."

DeVilliers half-rose, and then sat again. Thea found herself holding her breath. There was something between the two men, though no one quite seemed to know what it was. "Of course." DeVilliers picked up his cards with a practiced, negligent air. "Unless you've reason to mistrust your fiancée."

Jeremy took a step forward, his hands clenched, and Moira intervened. "Come, sir," she said, smiling winningly up at him, her eyes very green. "I intend to have you."

Jeremy looked down at Moira, startled for the moment out of his anger. "I beg your pardon?"

"As a partner, of course. For whist."

"Oh, of course. For whist." He gave DeVilliers one last look, and then escorted Moira to a table.

Thank heavens, Thea thought as play began, that DeVilliers and Lady Chatleigh were at her table. There would be no trouble between the two men tonight, but who could predict what the rest of the week would bring. It seemed as if DeVilliers were goading Jeremy for some reason, something that had to do with Evadne. And that was another thing, Thea thought, as he discarded a card. Jeremy's engagement was not yet broken,

103

but she suspected he was not pleased with his fiancée. That served her purpose quite well, though in this case he should know better. Miss Powell and Francis? Really!

"A good-looking young man, your brother," DeVilliers said after the game had been going on for a few moments.

"Yes, he takes after our father," Thea said absently, tossing down a card.

The duke grunted. "Really, Mrs. Jameson, I fear your mind isn't on the game," he remonstrated.

"Which is to our advantage, is it not, ma'am?" DeVilliers said, smiling across the table at Lady Chatleigh. "In fact, I believe we take this trick." He spread his cards on the table, and the duke rumbled again. "Miss Powell seemed quite taken with him."

Thea turned from saying something to Lady Chatleigh. "I beg your pardon, sir?"

"I believe Miss Powell is taken with your brother. She was flirting quite a bit with him this evening."

"Miss Powell flirts with everyone."

"So she does." DeVilliers glanced at Jeremy, who appeared amused by something Moira had said. "It could be useful."

"Sir?" Thea said, looking up.

"It is of no moment, ma'am. Our hand, I believe," he said, smiling, and laid down his cards.

"Oh, I say! We cannot let them get away with that, Mrs. Jameson," the duke protested, and all other considerations were forgotten in the competition to win at cards. It was only much later that Thea would remember, and wonder about, DeVilliers' words.

The morning dawned cloudy, and the members of the party held their breath, fearing that rain would again confine them indoors. There was a collective sigh of relief when the sun came out at midmorning. The expedition to the nearby ruins would not have to be canceled. The duke was the most delighted of anyone, arranging for transportation and a picnic with childlike glee. The older members of the party would travel sedately in several carriages; everyone else would ride.

The duke set himself the task of finding suitable mounts for everyone. Thus Thea found herself staring, her heart sinking, at a broad-chested, slightly sway-backed mare, whose gentle disposition made her perfectly appropriate for a lady's mount. The duke meant to be kind, she told herself, letting the groom assist her into the saddle. He probably didn't realize that she had been riding since she could walk.

Across the stableyard, Evadne was staring at her mount with like disapproval, though hers was more than evident in the frown on her forehead and her pout, not assumed for effect this time. She turned away as Lord Ware approached to help her mount. "No," she said, her voice loud in its petulance, "I won't ride that nag, I won't!"

"But, Miss Powell," Lord Ware remonstrated, "Daisy is perfectly safe and gentle—"

"Daisy! What a name for a horse!" She spun, pointing at a stallion just being led out from the stables, dancing and snorting. "I want that one."

"But, Miss Powell! That's my horse!"

"I don't care! I want it."

"Is there a problem?" Jeremy crossed the yard, having given the reins of his own horse, a black stallion named Lightning, to a groom.

"Oh, Stanton! They want to make me ride that poky old thing!" she declared, clutching at his arm. Behind her Lord Ware was frowning. "Please tell him to let me ride that one instead. Please!"

"You know I can't do that, Evadne," Jeremy said, patting her hand. "The mare doesn't look so bad—"

"Ooh!" Evadne stamped her foot. "You ride her, then, and I'll take yours!"

Thea, a fascinated bystander to this scene, had walked with her horse to the group. Evadne was playing into her hands. Let Jeremy see for himself what his fiancée was really like. "Dear, do you think you can handle him?" she asked, her voice sweet.

"Perfectly," Evadne said in clipped tones. "Can you handle yours?"

"Better than you can handle yourself," Thea muttered, wheeling away.

"Miss Powell, if you mind so much," Lord Ware began.

"Miss Powell will be perfectly happy to ride whatever you choose for her," Jeremy interrupted.

"Yes, well, I was going to say that we have other horses. They're not lady's mounts—"

"Oh, pooh!" Evadne tossed her head. "Who wants a lady's mount except older people? I'd like to look over the others, sir," she said, and placed her hand on his arm, walking away without a backward glance.

Across the yard, Thea, who had stiffened at Evadne's

last comment, turned and rode out into the lane, fuming. She didn't look up as the sound of hooves clopping next to her announced that she had company.

"So the little one has a temper," DeVilliers said.

"The little one is a spoiled baby," Thea answered, between clenched teeth.

"Oh, beyond a doubt. Come, pull up, Mrs. Jameson. It won't do to outdistance the others."

"On this horse? Hardly likely," she said, but she did slow her mount, easing over to the side of the lane to wait for the remainder of the party.

"Why did you not ask for another mount?"

"I thought I was being polite."

"A lesson for you, ma'am. Sometimes being polite is a mistake. Ah, here she comes now. On a more spirited nag, I see."

Thea turned, hoping briefly that Evadne was having trouble, but as she neared it was obvious that she knew how to handle her horse, a spirited bay mare. Lord Pelham was to one side of her, Francis on the other.

"I say, Thea, what is that you're riding?" Francis exclaimed as he passed by.

"A lady's mount," Evadne said before Thea could answer. "Do try not to fall behind too far, ma'am."

"Blast!" Thea exclaimed under her breath, and DeVilliers cast her a look of amusement and commiseration.

"I don't know what Stanton sees in her when he has you," he said, and she looked up in surprise.

"Sir?"

"Later, ma'am. If you will excuse me, I would like to speak to our hostess. Stanton is approaching, so you shall not be alone."

"Thank you." Thea looked after him, her brow puckered as she moved out into the lane, keeping to one side so that Jeremy could catch up with her. He gave her a quizzical look, but said nothing until they had been riding for a few moments.

"Did you put her up to that?" he said abruptly.

Thea looked up. "What? Who?"

"That." Jeremy pointed with his riding crop, and she saw that Evadne was riding quite close to Francis.

"Heavens, no! Why would I?"

"Jealousy."

"Oh, Jeremy!" Thea laughed, the last of her bad feeling finally dispelled. "I'm not jealous. I admit I was annoyed with her just now, but do you really think I'd use my own brother in such a way?" She smiled, secure that, in this instance, she was innocent. And, she thought, she had been right. Jeremy didn't like seeing Evadne with other men.

"No." Jeremy frowned. "Of course you wouldn't. Forgive me. I didn't think."

"Jeremy, is she giving you trouble?"

"Of course not." Jeremy's face was expressionless. "I am perfectly content with her."

"Oh." Thea rode in silence for a few moments. "She does flirt quite a bit," she ventured.

"She's young. She'll grow out of it," he said, with little conviction.

"Perhaps. Anyway, does it matter? You don't love her."

Jeremy hunched his shoulders, and his mount took exception to the movement, dancing sideways toward Thea. He took a moment to get the horse under control. "No."

Thea's heart contracted with sympathy. It was all very well to wish he'd see how unsuitable a bride Evadne was, but Thea hadn't expected that knowledge to hurt him. Impulsively she reached over and laid a hand on his arm. "At least, Jeremy, we'll always be friends."

Jeremy glanced down at her hand. "Yes," he said in an odd voice, and raised his eyes to hers. For a moment their gazes locked, and all knowledge of the world around her fell away from Thea. *Jeremy*, she thought, dazed.

"I say!" a voice came from behind them. "Hurry up, you two! You're holding everyone up, what?"

Jeremy glanced back. "My apologies, duke," he said to Rochester, riding close behind. "Come, Thea. Shall we ride?"

The sky brightened as the day went on, and by the time the party reached the ruins it was quite warm. Thea was glad to dismount, and she looked with interest at the remains of what had once been a considerable fortress, built just after the Norman conquest. One tower still stood, along with several of the walls, so that the layout of the castle was still visible. The spot was surprisingly peaceful, with green turf deep and springy underneath, and, over the crest of the rolling land, a glimpse of the distant Avon river, silver in the sun. Servants, sent ahead with hampers of food, were already busy setting up tables and serving the repast, cold chicken and ham, salad and a strawberry tart, and champagne.

"A simple alfresco meal," DeVilliers murmured.

Thea looked up, smiling. "Well, sir, you could hardly expect our host to slight us."

The breeze ruffled his thick, dark hair, sweeping the

109

curl away from his face, and he reached up to smooth it down. "No, indeed. I believe he is enjoying this party more than any of the guests." They both turned to look at the duke, whose thin face was beaming with pleasure as he looked down at his wife. "May I sit with you at luncheon?"

"Why, certainly, sir." Thea smiled again as she linked her arm through his. She glanced up as DeVilliers seated her, to see Jeremy, sitting some distance away. Evadne, by his side, was talking and laughing at something Lord Ware, on her other side, had said, but Jeremy, to Thea's surprise, was looking straight at her, frowning. With an effort, Thea turned her gaze away. At least Mr. DeVilliers found her attractive. Thea had no idea why he had chosen her, among all the ladies present, for a flirtation, but she was not complaining. His attention was balm to a soul wounded by Jeremy's engagement to another woman.

Beside her, DeVilliers congratulated himself on both his good fortune and his foresight. Mrs. Jameson wasn't the most beautiful woman present, but she was certainly one of the most pleasing. And no one's fool. With her he dropped his brooding air and took up, instead, a light flirtation that she appeared to enjoy. Stanton, he thought, not for the first time, was a fool. If a man had to marry money, he could do worse than Althea. And Roger had to marry for money. He hadn't thought of courting Althea, but it was a surprisingly pleasant idea. The extra advantage was that Stanton, by the looks of it, didn't like his being with her at all. No, not at all.

DeVilliers had no intention of revealing what was between him and Stanton, nor did he intend to forget it.

Originally he had hoped to use Evadne as his means of revenge, but she had made it clear, without words, that she wasn't the least interested in him. After all, he had neither title nor money, and Evadne was nothing if not shrewd. Althea, on the other hand, was, if more sensible, also perhaps more romantic. She would marry only if she chose, and not because of practical considerations. If he could take Althea for his own, revenge would be his, and it would be very sweet, indeed. He was very glad he'd come to this house party.

After luncheon the party broke up into smaller groups to explore the ruins. The sun began to hide behind ever-thickening clouds, and a cool breeze had come up, but the party was loath to leave. Like children released from the schoolroom, they trod through the castle, their voices echoing through ruined corridors and crumbling stairs. Thea was joined in her explorations by DeVilliers and Lord and Lady Chatleigh; the duke was with his daughter, and, surprisingly, Agatha Powell; Lydia, looking fetching in a mauve silk gown with a matching cottage bonnet, was with Lord Peter, the duke's brother. Jeremy took a long look at the dark shadows stretching upward in the tower, where several people had gathered, and then turned gallantly to Lady Pelham and her sister, offering to stay with them. Evadne, much to her surprise, found herself standing alone under a gracefully arched doorway. She was miffed. Having spent the better part of the day in the admiring company of Lord Pelham and Lord Ware, she found it quite lowering to be expected to explore some dull, dirty ruins by herself. She had just stamped her foot in annoyance and uttered a distinctly unladylike oath when Francis ambled up, his hands thrust into his coat pockets.

111

"Left alone, Miss Powell?" he enquired, and Evadne, too annoyed to remember to pout, frowned instead.

"Yes! Mr. Pelham is chasing after that insipid Lady Catherine, and I don't know where Lord Ware is!"

"I see." Amusement danced in Francis's eyes. He was not about to admit that he had disposed of both those worthy gentlemen by less than worthy means, having hinted to each that other ladies were interested in them. He had even gone so far as to sacrifice his sister to the cause. "May I suggest you make do with me?"

"I'll have to, won't I?" she said ungraciously, and turned away. "Come, if we have to explore these boring old ruins, let's get it over with."

"Very well." Francis followed behind her as she plunged inside the crumbling walls, allowing himself a smile at the way her skirts twitched from side to side. "When are you and Stanton to marry?" he asked as he caught up with her.

Evadne tossed her head. "It hasn't been decided yet. I expect before winter, though."

"Stanton is not rushing matters, then."

"He is a gentleman, sir."

"I'm not sure I'd be."

Evadne stopped, turning toward him. He was not her idea of the ideal gentleman; he was too tall for one thing, and though his coat could only have come from Weston, it still managed to hang loosely on his lanky figure. Besides, he had no title. However, the admiration of any man was better than nothing. "Why, sir, whatever do you mean?"

"Stop it." Francis reached out and touched one of her dimples. She drew back, startled by her reaction to the feather-light touch. "Save your flirtatious ways for someone else. You and I don't need to flirt, Evadne."

She backed away, her eyes uncertain, and then took refuge in anger. "I did not give you permission to use my name!" she exclaimed, and flounced away.

"You will," Francis called after her as she nearly ran from the ruins. He emerged onto the lawn where the picnic had been held, and Thea, looking harassed, approached him.

"Hide me," she said, putting her hand on his arm.

"Why?"

"From the duke and his son! Lord Ware has taken the most unexpected liking to me!"

Francis let out a laugh.

"It isn't funny, Fran, he has been following me around like a moonling all afternoon."

"I wouldn't worry about him," he said, and she followed his gaze to where Ware was gazing adoringly at a vivacious Evadne. Thea looked from the girl to her brother, and frowned at the sudden solemn look on his face.

"So Miss Powell has regained her admirers," she said lightly. "Foolish of me to expect to be popular when she's around."

"Yes, she is popular," Francis said, in such an odd voice that she sent him another swift look. "But, do you know, Thea, I don't think she's ever really gotten what she wants."

"Oh, Fran! She has everything. She's the most dreadfully spoiled girl I've ever seen."

Francis shook his head. "No, Thea, you're out there. Oh, I grant you she has everything, but sometimes everything isn't enough."

"Now what is that supposed to mean?"

"Nothing." Francis shook his head again. "Pelham and Ware are talking about visiting a local tavern to-night," he remarked offhandedly, not looking at her. Thea shot him a glance. She had nothing against Pelham, except his youth and immaturity, qualities that had led Francis into trouble in town. Pelham could afford to gamble; Francis could not. Everything in her longed to burst out against this proposed expedition, but for once she considered her words first.

"That sounds more interesting than playing cards for penny stakes," she said, her voice carefully neutral, and it was Francis's turn to look surprised.

"Perhaps. But it also means I'll have Miss Powell to myself." He bent to kiss her cheek. "If you'll excuse me, oh best of sisters, I'd like to speak to our host," he said, and walked away, leaving Thea to stare after him, surprised and mystified. Francis had indeed changed his ways, she thought, pleased. She only wished she could claim credit for it.

"Miss Powell claims another victim, I fear," DeVilliers said behind her.

Thea turned. "I beg your pardon, sir?"

"Your brother."

"Oh, I do hope not!" Thea stared after Francis, who was conversing with Lady Catherine, and shook her head. "No, I'm sure you are mistaken, sir."

"Are you?" Roger's smile was lazy. "No matter, ma'am, since she is already betrothed."

"Yes, of course." Thea glanced up at him, curiously. "Tell me, sir. Why aren't you one of her admirers?"

"An impertinent question, ma'am." DeVilliers waved

his hand languidly. "But, as you ask, I'll tell you only that I have, shall we say, more sophisticated tastes?"

There may have been a chance of mistaking his words; there was no mistaking the look in his eyes. Curiously, it only made her angry. "I'd rather not be caught between you and Stanton, sir."

Roger's eyes gleamed. "Perceptive of you. Actually, Althea—"

"Using Christian names so soon?" a voice drawled behind them, and they turned to see Jeremy. Thea started and pulled back, feeling guilty, though she didn't know why.

"Afternoon, Stanton," DeVilliers said. "As you can see, Mrs. Jameson and I are conversing."

"Yes." Jeremy looked from one to the other, his eyes hard. "I wouldn't have thought her your style, sir, unless you have other motives."

"Jeremy!" Thea protested.

"You are insulting, Stanton."

"Am I?" Jeremy's eyes remained fixed on his. "Do you wish to do something about it?"

DeVilliers glared at him, and then made a small bow to Thea. "My apologies, ma'am, but I fear I'm not welcome here anymore."

"But," Thea protested as he turned and walked away. She then turned on Jeremy. "How dare you chase him away! Who do you think you are?"

Jeremy shifted from one foot to the other. "Have you a *tendre* for him, Althea?"

"No! But whether I do or not is none of your affair."

"I would not see you with him, Thea—"

"My life is my own, Jeremy," she cut in, "and I do

not appreciate being made to feel like a bone pulled between two dogs!"

"What I did, I did for your own good."

His voice was icy, and that made Thea angrier. How dare he presume so much! "I'll make my own decisions, thank you!"

"Do so then, madam," he said even more frostily. "So independent, Thea, and so lonely, forever holding people at arm's length."

"I don't do that!" she protested again.

"Well, I wish you joy of your choice, madam, though I doubt you'll have it."

"Ooh!" Thea stamped her foot in frustration and whirled away, her arms crossed on her chest.

After a moment, Jeremy followed her. He cast an apprehensive eye up at the old stone walls, but when it became obvious that Thea planned to walk on the outside of the ruined castle rather than within, his shoulders relaxed. "Thea!" he called, and she turned. "Wait. I'll walk with you."

"I don't know why you'd wish to, if I'm so disagreeable," she said, but she stopped to wait for him.

"You know that wasn't what I meant."

Thea didn't answer for a moment. "I know," she said finally. "But everyone seems to think it strange of me that I live alone. Why cannot I live my life as I choose?"

"God knows," he muttered. "It doesn't seem to be the way in our world."

Thea looked up at him in surprise as they walked along. "You, Jeremy? But I thought you did exactly as you please."

He shrugged. "If I did—well, a man has to face up to

his responsibilities sometime. But that doesn't mean I'll forget my friends." He stopped, looking down at her. "Thea, you don't intend to marry him, do you?"

"Mr. DeVilliers?" Thea sounded startled. "No, of course not. I don't intend to marry anyone. But if I did, Jeremy," she continued, her voice growing stern. "It would be my choice."

"I understand that, Thea." He looked up again at the ancient stone walls that brooded beside him. "But please think carefully before you do anything. I don't wish to see you unhappy."

"I know Mr. DeVilliers hasn't the best reputation. But then, Jeremy, neither have you."

Jeremy winced slightly. "I suppose I deserve that. No, my life hasn't been blameless, Thea. Lord knows I've made my share of mistakes." He gazed down at her intently. "And there's one, if I could undo it—"

"Jeremy." Thea took a step back, unnerved by the way he was looking at her. There was a warmth there she'd never seen before. "Are you saying our friendship is a mistake?"

"Not our friendship, Thea." There was a wealth of meaning in his tone as he approached her, slowly, one cautious step at a time, as one might approach a frightened bird. "Maybe it was never meant to be just a friendship."

"Jeremy." She stepped back again. Why she looked up just then she never afterward knew, but look up she did, at the high stone wall behind them. What she saw made her freeze. High above, at the top of the wall, a block of stone tottered, teetered, and then fell free, directly above Jeremy's head.

"Jeremy!" she shrieked, and launched herself at him, throwing him to the ground, as the stone came whistling down.

Chapter 8

Bodies atop him, everywhere, and the smell of death in his nostrils. Nearby, a horse screamed, dying on the field of Waterloo, just as so many of his compatriots had died. Jeremy panicked. He had to get free, else he'd die here, suffocated by the press of bodies that had fallen on him when the shell had struck them. Someone screamed his name, a woman, though that was impossible, a dream, a dying wish. No, he was not going to die! Rearing up, Jeremy threw all his weight upward, and suddenly the suffocating pressure on his chest was gone.

"Jeremy!" The woman's voice spoke again, startled and frightened, and his vision cleared. He was not at Waterloo. He was, instead, within the peaceful precincts of a ruined castle, lying on thick, lush grass, unhurt except for having the breath knocked out of him. Just a few feet distant sprawled Thea, clumsily pushing herself up to her elbow and staring at him, her eyes wide, her face pale. Her dress was rucked up to her knees, he noticed almost dispassionately, displaying a lace-trimmed petticoat and an expanse of silk stockings.

"You have fine legs, Thea," he said.

She drew back, scrambling to her knees. "Jeremy!"

"What?" He braced himself on his elbows, and for the first time the strangeness of the situation struck him. "What the devil did you do that for, Thea, knocking me over like that? Don't you know I could have crushed you?"

"Oh, Jeremy." A hand to her mouth, she pointed. "It nearly hit you."

Jeremy turned his head. With that same strange feeling of unreality, he noted that there was now a huge block of stone embedded in the turf, just a few feet from where he sat. Now he remembered, the whistling noise he had thought was a shell, the thump that he had thought was the explosion of gunfire. It had been the stone, hurtling down from the castle wall. "What the devil—"

"I looked up," Thea babbled, rising up on her knees. "I looked up, and I could see it starting to fall, and I realized it was coming toward you, and—oh, Jeremy!" She launched herself on him again. He fell over, the breath knocked out of him again, her body a warm weight atop him. "You might have been killed!"

"But I wasn't." He was alive. Death had nearly caught him and he had cheated it again, all because of the woman soft and warm in his arms. Slowly he reached up and tucked a tendril of hair back behind her ear. "You saved me, Thea," he said gravely.

"I had to. Jeremy, I couldn't lose you, I—"

"What, Thea? No, look at me." He caught at her chin, forcing her to meet his gaze. Her eyes were vulnerable, turbulent and dark with emotion, the same emotions that were raging through him. In that moment they were completely open to each other, saying with their eyes all that they dared not say with words, sharing everything, holding nothing back. He might have been killed. He might have died, but instead, he was alive, gloriously alive.

His hand caught Thea about the neck in a grip that was almost savage, and his lips strained to hers. Thea made a startled sound in the back of her throat and pulled back, but he held her fast. Alive, he was alive, and the kiss celebrated that fact. No gentle kiss, of wooing or seduction; his mouth opened over hers, his tongue demanding that her lips open. Again Thea made a noise, and yet her lips softened, opened, her body relaxed upon his. He took immediate advantage of her surrender, plundering her mouth with his tongue, gripping her head so that their lips met just so. He wanted her with an ache he'd never felt before, not even in the frantic passion of the months after his return from the war. All those women, all those wasted nights. It was Thea. He'd been searching, and she'd been here all along. "Thea," he murmured, and she jerked her head back.

"Jeremy." The hands that had been cradling his face were suddenly pushing at his shoulders. "No, Jeremy, stop, this is wrong—"

"It was you, Thea." Denied access to her lips, he reached up to press hard kisses on her throat. "All along, it was you. Why didn't I see it?"

"Oh, Jeremy. No. No!" This as he reached for her mouth again. She arched her head away. "Jeremy, let me go."

"You feel it, Thea, too. Don't you?' His eyes burned

121

into her, an almost tactile sensation. "You feel what's between us."

"You're engaged, Jeremy," she said flatly, and pulled back. Perhaps because he hadn't been expecting it, his hands loosened and he let her go. She scrambled to her feet and then stood a few feet away from him, eyeing him warily as he rose. "No, stay away—"

"Oh, the devil." Tugging at his neckcloth, Jeremy wheeled away before she could realize the obvious effect she had had on him. "Damn it, Thea. I'm sorry." He turned his head. "I never meant to treat you like that."

"You're engaged," she repeated.

He closed his eyes. So he was. In the eyes of his world, that didn't always mean anything. There was no love between him and Evadne, while what he felt for Thea—well, what did he feel? Desire, certainly, but that wasn't new. This need, this strange new urgency, however, was new. He wanted her. God, he wanted her, not just for a friend, not just for an *affaire*. But what he could offer her he did not know. "I don't love her."

"I didn't love Hugh, but I stayed faithful to him."

"No one would think anything of it, Thea."

"I would. And so would you."

"Would I?" He considered that for a moment. In the past, he wouldn't have thought twice about entering into an *affaire*. Now, though, she was right. It would bother him to be unfaithful to Thea. To Evadne, he corrected himself. "You're right. God help me, I don't know why, Thea, but you're right. God." Pulling at his neckcloth again, he moved in the direction of the block of stone. His legs, he noted dispassionately, weren't very steady, whether from his brush with death or passion, he couldn't say. "How the devil did this fall?"

Thea hesitated, and then walked over to him. In the light of what had just happened between them, the stone seemed a safe subject. "It must have been just ready to drop. Of all the miracles—"

"Unless someone pushed it."

Thea drew in her breath. "Why would someone do such a thing?"

"I don't know." Like the soldier he had been, he studied the wall, looking for other signs of crumbling and decay. "I'd wager there are stairs on the other side."

"But why, Jeremy? And who?"

"I don't know," he said again. "But we were lucky." His eyes caught hers, and again that silent communication passed between them. Thea, as lost to him as if the stone had found its mark. "Perhaps we'd best return to the others."

"Yes." Thea's voice shook a bit. "I think that would be best. Oh, dear, Jeremy, you're covered with mud."

"It can't be helped. Shall we?"

Thea hesitated, and then put her hand on the arm he held out to her. "Yes."

The sun had come out again, its rays golden as it touched on the ancient stone, making the turf glow a brilliant emerald. It illuminated the group that had gathered some distance from the ruins, highlighting the bright pastel frocks of the women and glinting off gold watch fobs. Lord Pelham and Lady Catherine were missing, Thea noted, likely still exploring the ruins. Everyone else was present.

The duchess was the first to see Thea and Jeremy, glancing toward them as they neared. Her eyes, usually so heavy-lidded, widened as she took in their appearance, and she hurried over to them. "Good heavens, what happened to you two?" Her smile turned arch. "We were wondering where you were."

"A stone from the ruins nearly fell on us," Jeremy said curtly, and startled exclamations broke out from the group. If he looked just a little harder at people, only Thea seemed to notice. "No, no, we weren't hurt. Mrs. Jameson is a bit shaken up."

"Of course, who wouldn't be?" Moira took Thea's arm. "Come, my dear, what a nasty experience for you."

"Yes," Thea murmured, watching Jeremy as he crossed to his fiancée. Just a moment before he had been kissing her as if she were his only hold to life, and now it was as if she didn't even exist. It hurt. It was as things were, as they should be, but it hurt.

"Stanton!" Evadne pulled back from the hand Jeremy held out to her. "But you're covered with mud!"

Jeremy dropped his hand and stepped back, a cool smile playing about his lips. "Forgive me for appearing before you like this. I'll change when we return to the castle."

"I should hope so! Why, if I got mud on this gown Mama would be furious."

"He could have been killed!" Thea exclaimed. Her voice was under control, but now that he was safe, now that they were back among other people, she kept seeing the stone falling, and Jeremy helpless beneath it. "And you complain that he's dirty—"

"Well, he wasn't killed, was he?" Evadne glanced at Francis, who was frowning. "He says he's not even hurt."

"Of course he would. It's a miracle he wasn't."

"How did it happen?" DeVillers asked.

"Ahem." The duke cleared his throat. "Afraid stones come loose from time to time. Ruin's not safe anymore. My apologies, ma'am, that it happened when you were near."

"Well." Moira spoke briskly. "Stanton and Mrs. Jameson won't wish to be kept standing around discussing it. It's time we returned to the castle. Come, Lionel."

"Yes, m'dear," the duke said, surprisingly meekly, and turned to follow her.

"What about me?" Evadne said, stamping her foot, and Francis, taking Thea's arm, turned.

"Oh, by all means, Miss Powell," he said coolly. "Come along, as well."

"But—" Evadne protested, staring after them. Moira led the way over to the horses and the others followed. No one was left to take her arm. "Oh, very well," she said, though there was no one to hear, and followed behind them, pouting.

"Damned odd thing to happen," Chatleigh commented to Jeremy as they mounted their horses, held by grooms. "Damned odd house party, if you ask me."

"Rather." Jeremy turned to ride beside Chatleigh. "Did you happen to notice where DeVilliers was when all this was going on?"

"So that's the lay of the land, is it?" Chatleigh glanced toward DeVilliers, who was helping Thea to mount her horse. "Sorry, Stanton. Afraid I don't pay too much attention to him."

"Neither do I, usually. But the stone could easily have fallen on Thea. Mrs. Jameson, I mean."

Lady Chatleigh, riding at her husband's side, leaned

forward, her auburn curls dancing with the motion. "Then you must watch out for her, sir."

Jeremy's eyes were grim as he followed Thea and DeVilliers with his eyes. "I intend to."

By Saturday afternoon, tensions were running high in Rochester Castle. Both Lord Pelham and Lord Ware continued to pay court to Evadne, which upset Lady Catherine considerably and annoyed the duchess; both saw Lady Catherine's chances of at last marrying slipping away from her. Francis, who before had been one of her admirers, now tended to stay with the other men, playing billiards or cards or even listening to the duke telling one of his interminable hunting stories. The Chatleighs were bored, though of course they took great pains not to show it, and Thea kept to herself, very quiet. Only Evadne seemed untouched by the tension, and there were few who thought that was to her credit.

Jeremy sought escape from the group in his host's large, well-stocked, and little-used library, hoping to find peace and instead mulling over the situation. Thinking about what might have happened, and how it had made him feel; thinking that he had wasted his life this past year and that it was time to grow up. Remembering how Thea had reacted to the fall of the stone, and contrasting that with Evadne's reaction, and wondering if he had made a horrendous mistake. Usually he didn't let himself remember what had happened to him at Waterloo. Usually, he suppressed all memories of the shell, ironically from the British side, that had wreaked such havoc, wounding him, killing his horse, and burying him beneath a pile of dead and dying men. Trapped at

126

the bottom, there Jeremy had stayed, in pain, sweltering in the heat, and, to his eternal shame, panicking. It had been hours until the bodies above him had been removed, hours in which he had suspected he would die, too. That first breath of fresh air had been very, very sweet.

Since then he had found he could not abide crushes, the crowds fashionable London hostesses were so proud of attracting to their balls and routs. Nor did he enjoy being indoors when he could be out, and, in a place such as Rochester's ruins, he felt no awe, only a sense of the walls closing in on him. He knew now why he had been so restless the past few months. A woman's hand clinging to his arm suffocated him; a woman's demands made him feel trapped. Unless that woman was Thea.

The incident at the ruins had been passed over as an accident. A terrible accident, of course, and much discussed, but surely nothing more than that. If Jeremy had his suspicions, he kept them to himself, glancing only occasionally at DeVilliers. Even he, however, found it hard to believe that DeVilliers would do such a thing deliberately, for revenge. Unless, Jeremy mused, there was another motive.

Frowning, he rose and left the room. Earlier in the day he had heard Thea offer to help arrange flowers for the ball to be held that evening, and so his steps took him down the corridors leading to the ballroom. The great castle was eerily quiet; like him, most of the others had sought their own counsel. Today was the last day of the house party. The ball would be held tonight, and by tomorrow the guests would start to leave. Jeremy would be glad to return, at last, to Moulton Hall, his estate on the Kent coast.

He paused at one of the doors leading to the ballroom, and looked into the room. The french windows were open, the drapes drawn back, dust motes dancing in the golden light of late afternoon. From his vantage point Jeremy could see Thea, not only from the back, but reflected in the pier glass hanging above the marble shelf, where she stood arranging flowers in a brass urn. Her slender figure moved gracefully as she set stalks of lilies and irises into the urn, and the sun touched lightly on her hair, turning it to a flame whose brightness outshone the gilt of the mirror. She was frowning slightly with concentration, her lower lip caught between her teeth, and Jeremy was transfixed.

He had made no sound, but suddenly Thea looked up. Her startled eyes met his, reflected in the mirror, and she turned. "Jeremy! I did not hear you come in!"

"My apologies, Thea." He crossed the room, the heels of his Hessians clicking on the parquet floor. "I didn't mean to startle you."

"You didn't." She picked up another lily, concentrating on it instead of him. "How is it you are here, this time of day?"

"I came to talk to you, about the other day."

"Oh?"

"Yes, I—damn it, Thea, I'm trying to apologize. The way I behaved—it was unforgivable."

Thea's eyes were wary. "Very well," she said finally. "We'll forget about it, then."

"No, damn it, Thea, I don't want to forget."

"I think you haven't a choice, sir." Studiously

avoiding looking at him, she placed another flower in the urn. "You're engaged."

"And you are carrying on a dangerous flirtation."

She looked up quickly. "What are you talking about?"

"You and DeVilliers. Don't pretend, Thea. I've seen you two together."

"I wasn't aware it was any of your business."

"Oh, very cool, Thea. I am aware I gave up all right to speak out some time ago."

"Yes. What have you against Mr. DeVilliers, Jeremy?"

Jeremy shifted to his other foot. "Let us just say I know things about him to his discredit. Believe me, Thea, I wish only to spare you pain, but if you care about him—"

"Do not be more foolish than you can help!" she exclaimed, thrusting a flower into the urn with unnecessary force. "I do not care a fig about him! But it is very pleasant to be courted, Jeremy."

"Are you so desperate you'd settle for him, Thea?"

"Jeremy!"

"You are an attractive woman, Thea. You could do better."

But I couldn't, she thought, her heart suddenly aching. *Not now.* "Why are you saying these things to me?"

"Because I care about you." Thea's eyes flew to his. "Thea—"

"Oh, Stanton, there you are!" Evadne called from the doorway. Thea started and dropped the remaining flowers, and Jeremy turned and watched as Evadne floated across to them.

"Evadne," Jeremy said, bowing slightly. "I thought you were resting."

"Oh no, I couldn't, I'm much too excited! I thought I would come and see what you are doing, sir." She wrapped her hand around his arm and smiled coquettishly at him, batting her eyelashes.

Jeremy did not return the smile. "As you see, I am here."

"Oh dear, Mrs. Jameson, that is not the way to arrange flowers at all!"

"I realize that," Thea said through gritted teeth as she rose, holding the flowers she had dropped. "But someone must do it."

"I quite admire you, ma'am. Yes, I do! You are so industrious and sensible. How wise you were to wear such a dark dress, it won't matter if the flowers stain it! I'm sure I don't have a gown that color."

"I'm sure you don't," Thea muttered, stabbing flowers at random into the urn.

"But, ma'am, do you not think you should be resting?" Evadne asked solicitously. "After all, tonight will be a late evening and you do look fatigued."

Jeremy choked. "Come, Evadne, let us go and see if the duke has anything else planned for this evening."

"Oh yes!" Evadne gazed up at him. "I so enjoy the duke's entertainments, don't you?"

"Yes, he quite enjoyed having rocks fall on him," Thea muttered.

Evadne threw her a quick, limpid-eyed glance. "But I am persuaded that was an accident, and it will not happen again. I shall make sure of it."

"Oh?" Jeremy glanced helplessly at Thea's bent head

130

and then turned away before Evadne could do any more damage. "And how do you plan to do that?"

"Why, by staying quite close to you, sir, of course! I cannot wait for you to see my gown, Stanton, it is of white silk," she went on as Jeremy led her away. "Mama says I may wear it since no one has seen it in London yet. I suppose you'll be wearing your burgundy, Mrs. Jameson?"

Thea glanced up to see in the mirror that Evadne was looking back over her shoulder. "Yes, Miss Powell."

"You· are so sensible! But then, perhaps you don't mind wearing the same gown so often? Of course, no one here matters. You'll quite like my gown, sir," she chattered as Jeremy finally led her out of the room. "It has *dents de loup* about the hem, and it is embroidered in silver—"

"And it is undoubtedly hideous!" Thea exclaimed to the empty room as Evadne's voice trailed back to her. "How can he *stand* that little ninny?" She shoved the remaining flowers in at random and then turned away, dusting her hands together. " 'So sensible,' " she mimicked as she strode across the room. " 'Shouldn't you be resting, Mrs. Jameson?' and 'Are you wearing the burgundy?' Well, no, I am bloody well not wearing the burgundy!"

"Ma'am?" A footman in the corner stared at her as she emerged from the ballroom.

Thea colored, but held her head high. "I don't believe I should wear burgundy tonight, do you?"

"No, ma'am," the footman stuttered.

"Good." She stalked past him and ran up the stairs to her room, not caring what anyone might think. Without speaking to her startled maid she crossed the room and pulled a gown out of the wardrobe. "I'll wear this to-night, Betsy."

"But, mum," Betsy protested, "the burgundy silk, I've pressed it already."

"Burn it. I never want to see it again."

"Yes, mum." Betsy's eyes were wide as she dropped a curtsy and then scurried out of the room, the gown Thea had chosen draped over her arm.

"Fatigued, am I?" Thea glared at her reflection as she stood in front of the dressing table, scattering hair pins and drawing a brush ruthlessly through her hair. "Oh no, Miss Powell, you'll see. And so will Mr. DeVilliers, and so will you, Jeremy, you idiot! I can have suitors if I want them and I do not need anyone to tell me how to run my life, and I do not hold people at arm's length!" She stared defiantly at her flushed cheeks, and then held up her hand in a mock toast. "Tonight, my girl, will be yours."

Chapter 9

Long before the appointed hour, carriages began streaming toward Rochester Castle, lit on this festive night from the highest tower to the lowest cellar, for the first grand ball held there in many an age. The presence of so many stylish ladies and gentlemen at the castle had excited a great deal of interest for miles around, and invitations to the ball were a much-coveted item. As the day drew near excited young misses and anxious young men scanned the leaden skies, fearing the weather would interfere with their plans, but the night of the ball was quiet and balmy, with a full moon to light the guests on their way.

The duke and his family stood near the doorway leading into the ballroom, brilliantly lit by hundreds of wax tapers gleaming in the crystal chandeliers and reflected in the pier glasses that lined the walls. The french windows leading to the terrace were open, and already the room was awhirl with color and movement, gentlemen in proper black and white or colors that rivaled the silks or satins or muslins of the ladies' gowns. Precious jewels glittered and flashed in the light, as sparkling as the conversation. Such an occasion was becoming rare in this part of the world. It was a night most of the guests would long remember.

Jeremy glanced up again as yet another young lady flitted into the room, her face flushed with excitement, and then looked away. Not Thea, though why he so badly wished to see her he couldn't say. He wished of course to apologize for Evadne's rudeness of the afternoon. And yet he had not quite shaken from his mind the image of her as she had appeared in the glass, slender, graceful, with an uncommon beauty. He didn't understand it. Thea, of all people, his friend, and yet his need to see her was almost overwhelming.

". . . and I am so glad you wore that coat tonight, Stanton, it quite sets off my gown," Evadne chattered, and Jeremy pulled himself from his musings.

"Glad to oblige," he said ironically. He was wearing a coat of darkest blue velvet, with white satin knee breeches and a waistcoat figured in light blue and silver thread. His intention had not been to act as a foil for Evadne, in her evening gown of white watered silk, but that was the role she had assigned him. It was, he realized without much surprise, the role he had played since their engagement. Why hadn't it bothered him before?

He became aware that Evadne was staring at him, and he realized that he had missed what she'd said. "You look very lovely, my dear," he asserted, and her face cleared. One would never go wrong complimenting Evadne, and in truth, she did look lovely, young and innocent and almost sweet. He wondered, however dispassionately, why he had never before noticed that her eyes bulged a bit.

There was a sudden buzz of excitement at the door,

and he glanced toward it, unable to see what was causing the commotion. "Is that the duke coming in at last?" Evadne said, craning her head to see. "I do wish he'd hurry and open the ball so I could dance!"

"He must greet his guests," Jeremy said absently, still looking toward the doorway. He was about to turn away when the crowd parted, and he saw what was causing the stir.

Thea. Good God. Beside him, Evadne suddenly gripped his arm, but he hardly noticed. For the life of him, he could not look away. Was it really Thea? She was not, tonight, merely a sensible, almost plain widow. Instead she was radiant, smiling, and beautiful. Jeremy's mind caught at the word and held it. Yes, beautiful, though he'd never before realized it. Her gown was of sapphire blue satin, glowing and glistening, a color he had never seen on her. Her hair had been styled differently, too, framing her face more loosely, with one curl escaping to fall upon a creamy shoulder, left bare by the low-cut gown. The heavy, rich fabric draped over her curves, falling straight to the floor with neither flounce nor rouleau. It was, perhaps, too severe in its simplicity to be stylish, but it suited her. It made her alluring, desirable, no longer simply the friend he sometimes took for granted, but a woman whose attraction was undeniable, a mysterious stranger whom he suddenly wished very much to know.

As if drawn by a magnet he stepped forward, and Evadne's hand caught at his arm. "There, the duke is coming in now! I do hope they play a waltz," she said.

"Not for the first dance," Jeremy said absently, his eyes reluctantly leaving Thea. He was not the only one to discover her beauty; several gentlemen were clustered around her, among them Lord Ware and Lord Pelham.

"He is an old prude!"

"Now, girl, that's not the way to talk of our host," Agatha Powell said coming up to the couple. She had seen the way Jeremy had looked at Thea, and she was not pleased. Evadne had best be careful or she would lose him. "I'm sure Stanton would be happy to lead you out, no matter what the dance."

"Hm?" Jeremy turned to see mother and daughter regarding him, and he blinked. For a moment, they looked so alike—but that was ridiculous. "Oh, of course. Miss Powell?" He gestured toward the floor as the orchestra began to play a cotillion, and she simpered up at him.

"I would be motht pleathed, my lord," she said, and let him lead her out, blissfully unaware of the way his lips twitched in annoyance at her lisp.

"You look beautiful," Lord Pelham said fervently to Thea across the room, causing her to look at him in surprise.

"Oh. Thank you, sir," she said, and looked again at Jeremy and Evadne dancing, forcing her clenched fists to relax. "But Miss Powell is radiant, is she not?" She rushed on before Lord Pelham could answer. "And of course, she does have a good dowry."

Lord Pelham looked at Evadne. "Does she?"

"Yes, so I'm told. And the Powells are a good family."

"Of course," Lord Pelham said absentmindedly. Thea was briefly annoyed, and then amused, at how quickly he changed allegiances. "Excuse me."

"Of course, sir." She had accomplished her goal. For one dance, at least, Jeremy and Evadne would be apart, and she had planted the seeds of greater interest in Lord Pelham's mind.

"Bravo," a voice said behind her, and she turned to see Roger DeVilliers grinning at her. "Well done, Althea."

Thea colored, but she held her head high. "I don't know what you mean, sir."

"Don't you? I fear you're doomed to failure. The little one has eyes for no one but Stanton."

"For now," Thea murmured. "You do not dance, sir?"

"I was hoping you would be free, ma'am."

She made a little pretense of checking her dance card. "Why, it just so happens I am, sir."

"Then I would be happy to lead you out." He held out his arm and she let him lead her onto the floor, joining one of the sets just forming. She felt different tonight, younger, freer, and life seemed open to her with boundless opportunities, as it had not since before her marriage. It was the dress, she decided. It not only made people, especially men, look at her differently, it made her feel different, as if there were another person inside her, whose presence she had never suspected. It was a different Thea, a Thea who laughed and smiled and flirted with the gentlemen, a Thea who held no one at arm's length. She wondered if Jeremy had noticed.

"Jeremy, you danth tho well," Evadne said, batting her eyelashes again. Jeremy's answering smile as he escorted Evadne from the floor was remote. Across the room from him he could see Thea, in that remarkable gown, laughing up at DeVilliers, who was clearly ogling her bosom. His hand suddenly tightened on Evadne's. "You're hurting me!" she hissed.

Jeremy looked blankly at her and then loosened his grip. "My apologies," he said absently.

Evadne threw him a look that was not at all flirtatious and then followed his gaze. That hateful Jameson woman! Evadne wanted to stamp her foot in anger and frustration. Tonight was supposed to be *her* night, and instead Mrs. Jameson was getting all the attention. How dare she wear such a gown. She was too old! Why, even Lord Ware and Lord Pelham gazed at her as if she were a goddess. Evadne hadn't minded Mrs. Jameson when she was dressed in her sensible, high-necked gowns in plain, dull colors. Stanton would soon tire of her and, even if he didn't, it would remove an onerous wifely duty from Evadne. But now! Now she had every gentleman in the room clearly besotted with her. It wasn't fair.

The orchestra began to play a waltz, and Evadne turned toward Jeremy eagerly. His name was not on her card for this dance, but she didn't care. It was time she showed Mrs. Jameson, and everyone else, just who mattered in Jeremy's life.

"My dance, I believe, Miss Powell," a voice said beside her, and she turned to see Francis Thorne. Her breath caught in her throat. How absurd! Certainly he was handsome, in a fair-haired, understated sort of way, but nothing to compare with Stanton. He always dressed so carelessly, too, in coats that, though undeniably well-made, never hung quite right on his tall, lean frame. Even tonight his neckcloth seemed limp, in need of another coat of starch. But the shoulders that filled out his coat were his own, unpadded, his legs, in white silk stockings that needed to be straightened, were lean and muscular, and his hand, held out to hers, was broad, strong, and capable.

"I—believe it is," she said, more breathlessly than the moment seemed to warrant. "You'll excuse me, sir?"

Jeremy smiled down at her and then looked at Francis. "Evening, Thorne."

"Sir." Francis briefly shook his head. "May I have Miss Powell for this dance?"

Jeremy nodded, his gaze involuntarily returning across the room, where Thea still stood with Roger DeVilliers. "Of course."

Francis's eyes followed. "You needn't worry about him."

"Needn't I?" Jeremy turned back. "He bears watching. Still." He smiled at Evadne. "Best have your waltz now. We are lucky the duke is allowing it."

Evadne gave Francis a smile, not her most charming one, and held out her hand. "I would be honored, sir," she said, with no trace of a lisp, and let him lead her out to the floor. She was not quite able to explain, even to herself, why she was so reluctant to waltz with him.

Jeremy watched Francis and Evadne begin to waltz, and then turned, feeling at loose ends. He had engaged to dance with few ladies this evening, and so his time was his own. He could wander into the card room, he supposed, or join the group of which Chatleigh was a part and talk politics, but neither interested him. His restless gaze went about the room and settled on Thea.

Again his breath stopped. She was listening to something DeVilliers was saying with every appearance of interest, and the look of serious concentration on her face was as appealing as her smile. She didn't flirt, his Thea; she didn't pose or tease or lead a man on. She was just herself, and that was why her present behavior was so disturbing. Was she acting tonight, or was this just a side of her he hadn't seen before? He had to know.

Nodding and smiling to other acquaintances, he crossed the room. As he reached Thea's side, DeVilliers gave him a cool, measuring look, which he ignored. "Good evening, ma'am." He bent over her hand in its white kid glove for a fraction of a second longer than usual, and felt her start of surprise in her fingers. "And may I say how lovely you look tonight?"

"Thank you, sir." She gave him a brilliant smile that briefly made his head spin. "You are enjoying the evening?"

"Quite."

"I see your fiancée is waltzing with someone else," DeVilliers said, and Jeremy's hand tightened on Thea's arm.

"Why, she is with Francis!" Thea said in surprise.

"Yes. They look well together, do they not?"

"Yes." Thea frowned a little, unaware of the way the two men looked at each other. Francis and Evadne did look well together, surprisingly and disturbingly so.

"Are you engaged for this dance, ma'am?" Jeremy said abruptly, and she came out of her daze.

"No, sir, I am not, but Mr. DeVilliers—"

"Go on, Althea." DeVilliers waved his hand lazily. "We can talk more later."

"Very well. Then I would like to dance with you, sir." She glanced up in time to see Jeremy give DeVilliers another steely-eyed look. In return, the other man simply smiled and bowed.

"You are behaving strangely tonight, Thea," Jeremy said in a low voice as he led her onto the floor.

Thea stopped. "Are you going to lecture me again?"

140

"No, but—"

"Because if you are, I think we should talk someplace a bit more private, don't you?"

Jeremy stared at her, not quite believing what she had said, or the coquettish tone of her voice. This was not at all the Thea he knew. The thought was oddly exciting. "Very well, Thea. Shall we go out onto the terrace?"

"Certainly, sir." She placed her arm through his and they crossed the crowded ballroom. Outside on the flag-stoned terrace the air was soft and balmy, and a full moon rode in the sky above a scattering of clouds and a sprinkling of stars. Thea leaned on the stone balus-trade, looking out into the midnight darkness of the garden. "It is a beautiful night."

"So it is. Have you ever heard of being moonstruck, Thea?" Jeremy said, his voice husky.

Thea whirled, but in the dim light she couldn't see the expression on his face. "I—don't know what you mean."

"That is a most remarkable gown you are wearing, you know."

"Yes, I know. Mr. DeVilliers thought so, too."

If she had hoped to bring him down to earth, she couldn't have chosen a better way. He scowled. "Stay away from him, Thea."

The old Thea would have bristled at his proprietary tone of voice; this new Thea, who enjoyed wearing such a daring gown and receiving so much masculine atten-tion, merely laughed. "Jealous, Jeremy?"

"No!" he denied, a little too vigorously. She simply looked up at him, and after a moment, he let out his breath.

"Yes, damn it. I know I've no right, but I don't like

seeing him look at you as if he's starving and you're a particularly dainty morsel. Damn it, Thea, that's not funny!"

"Yes, it is!" Thea laughed. "Jeremy, if you could only hear yourself! You are correct, you've no right to say such things." She grew serious. "You are engaged, as I recall."

"I haven't forgotten." His eyes were steady on hers. "But that doesn't mean I can stop caring, or that when you look as you do I'm not attracted. And, yes, I do get jealous when I see leeches like Roger DeVilliers drooling all over you!"

"Jeremy, what on earth is between you two?"

"It doesn't signify. What does is that I would not see you hurt."

"I won't be." She laid her hand on his arm. "Jeremy, this does no good. The fact remains that you are engaged."

Jeremy's answer was a long time in coming. "Yes."

"And I will be no man's mistress. Can we not continue being friends?"

"Friends!" He paced a few steps away and then turned, glaring at her. "Of all the damned, unrealistic things—"

"It was what you yourself suggested," she reminded him.

"I was a fool." He spoke crisply.

"Perhaps. But I see no other way, Jeremy. You cannot have both of us." The words hung on the air, and she waited for him to answer, to say—what? Surely she didn't want to marry again, him or anybody. Only her pride would be salved if he chose her over Evadne, a most unlikely circumstance. "I think we'd best go back in."

Jeremy let out his breath again and then held out his arm. "My apologies, Thea," he said formally. "Come, I'll escort you inside."

Francis slid an arm about Evadne's waist as they began to waltz, and, for all his leanness, held her quite firmly, though at the correct distance. Evadne glanced up at his face. He was looking at her, but instead of the fatuous smile she was accustomed to seeing on young men's faces, his wore a puzzled frown. Evadne's temper, already exacerbated by Thea's behavior that evening, soared. "You are perhaps angry with me, sir?"

"And if I am, would you care?" he demanded.

Evadne's eyes widened in surprise, and then she pouted. "What have I done to detherve that, thir?"

"Stop it," he said sternly. "Save such tricks for other men. I'm onto them."

"Why, thir, I don't know what you mean—"

"I know you better than that, Evadne. You don't have to put on a pretense with me."

"It'th not a pretenth! I mean, it isn't a pretense. Why do you talk to me so?"

Francis gave her such a long, hard look that she shrank back. "God knows why I care so much about you," he said in a low voice. "You're selfish and shallow and spoiled, and no man in his right mind would want you for his wife."

Evadne tossed her head, making her curls dance. "You are insulting, sir."

"No," he said slowly. "At least, I don't mean to be.

But I know you, Evadne, and I know there's another person hiding inside you."

"I don't know what you mean," she said, puzzled, and Francis let out his breath.

"I feared so. But she is there, and that's the girl I care about. The one no one sees, the one who is afraid no one will ever care about her—"

"No!" Evadne tried to pull free from him, but his hands held her fast.

"—the one who flirts so people won't ignore her. Why are you marrying him?"

"You've no right to quiz me so!" Evadne exclaimed, honestly frightened. How did he know such things about her? "It's none of your concern!"

"Oh yes, Evadne, it is. Stanton's too old for you. He doesn't even like you."

From somewhere Evadne found the courage to confront him and stifle all the old insecurities and fears that she thought she had vanquished. She raised her chin and returned his look coolly. "Stanton suits me quite well. I expect I shall enjoy being a viscountess."

"So that is all that matters to you? His title? I might have guessed," Francis said bitterly. "It doesn't matter that my family is as old and respected as his?"

Evadne tossed her curls. "No, sir, why should it? You have no title."

Francis glanced down at her, momentarily speechless with anger. "Perhaps I was wrong about you. Perhaps there is nothing more to you than a shallow, spoiled girl."

She gave him a cool smile. "Perhaps."

"Marry him, then! But you'll live to regret it."

"Why, I don't think so. I shall have everything I want."

"Except love."

Evadne batted her eyelashes. "Perhaps even that, too."

Francis stopped still, in the midst of the whirling dancers, staring down at her. Then, without a word, he released her and walked away, leaving her stranded and feeling as wretched as she ever had in her life. She wanted to cry. Instead, she stamped her foot and stormed off the floor, ignoring the curious gazes of the people around her, until she saw Lord Ware, talking with a young lady. Her determination returned. There was someone on whom she could rely. But, as she crossed the room, Lord Ware raised the girl's hand to his mouth and then turned away, leading her, apparently, to the supper room. Evadne was, again, alone, and she didn't like it one bit.

"All alone, Miss Powell?" a voice said by her side. Evadne started, and turned to see Mr. DeVilliers, smiling at her quite kindly. Everyone knew. Everyone pitied her.

"No, of course not," she said coolly, raising her chin. What did she care what he thought, anyway? She had to admit that his thick, dark hair and his brooding face were wonderfully romantic, but he was old. Older than Stanton, even, with neither title nor fortune to recommend him, and so she hadn't paid him much heed during the week past. He was, however, the only person in the room who was paying her the slightest bit of attention. That was, for the moment, enough.

DeVilliers continued to smile, not at all discomposed by her haughtiness. In her fluffy white gown, she looked like nothing so much as a kitten in a temper. Not his type at all, but she had possibilities, and he'd been blind not to see them sooner. For, if a kitten had claws, she also could be gentled with the right stroking. He'd been a fool to ignore her.

During the last few days, DeVilliers's dislike of his erstwhile rival had grown to enormous proportions, until he was alive to anything that might cause Jeremy harm. To that end, he had concentrated on charming Mrs. Jameson, something Stanton obviously disliked. Now he wondered if he'd made a mistake. By the look of things, Thea was holding Stanton at arm's length. He should have been concentrating on Miss Powell. He doubted that Stanton was seriously attached to the girl, but her potential to cause him embarrassment was considerable. Not to mention that she was an heiress. He had been remiss not to focus on her sooner.

"But you're not dancing," he went on, still with his most charming smile, and at last was rewarded by a smile from her. A calculating smile, which intrigued him. This kitten did, indeed, have claws, and that served his purpose well.

"I fear not." Evadne sighed. "Someone signed my dance card, but he is not here. Can you make out the name, sir?"

DeVilliers shook his head over her card. "No, I cannot. He is foolish, whoever he is, to leave you standing alone."

Evadne dimpled up at him. "Thank you, sir, that is very kind of you to say."

"Not kind," he protested, holding up his hands. "Honest, my dear."

At that, Evadne's smile grew wider. Tonight had not

been to her liking at all. Not only had Francis walked away from her—and no man had ever before done that!—but she had seen her fiancé return from the terrace with that hateful Jameson woman. None of that mattered now, however. She was being admired by the most sophisticated, mysterious gentleman she had ever met. It did not matter that in the past weeks he had ignored her or, at most, given her an indulgent smile. He was with her now, and that went a long way toward healing the wounds the evening had inflicted upon her.

"I appreciate your honesty, sir," she said, tilting her head to the side as she looked up at him.

He laughed. "You are quite vain, little one. But then, so am I. I think we shall suit." His smile was slow and intimate. "Yes, I think we shall suit quite well. Come." He took her arm and began to walk, slowly, toward the windows. "Since your partner has been fool enough not to claim you, may I sit out this dance with you?"

"By all meanth, thir."

DeVilliers blinked in surprise. "But I find it a trifle warm in here, do you not? Shall we go out onto the terrace?"

Evadne's smile momentarily stiffened. She had been warned against such behavior, and her common sense told her it was dangerous. But she was tired of obeying society's dictates. "Yeth, why not?" she said, and let him lead her outside. That would show him, she thought, and didn't know if she meant Francis or Jeremy.

Jeremy and Thea returned to the ballroom in time to see Francis stalk from the floor, leaving an obviously

147

astonished Evadne alone. "I wonder what that was all about?" Thea said.

Jeremy shrugged. At the moment he was not concerned about Evadne. "Perhaps she finally flirted too much," he said, and Thea sent him a swift glance. She had never before heard him express disapproval of his fiancée.

"Well, in any event, she has made a quick recovery." And Thea nodded toward Evadne, who had been joined by Roger DeVilliers. Evadne was talking and smiling at him with such vivaciousness, one would have thought the incident on the dance floor had never happened. Thea expected Jeremy would now leave her in favor of Evadne, but to her surprise he made no attempt to leave her side.

"I have no worries about her." Jeremy gave her a searching look. "I must leave you. I am promised to the duchess for this next dance."

Thea bore his gaze with equanimity, though it was hard not to look away. "Then you must not slight her, sir."

"We'll talk later."

"Perhaps," she said, and with an enigmatic smile turned to greet the local vicar, who had secured for himself the next dance with her. What else, she wondered, would happen this evening?

Chapter 10

It was late. The last guest had departed hours ago, the moon had set, and most of the inhabitants of the great castle were asleep. Thea, however, was unable to sleep. In her mind she kept going over the evening and reliving different incidents: Francis and Evadne; Mr. DeVilliers and the enmity between him and Jeremy; her own daring in wearing such a gown. She had felt different, freer. Now, though, the evening was over. She was simply herself again, Althea Jameson, plain, quiet, widow. She felt flat, let down, and also very lonely. For a few heady moments that evening she had thought Jeremy cared, until he had walked away.

At last she gave up on sleep, and, picking up her taper, left her room, not caring that she wore only her nightgown and wrapper, or that her feet were bare. No one would see her. She would go to the library and find something to read and then return to her room. At least, that was her intention. But as she came to the end of the corridor, she found a massive oaken door, bound in iron, standing open. Within, lit by torches, was a winding stone staircase, looking medieval and romantic, perhaps leading up into one of the castle's towers. For a moment, the magic of the night returned. A tower in a castle. What could be more appropriate? Without stopping to question herself, Thea turned and began climbing the stairs. On such a night, anything might happen.

Jeremy couldn't sleep, either. Restlessly he paced his room, still dressed, though he had discarded his coat and waistcoat. It had been an odd, unsettling evening, not the enjoyable social event he had hoped for. It had been rather a shock, discovering that his intended's behavior was beginning to grate on his nerves. It was even more of a shock, however, that the person he kept thinking about, the one he couldn't get out of his mind, was Thea. Thea, as she had looked in that remarkable gown, cut almost too low for modesty. Thea, teasing him about being jealous. Thea, so near, and yet so unattainable. It drove him to distraction, until, with an oath, he picked up his candle and left his room. He'd go for a walk, work off some of his energy, and perhaps then he'd be able to forget about Thea. Perhaps.

The heavy door standing open to the tower made him stop, and he peered up the stairway. Unlike Thea, he'd noticed it before, though he'd never had the desire to explore further. The stairs were hollowed in the middle, as if worn by the steps of thousands of feet; the tower, made of stone blocks, was narrow. All that stone, pressing in upon him. But the lighted torches took away the darkness and made the heaviness bearable. Lured by a compulsion he didn't understand, Jeremy turned and began to climb the stairs.

Light spilled out from another opened door, this one at the top of the stairs, the only room in the tower. Pausing for a moment on the landing, Jeremy glanced around, feeling again that oppressive sense of the walls closing in on him. Then, shaking it off, he stepped through the door and stopped, momentarily speechless.

It was a room from a fairy tale, though not a European one. It was a room from an Oriental dream, and one that was obviously not intended for display. The harsh stone walls were covered with silk hangings woven in exotic designs with every hue imaginable, creating a rainbow even in the darkest night. To his left, a brazier of brass and iron glowed with heat, while, underneath, a thick rug of Persian origin muffled his footsteps. Most startling of all, however, was the room's main piece of furniture, across the floor from him. It was a huge divan, upholstered in crimson brocade, with silken cushions scattered upon it in great profusion. Next to the divan, staring at it with wide-eyed astonishment, was Thea.

Jeremy's heart, which had returned to normal, began pounding again. She was the last person he had expected to see in such a place, and ordinarily he would have said she didn't belong here, in this Oriental bower. Yet tonight, in her blue gown, he'd seen another side of her. A side he very much wished to know better. A side that did belong here. "Thea?"

Thea spun around, her hand to her heart. "Jeremy! Oh, you startled me."

"My apologies, Thea. I didn't know you were here." He looked around the room. "What is this place?"

"I'm not sure. The door was open, and so I decided to see what was up here." Her smile was shy. "I couldn't sleep."

"Neither could I." And here, standing before him was the reason why. She looked different than she had earlier; her nightgown and wrapper covered her completely, and her hair hung over her shoulder in a thick plait, not at all seductive. For all that, though, there was something very sweet and appealing about her as she stood before him, looking up at him almost shyly, one bare foot crossed over the other. "Rather a romantic idea, isn't it? A hidden boudoir in a tower."

Thea's startled eyes met his. "Jeremy, do you think—"

"That we interrupted a tryst? I doubt it. There's just one set of stairs. We would have seen anyone who was here. But still." He prowled around the room, studying the hangings, grinning down at the luxurious divan, and all the time coming closer and closer. "I can't imagine what else this room is used for, can you? Or why it's lighted?"

"Oh. Then I'll go. If you'll hand me my candle—"

"No, don't." He reached out and caught her arm. She stopped, very still, glanced at his hand and then raised her eyes to his face, looking at him searchingly. He returned the gaze, conscious of her warmth under his hand. "Thea."

"Jeremy, I'd best go—"

"No. Not yet." His hand loosened, but instead of releasing her it slid up her arm, ever so slowly, until it reached her shoulder. Thea swallowed, hard, and with his other hand he traced a line softly along her jaw. "Do you know, when I saw you at the ball, Thea, I felt I'd never seen you before," he said softly.

"Maybe you hadn't," she answered just as softly, fighting the treacherous urge to lean against the fingers that were now stroking her cheek.

"Maybe. But now . . ."

152

"Now?" she prompted.

"I've been blind. So blind." His thumb brushed across her lips, and then his hand slipped down to hold her other shoulder. "And every kind of a fool."

Thea watched, standing quite still, as his face came closer. She should leave. She should, but something held her. It was the magic of the night, of the room. Her eyes closed as his arm slipped around her waist, his fingers tilted up her face. This was real, this was right. She raised her lips to his and felt his kiss upon her lips.

Something happened within Thea as Jeremy's lips touched hers, something new to her. Her body went languid, her limbs weak, so that she had to cling to him, lest she fall. Her arms wrapped about his neck, her hand thrust into his hair, her body molded itself against him as the kiss lengthened and deepened. Never had she felt anything like this, this wanting, this need, and when his tongue probed against her lips in an unspoken command, they parted for him.

"Ah, Thea," he gasped, abruptly breaking the kiss and pulling her close against him, his heart racing, his breathing ragged. "This is madness."

"Sweet madness," she whispered, raising her lips to his. He could not resist their invitation, and with a groan he bent his head to taste of them again.

"Sweet, so sweet," he muttered against her lips, pressing quick, hard kisses on her cheeks, her brow, her eyes. She shifted against him, and his hand slipped down to untie the sash of her wrapper. And then he was touching her, his hand curved about her breast. Sensations she had never before felt came alive in her at his touch, emotions rioted within her. Her knees abruptly gave way and they sank together onto the divan. Thea let her head drop back as he bent to kiss her throat, luxuriating in the sweet sensations flooding through her. A man's arms about her before had been a trap, but, held close to Jeremy, she felt safer than she had ever been.

The scents of the Orient that perfumed the room, jasmine, gardenia, plumeria, spicy and seductive, combined with the glowing warmth of the brazier and the jewel colors of the silks to make this a moment out of time, a place that existed only for them. A place that was as real and as right as the emotions each awoke in the other, and as exotic. Jeremy murmured words to her as he pushed the wrapper from her shoulders and slowly unfastened the buttons of her gown, and like a harem girl, she stretched sinuously under the touch of his hands. She was no longer Thea, but something more elemental, more basic. She was a woman in the arms of her lover, the taste of brandy on his tongue and the aroma of his cologne as compelling as any Oriental spice.

Jeremy tugged, and her nightgown slid down past her hips. For a moment sanity returned, and with it, doubts. This wasn't like her, she shouldn't be doing it, but then he kissed her again, and her doubts drowned in the rising tide of sensation. The silk brocade of the divan was deliciously cool under her heated flesh; and once he removed his own garments, Jeremy's skin was soft, supple, and warm under her fingers. She gave herself to him as she had to no other. She winced at their joining, for it had been so long, but then he was one with her, and it was magic. There was no pain—no pain!—only a giddy pleasure she could never have imagined and an urgency she had never before felt. Under the coaxing of his hands, strong and sure but gentle, she moved, smoothly and fluidly, with him in ways that were unfamiliar to her but that her body somehow knew, reaching for something just beyond her grasp. In the mad, magic moments when she spiraled out of herself, she became his, as she never had been anyone else's; she became more fully herself, as she never before had been. And, as she slowly drifted back to earth, held safely in Jeremy's arms, she knew, at last, what it meant to be loved.

Jeremy stirred, the muscles of his shoulder, cushioning her head, rippling slightly. She made a little sound of contentment and nuzzled against him, knowing she had finally found the place where she belonged. "Thea," he said, his voice husky. "Did I hurt you?"

Her eyes still closed, she smiled. "No."

"I didn't mean for that to happen."

"Mm." Neither had she, but it had, and she wasn't sorry.

"I don't want you to think that I followed you up here just for that. It's just that, when I saw you here— Thea, I've wanted you for so long."

She had wanted him, too. She could admit that, now. The woman she had been was only a facade for the Thea that had been hiding all this time. There was, indeed, fire inside her. "We were meant to be together. I think I've always known it."

Beside her Jeremy shifted and then rose, leaving her alone on the divan. Thea smiled to herself, her eyes closed, a voluptuous smile of satisfaction and contentment. She and Jeremy. Why had she not seen it before this? Of course it would be difficult for him to break his engagement. He was an honorable man, and that honor would not permit him to marry one woman while loving another. It had to be love that was between them. Never before had she felt like this. She suspected he hadn't, either.

"I didn't mean for it to happen," he said again, his voice tight. Thea raised her arm from her eyes to see him standing across the room from her. He was dressed, but, even through the fine lawn of his shirt she could see that his muscles were bunched with strain. Abruptly she realized that she was lying in a most immodest pose. A moment ago it hadn't mattered. Now it did, though she wasn't sure why. Unease stirred within her as she pulled her nightshift on. "Jeremy?" she said, her voice sounding very young and uncertain, and he wheeled to face her.

"Damn!" He drove his fist into the palm of his hand. "If I had it to do over again!"

"You wouldn't? Is that what you mean?"

"No, Thea, I didn't say that."

"No, you didn't." The unease tightened within Thea as she rose from the divan. Something was happening here she didn't understand, and yet knew all too well. It was important she remain calm. The cool Thea, the Thea the world knew. "Jeremy, you didn't force me, you know."

"I know, Thea, but don't you see that makes it worse?"

"Makes what worse, Jeremy?" she said carefully. "We've found each other. What is so very bad about that?"

Jeremy faced her from across the room, a strange look on his face. It was as if he had tasted something he usually considered a treat, and found it bitter. "Thea, I don't want to lose you."

"I wasn't aware I was yours to lose," she said tartly, annoyed with his careful choice of words and the way he avoided her eyes.

"But you are." His eyes bored into hers, looking deep into her soul, connecting them again as inexorably as they had been joined just a moment before. "Aren't you?"

She wavered, glancing toward the door, and then gave in. "Yes," she said in a rush, overwhelmed by the feelings that flooded her. "Yes, Jeremy, I—" She clutched at his shoulders as he crossed the room in several long strides and caught her up against him. "Yes, I'm yours, I'll always be yours—"

"Thea." His voice was a groan and he kissed her, her eyelids, her cheeks, her mouth. "You won't regret this, darling. I promise."

"No," she murmured, holding to him, feeling at last alive and safe, giddy with joy. "No, I won't."

"I'll take care of you. You'll be my wife in every way that matters."

The room was suddenly very cold. Thea's hands went still and her eyes opened, no longer drugged by love and dreams. It wasn't forever he was offering her, it wasn't the honorable choice, but something that appalled her to her soul. "Jeremy." She looked up at him, though his arms were still around her. "You'd do that to Evadne?"

Jeremy made an angry little gesture with his hand. "She doesn't matter. I'm honor-bound to marry her, but—"

"But what does your honor owe me, Jeremy? Or yourself?" With a little tug she pulled away from him. "According to honor, I should be your wife."

157

"Thea." He strove to sound reasonable. "You've been married already, and—"

Her eyes flashed with the fire that she had found blazed inside her. "And what? Do you think that means I'll accept any offer you make me? No, Jeremy. No." She wrapped her arms around herself, to ward off the chill that had overtaken her. "I will not be your mistress."

"It's all right, darling." He brushed a feather-light kiss on her nape, left defenseless by her bent head. "No one will know."

"I'll know. And I cannot do it." She whirled to face him. "Listen to me, Jeremy. My husband kept mistresses from the beginning of our marriage. Do you have any idea what that did to me? I died a little inside each time he went to someone else. And when he died, it was fighting for the honor of another woman. Not me." Her eyes were huge and dark with remembered pain. "I swore, Jeremy, that I would never put another woman in that position. I value myself too highly."

"Thea." He reached out to grip her shoulders, and let his hands drop when she stiffened. "I don't love Evadne. She doesn't love me. This is the way things are in our world."

She shook her head. "Not for me, Jeremy."

"I can't offer you marriage, Thea," he said, his eyes steady on her.

"And you wouldn't if you could. Don't deny it, Jeremy, I know I'm not what you want in a bride. You want someone young, someone you can mold to your liking. Well, good luck to you," she said bitterly. "Evadne will fight you every step of the way." She bent and picked up her discarded wrapper, thrusting her arms

158

into it, her movements jerky. "I must have been mad, to stay here with you."

"Damn." Jeremy thrust a hand into his hair. "Thea, I mean no harm to you."

She wouldn't look at him. "I know."

"Thea. Don't go," he urged, and she paused by the door, her head slightly turned. "I know this isn't what you want, but it's the best I can offer you. Stay with me. Let me love you. I promise you won't regret it, I promise no harm will come to you." He paused. "Stay."

Thea squeezed her eyes shut. She wanted to. Oh, how she wanted to. "I can't." She reached for the doorknob. "I'll be leaving for Linwood tomorrow."

"Thea. What if there's a child?"

Thea's shoulders stiffened, and her head rose. "I'm barren," she snapped, and whisked out the door, leaving Jeremy to stare after her in shock.

The house party was over. With many regrets and words of gratitude, the guests departed, some to return to London, to attend the wedding of Princess Charlotte, others to go to their homes. Mrs. Jameson and her party had left the day before; everyone else was leaving today. Guests and hosts alike heaved a tremendous sigh of relief. It had been a pleasant time, but all were glad it was over. There had been some ticklish moments, the duchess reflected as the door closed behind the last guest, and some entertaining ones, as she had hoped when she had planned her guest list. Perhaps a bit too entertaining, considering some of the incidents. Thank heavens the party had ended without anyone being killed.

* * *

Jeremy rode his horse alongside the Powells' traveling carriage, lost in thought. It was high time he made more of an effort with Evadne, instead of leaving her to her own devices. It might be the way of most *ton* marriages, but it was not, he had found with some surprise, what he wanted for himself. He wanted at least companionship with his wife. To that end, he had invited the Powells to stay at Moulton Hall, his home on the Kent coast. There, without other people around to act as a distraction, he would have the chance to get to know Evadne, and she to know him. She would be acquainted with his home beforehand, and with his daughter. At last he was giving Gillian a mother.

They had been on the road for two days, and now were nearing Moulton. Jeremy should have been happy, but he wasn't. He had lost Thea. Lord, he'd made a mull of it, and all because when he had most needed to, he hadn't controlled himself. Women were easily available to a man who was passably good-looking, passably charming. Friends that one could trust, though, were in lamentably short supply. He had never realized how much he had come to depend on Thea, until he had lost her.

Not for the first time, he reviewed all that had happened in the bizarre tower room at Rochester Castle. At the time it had seemed right, so right, as nothing in his life ever had before. Never had he known such closeness with another; never before had he wanted a woman so much, but not just physically. He wanted more with

Thea, he wanted to possess her, to know her; and, at the same time, take care of her. It could have been so good, so right, if she had only relaxed her scruples.

And yet . . . And yet, for a moment when he thought she had done just that, when he was astonished that she had given herself to him without marriage and seemed to be giving into his wishes, he had felt a strange mixture of emotions. Happiness, of course, and triumph, too, but mixed with them had been disappointment, surely an odd thing to feel when he had won what he desired. Disappointed he had felt, though, in her and in himself as well, though that was harder to admit. Disappointment that she would so easily give up her principles; disappointment that their relationship would never have the bond, or the blessing, of marriage.

Perhaps then it wasn't so strange that he'd felt almost relieved when she had refused his offer to take care of her. No one would care if she carried on a liaison with him, so long as it were discreet. He didn't think even Evadne would mind. He would, though. It wasn't what he wanted. And Thea had every right to live her life as she chose. He had no right to force her to something she didn't want. Like it or not, she'd made the right decision.

Life was back to normal, then, or almost normal. For, try though he might, he couldn't help seeing himself just a little differently, and he didn't like what he saw, a man who looked to his own pleasure without regard for others' feelings. And, try though he might, he knew he could never again regard Thea as simply a friend. What had happened between them had changed everything.

Shifting uneasily in the saddle, he turned to look at

the carriages following behind him. He would have to make do with Evadne, though he could not imagine experiencing the same rapture with her that he had felt with Thea. He could not imagine wanting her in the same way. But then, she would be his wife. One didn't feel that way about a wife. It wouldn't be proper. One found that kind of satisfaction elsewhere. At least, he had. Now, however, he recoiled from that idea almost as much as he had from the thought of turning to Evadne. It was Thea he wanted, and it was Thea he could not have.

A breeze came to him, bringing with it a special tang that made him lift his head sharply. The sea. They were near home. Something within him quickened at the thought of being home, close to the water again, and he rode a little ahead of the carriage, to the top of the hill. There, below him and to his right, was Moulton Hall, only its chimneys visible. Beyond lay the Straits of Dover, deceptively blue and peaceful looking on this clear day. Home. Jeremy gazed at it a moment longer before spurring Lightning forward. He was home, and nothing would ever again be the same.

"Whoa, boy." The rider pulled the horse to a stop at the crest of the hill and surveyed the view below. Clouds sent dappled shadows over the old, half-timbered manor house, the paddocks where mares and foals roamed and played, the hayfields rippling in the breeze. The horse nickered as if in appreciation, and the rider leaned over to pat its neck, settling long legs clad in breeches and boots more firmly in the stirrups. "Yes boy, home," Thea said softly, and flicked the reins. Obediently the horse set off down the hill.

The horse was heading for home and food; Thea was heading for peace, and she felt it settle upon her as she descended into the valley. After the fiasco at Rochester Castle, she had had only one thought, to come home, where she would be safe. Thea had come to regret her choice of husband during the years of her marriage, but for one thing she would always be grateful. Hugh had left her Linwood.

At the stables she dismounted, handing the reins to Michael Keenan, her head groom and manager when she could not be on the estate. "You've trained him well," she said, lightly slapping the horse's flanks. "Though I don't think we'll try him at Newmarket."

"No, sure and he'll never win any races," Keenan said, leading the horse away, "but he'll do for hacking around."

Thea nodded agreement and turned away, going into the office where Francis was bent over the stud book, concentrating on the entries. Already he was looking better, without the long nights of gambling and carousing to take their toll on him. They spoke a little bit about the stud's operation, and then Thea walked back to the house, tapping her riding crop lightly against her boots. Her hair, held only by a ribbon, swung back and forth. On the surface, her life was all she could wish. Underneath, however, was quite another story.

Stepping into her study, which she used as an office, she sat at the large mahogany partners' desk to deal with the correspondence that came with operating a successful stud farm. In the act of slitting open an envelope, though, she set down the pen knife and put her head in her hands. The peace she usually found at Linwood was missing this time, and not because the farm itself had changed. It was what was in her that cut up her peace, the memory of those mad moments with Jeremy that tormented her endlessly. In returning home, she had thought to outrun her demons, but with no success. They hadn't followed her here; she had brought them with her.

They tormented her, those demons, when she lay awake and vulnerable late into the night. They reminded her ceaselessly of Jeremy's voice, his caressing hands, the splendor and the rapture of being one with him. They told her that what had happened was rare and precious, and that she shouldn't have given it up. Nothing mattered but the two of them, and the world was well lost.

Other demons would chime in at that point. The trouble was, there was more involved than just she and Jeremy. There was the world she lived in, which delighted in scandal and would think nothing of discussing her reputation and shredding it to tatters. More importantly, though, there was Evadne. Thea could understand, in a way, why Jeremy had acted as he had. He was a man with a willing woman. A very willing woman. Thea could not deny that she'd been that. Very few men would ignore such an opportunity, especially a man who had gained himself a reputation as a rake. Nor did he love Evadne. The fact remained, though, that he was promised to her, and, in spite of it, Thea had let him make love to her. No, she thought, brutally honest. She had encouraged it. She, who knew too well the pain of living with an unfaithful husband, who had sworn she would never put another woman in the position she had found herself in, had done that very thing. Her conscience would not let her forget what she had done, or that it was wrong, no matter how right it had seemed. Of all the demons she faced, that one was the worst.

There was one other demon, though, that was nearly as bad, and that was the memory of Jeremy, telling her that he would still marry Evadne. That hurt. Oh, it hurt. For the first time she forced herself to face that fact, fully. Jeremy would take another woman to wife. Another woman would run his home, bear his children, be his companion into old age. Not her. All her fine, high-flown ideas about saving him from Evadne had been just that, ideas. She had no real desire to save him, unless it were for herself. She was, as he had once accused her of being, very jealous indeed.

Thea raised her head and stared ahead of her unseeingly. There was nothing she could do, nothing. In the hours after their encounter she had paced her room, determining at one moment that she had done the right thing, deciding in the next that she hadn't. She wanted him so. She wanted to be with him, on any terms he offered. No matter the consequences; even if it meant the loss of her self-respect.

And that, at last, was what had stopped her. It was the only thing now that kept her sane, in spite of all the demons. It would be the veriest bliss to be with him, but eventually it would destroy her. Eventually he would tire of her and seek another mistress. She could not bear it. She had worked too hard, too long, to be true to herself, to like and respect herself again, after her husband's death, to throw it away so easily. If she had nothing else, she would have herself.

Except that she was not quite the person she'd

thought. She'd made a bad mistake, and the consequences were bitter. She'd lost Jeremy; she'd lost her comfortable view of herself. She was not the cool widow she'd thought, nor was she as upright and moral as she'd once believed. It was a hard lesson to learn. How she was going to live with this new knowledge of herself, she didn't know.

Wearily Thea picked up the penknife again and began to open her letters. Life went on, and she supposed she would survive. It would, however, be very hard. Very hard.

Chapter 11

Evadne's mother glanced out from the Powell's carriage as it turned into the drive of Moulton Hall. "Why, I think we must be there, my love. I can just see the chimneys."

"Thank heavens," Evadne, sitting across from her, said fervently. "I'm tired of this stuffy old carriage."

"Now, my love, we've spoken on this before. A lady expresses herself more elegantly. Quite an estate," she added, looking out again. "I wonder what the income is?"

"Oh, Mama." Evadne moved restlessly on the seat. "I wish I could have brought Fluffy."

"Now, girl, there'll be no more of that. Imagine bringing that cat on a visit." She shuddered. "You may be certain Stanton would not be pleased."

Evadne's lips set in a mulish pout. "I don't care."

"We'll have no more of that, girl," Agatha said sharply. "Stanton is doing you an honor by marrying you and you're to behave in his home."

"My home. Well, it soon will be, Mama." Her eyes, candid and very blue, met her mother's.

"As you say." Agatha turned away, feigning indifference to her daughter's sudden attempt at dominance. Thank heavens the chit would soon be married and off her hands.

The carriage rolled to a stop, and a footman approached to open the door. Agatha Powell emerged, followed by Evadne, who stopped and stared for a moment at her future home. Of rosy brick, with ivy-entwined walls and black shutters, Moulton Hall was a comfortable house, dating back to Queen Anne. There was no great entranceway, only a modest portico jutting into the drive of neatly raked gravel. Flowers bloomed in borders bright against the brick. It was a charming house, but compared with Rochester Castle it was tiny. "Why, it's a poky old place!" Evadne exclaimed just as Jeremy descended the stairs.

"Welcome to Moulton," he said, holding out his hand to Evadne. She gave him a ravishing smile, which he did not answer. He had heard her comment on his home, and he was in no mood at the moment to deal with her petulance or flirtatiousness. "Come." He took her arm and led her inside. "My staff is waiting to meet you, as is my daughter."

"Oh yes, I cannot wait to meet the dear little thing!" Evadne gushed.

Inside the hall she stopped and looked around. Ahead of her was a wide, straight staircase, its banisters curved and polished with the touch of time. Lined up nearby, on the polished parquet floor, were the servants, Gregg, the butler, and Mrs. Gregg, the housekeeper, by his side; several footmen and maids, and the cook. Evadne smiled at them, holding to Jeremy's arm with a possessiveness that was not lost on any of them. "What a charming home, Stanton," she said when the staff had been introduced. "But where is your daughter?"

Jeremy looked up and grinned. "Here she comes now," he said, and went to stand at the foot of the stairs, arms akimbo. Coming down the stairs was a small girl, one hand clinging to her governess, the other holding a large piece of paper. The governess was a tall, thin woman of uncertain age, a cap set upon her graying hair, and though she was plain there was a humorous twist to her lips. Evadne dismissed her from her thoughts immediately. But the child! Lord, she'd rarely seen such a plain little girl. Like her father she was dark, with the same penetrating blue eyes, but the features that made Jeremy handsome were too heavy for a little girl's face. Evadne's lips twitched with annoyance. There were definite disadvantages to this marriage. However, she was certain she could soon persuade Jeremy to send his daughter to school. Then, Evadne thought, she wouldn't have to look at her.

The child's eyes were wide and solemn as she reached the floor and, prompted by her governess, curtsied before her father. Jeremy watched with no expression until suddenly he dropped to one knee and opened his arms. "Well?" he said, and Gillian crashed into his arms, nearly toppling him over. He gathered the small, wriggling body close to him, fighting a surge of emotions and an absurd lump in his throat. "Got a kiss for your father?"

Gillian pecked him on the cheek, and then pulled back, her face wrinkling. "Your face is scratchy, Daddy."

Jeremy passed a hand over his chin; he was heavy-bearded and needed to shave twice a day. "So it is. My apologies, Miss Vernon," he said, and Gillian giggled at being addressed as if she were a grown-up lady. "What is that, Gillian?" he asked, motioning toward the piece of paper she held in her hand.

"A picture. I made it for you, Daddy," Gillian said shyly, handing him the paper and then standing with her hands behind her back.

"Well, it's fine." He smiled at the childish painting of a red boat with a triangular sail floating above waves of deep blue, under a blazing yellow sun. Jeremy pointed to the stick figure on the boat. "Who is that, poppet? The Prince Regent?"

"No, Daddy! That's you!"

"Hm?" Jeremy reared back and pretended to study the picture again, a frown on his face. "Looks like Prinny to me."

"Oh, Daddy!"

"Do you sail, Stanton?" Agatha asked, and Jeremy rose, tucking Gillian's small hand in his.

"Yes. Would you like to try it sometime, Evadne?" he said, turning to her.

Alarm flashed briefly in Evadne's eyes, and she lowered her head. "Yes, Stanton, I would. But, sir, you've yet to introduce me to your daughter."

"My apologies, Evadne. Miss Powell, may I present to you Miss Gillian Vernon." He nudged Gillian in the back and she dropped a quick curtsy before returning to his side.

"Why, hello, Gillian," Evadne said, her voice unnaturally high as she smiled and reached out to pat the little girl's head. "How pretty you are." Gillian squirmed against her father, her eyes wide, and popped her thumb into her mouth.

"Come, Miss Gillian." The governess stepped forward. "It's nearly time for your tea. If we may, my lord?"

"Yes, Miss Moffett." Jeremy rumpled his daughter's hair, and she smiled up at him. "I'll want a word with you later."

"Of course, my lord." Miss Moffett and Gillian both dropped curtsies and then went upstairs, the slump of Gillian's shoulders showing undoubted relief.

Jeremy looked at them speculatively for a moment and then turned back to his guests. "Shall we go into the drawing room?" he said, indicated a door to his right. "I believe it's time for tea."

The following morning Jeremy walked toward his stables, accompanied by Evadne, fetchingly clad in a sky-blue riding habit with a frill of lace at the neck. He hardly listened to her chatter about Moulton or the changes she would make once they were married; all his attention was centered on Gillian, walking on his other side and clinging to his hand. Her silence bothered him. She was a well-mannered child and would not talk when an adult was speaking, but this went deeper. It was a sullen silence, broken only by the monosyllables she gave to any question asked her. Odd, but it was almost as if she disliked Evadne, and for the life of him he could not imagine why. Evadne certainly was nice enough to her, smiling at her and talking to her, but Gillian had not responded. Instead, she tended to cling to him or to her governess, her eyes wide, her thumb in her mouth, a habit he thought she'd broken long ago. Gillian, raised with only adults for company, was usually friendly and at ease with people. Jeremy, remembering a childhood spent isolated from his parents, had always allowed her to talk, instead of sitting mute like a little doll. There was no excuse for her acting this way. He would have to speak with her later.

". . . and of course, we'll be spending winters in London," Evadne chattered on. "And you'll be taking your seat in Parliament."

"I will?" Jeremy said, startled out of his thoughts.

"Yes, of course. It's your duty, and Mama says one must always do one's duty."

"Certainly, but I have no interest in politics, Evadne."

"None?" Evadne stared up at him in surprise. "But that's silly! If I were a man, I'd want to be in Parliament."

"Would you?" Jeremy said, biting his lips to hold back a smile. Evadne, an M. P.? Absurd! "I assure you you'd find it quite boring."

"Daddy." Gillian tugged on his hand. "Can't we go sailing?"

"I told you no, poppet. We're going to select a mount for Miss Powell."

"Do you like horses, Gillian?" Evadne asked, her voice high.

"No."

"No? But that's silly! Everyone likes horses."

"I don't. I think they're stupid!"

"Gillian!" Jeremy exclaimed. "Apologize to Miss Powell at once!"

Gillian looked down and dug one toe into the ground. "I'm sorry," she muttered.

"That's quite all right, dear. Do you ride?"

"My groom has been trying to teach her," Jeremy

said when Gillian didn't answer, "but without much success, I fear."

"I expect she'll learn. My, what a fine stable," Evadne said as they passed under the archway into the stableyard.

"I think so. That's Follett, my groom, holding that bay mare. I think you might like her."

"Yes, she's a beauty." Evadne approached the mare.

"Daddy." Gillian stopped short, dragging Jeremy back. "May I go back to the house?"

"Not yet, poppet. See, Follett's saddled Pepper for you. I thought we'd show Miss Powell about the estate."

"I don't want to ride, Daddy."

"I don't care for it when you whine, Gillian," he said, his voice crisp, "and—"

"Jeremy!" Evadne called, her voice high with delight, as the groom helped her into the saddle. Jeremy looked up, and Gillian took advantage of his distraction to free herself. "Oh, she's a darling!"

"Yes, isn't she?" Jeremy strode forward, noting from the corner of his eye that Gillian was sidling toward the fence.

"She's a spirited one, isn't she? Let go her head," Evadne commanded the groom, and the mare, let loose, danced a few steps sideways. "What fun!"

Gillian had scrambled up to the top rail of the fence and now was sitting there, eyes huge in her pale face. Jeremy frowned slightly and crossed to her. "Come," he commanded, holding out his hand. "I'll help you mount Pepper."

"No, Daddy, don't make me—Daddy!"

Her words ended on a scream. Jeremy whipped

around in time to see the mare rear. He raced forward, but Follett had caught hold of the bridle, bringing the mare down and soothing her with soft words and a gentle touch. "Good God!" Jeremy exclaimed. "Are you hurt?"

Evadne's cheeks were flushed, her eyes bright. "Oh, that was splendid!" she exclaimed. "I shall expect a fine ride."

Jeremy stared at her and then turned back to see his daughter running out of the stableyard toward the house. "Gillian!" he called, and started after her.

"Let her go, Stanton." Evadne walked the mare, now well under control, to his side. "She'd only hold us back. It's stupid to be so frightened by a horse."

Jeremy turned cold, hard eyes on her. "Gillian is not stupid."

"No, did I say so? Come, Stanton, mount up! I want to ride."

Jeremy looked at her a moment longer and then turned toward his horse. For a moment his eyes met Follett's, and then he mounted. The pleasure had gone from the morning for him. He was not, at the moment, pleased either with his daughter, or with his future bride.

Several days later, Jeremy sat in his study, a sanctuary from the bedlam his house had become, and wondered about the wisdom of bringing Evadne here. Since his wife's death, Moulton had been a place of peace and relaxation for him, a haven from the hectic life led by the *ton*. Here he could follow his own pursuits, whether riding or sailing or just being with his daughter. Here he could breathe freely. The Powells' visit had changed all that. He felt he might never have any peace again.

Matters had gone wrong almost from the beginning. First, Evadne hadn't liked her room, the best guest bedroom at the front of the house, claiming the early morning sun would awaken her. Mrs. Gregg had taken exception to Evadne's tone of voice, and though Jeremy had managed to soothe his housekeeper's ruffled sensibilities, she was not the last of his staff to be annoyed by the visitors. Both Agatha and Evadne had an unfortunate way of ordering the servants about, and Jeremy, who liked his home to run in an easy, relaxed way, had finally been forced to speak to his fiancée. That had led to her pouting and flouncing angrily away. The whole of that evening she had ignored him, instead concentrating on the new vicar whom Jeremy had invited to dinner, to that young man's considerable embarrassment.

Jeremy had been out of patience with her then, but the next morning she had come downstairs in such a sunny mood and asked his forgiveness so prettily that his annoyance had melted. She was young, he'd thought indulgently. She'd soon settle down. However, matters had not improved, and the incident at the stables hadn't helped. Evadne hadn't meant to frighten Gillian, though she should have known better than to let her horse rear, he thought, with a return of the annoyance he'd felt yesterday. Of course, she hadn't realized just how frightened Gillian was of horses.

To tell the truth, he hadn't, either, and it bothered him. Strange, for she was so intrepid in the boat with him, and was turning into a creditable sailor. Evadne, on the other hand, when they had gone out the previous afternoon, had turned green when they were not twenty feet from shore. Of course, that wasn't her fault. In all fairness, much of what had happened hadn't been. He could understand she might find life here a trifle flat, after the excitement of London and Rochester Castle. Nor did she seem to know how to handle children. But this was his life. She'd best become accustomed to it, as Iris, his first wife, never had.

That made him frown. Lord knew he didn't want to make another such mistake. Certainly he needed money, but not so badly that he'd throw himself into another bad marriage to get it. Nor did he have the excuse this time of being in love; he thought he saw Evadne very clearly indeed. Yes, she was a flirt. Yes, she liked the excitement of town life. But she was young, he told himself once again, and malleable. Surely he would be able to mold her to his liking.

His musings were interrupted by the sound of carriage wheels rumbling on the drive. Glad for the interruption, he rose and looked out the window, to see a Powell footman descend from a traveling chaise, holding, at arm's length, a large box with holes cut into its sides. Curious, Jeremy crossed the room and went out into the hall, just as Gregg opened the door. From the box issued an unearthly howl that made Jeremy's hackles rise and caused Gregg to step back in surprise.

"What the devil?" Jeremy said, and the footman turned to him looking vastly relieved.

"Miss Powell sent for this, my lord," he said, thrusting the box at an astonished Gregg and fleeing. Jeremy and his butler exchanged mystified looks, and at that moment Evadne tumbled down the stairs.

"Fluffy!" she exclaimed. "Is that Fluffy? Oh, do put him down, Gregg!"

"Yes, miss," the butler murmured, setting the box down with a thump as another howl filled the hall.

"Evadne, what on earth?" Jeremy said.

"It's Fluffy." She fell to her knees and tugged at the latches, opening the box. Immediately the huge, brindled cat Jeremy had seen on his occasional visits to the Powells' London home emerged, snarling and spitting, in spite of Evadne's efforts to calm him. Jeremy and Gregg took an involuntary step back. "Mummy's little precious," Evadne crooned. "Pretty little kitty."

"Good God!" The cat looked, if anything, more disreputable now that it had in London, where it apparently had had a fine time. Its nose was scratched, and there was a bald patch on his neck. "You don't mean—is that deuced animal staying here?"

"He's mine!" Evadne said defiantly, clutching the cat closer. The animal let out a long, low growl. "I want him to stay."

Jeremy gave her a long, hard look, and sneezed. "That tears it. Gregg, I want that animal out of here immediately," he said, and stalked into his study.

"No!" Evadne cried, and followed him without knocking on the door. "Fluffy is staying."

"No, Evadne." Jeremy turned from his desk, gazing at her coolly. "I do not like cats. The creature will have to go."

Evadne gazed up at him, and the laid her hand on his sleeve. "But he's such a nice cat," she said coaxingly. "Pleath? Pleath let him thtay?"

"I'm sorry, Evadne." Jeremy's voice was firm, but kind. "I can't have a cat in the house. He can't stay."

Evadne pulled back, her eyes filling with sudden tears as she stamped her foot. "You—you beast!" she cried, and ran from the room.

Jeremy looked at the study door for long moments after it had closed, and then walked out into the hall. "Gregg?" he called, and the butler came forward, looking sheepish. "Did you do as I asked?"

"No, my lord. The young lady was powerful upset," he went on, before Jeremy could say anything. "She took the—creature and went upstairs with it, sir."

Jeremy stared at him for a moment and then turned. "Oh, very well. I shall be in my study if I'm needed."

And pray God he wasn't, he thought, sinking down behind his desk. He needed a rest from his guests, from the entire situation. There was no denying the fact: Evadne's visit was not going well. If only Thea were here, he thought wistfully, and then banished the thought. Thea was lost to him. He would have to make do with Evadne.

His fingers, which had been toying with a pen, stilled. That didn't mean he had to spend the rest of his life like a monk. Nor did it mean he couldn't see Thea, even if he had lost her friendship. When they were in town for the season they'd be bound to run into each other. There'd been too much between them, even before that night at Rochester Castle, for him to forget her. He missed her, damn it! He missed her serenity, her intelligence, her calm beauty. He wanted to see her again. He wanted, if nothing else, to apologize for his behavior. He could not go on, the rest of his life, being at odds with Thea. With anyone else, but not with her. He had to see her, and he thought he had the perfect excuse.

It was Evadne, surprisingly, who had given it to him. Evadne, who belied her femininity by riding like a demon and by driving to an inch, had looked over all his horses and declared that he didn't own one good team of carriage horses. At the time he had been annoyed, but soon he had resigned himself to the idea of buying her whatever she wished, giving her things to make up for the one thing he couldn't give her. In town he would have gone to Tatersall's, but that wasn't possible now. However, Linwood, Thea's stud farm, was just a few hours distant. He could ride over to see what she had available, could he not? There was surely no harm in that.

With sudden energy, he rose from his desk. Yes. That was what he would do. If he accomplished nothing else, at least he would escape for a time the uproar Evadne's visit had caused in his house. Perhaps he was making a mistake, but it felt like the first right thing he'd done in a long time. He was going to see Thea again.

"Whose carriage is that, Keenan?" Thea asked as she rode into the stableyard, her trim figure attired in breeches and shirt, tall and erect in the saddle. Riding alone over her land she had escaped for a time from herself. Now her interlude was over. Time was beginning to heal her, though. She no longer winced when she thought of what she had done; that particular sore spot wasn't so tender anymore. She was human, and she'd made a mistake. A bad one, certainly, but she needn't atone for it the rest of her life. At the same time, she didn't regret what had happened. There was a woman inside her whose presence she had never suspected. Jeremy's passion had brought her to life, making Thea feel whole. Though it had been a long time since she'd been a girl, she felt as if she'd grown up in the last month. She had learned a great deal about herself and had survived. If there were times when life seemed empty, lonely, she ignored them. She had everything she could want. It was time to go on with her life.

"Visitors, ma'am." Keenan took Daffodil's reins as she swung down to the ground. "Interested in our horses."

"Oh? Customers, do you think?"

"Sure, and they might be. A gentleman and two ladies."

Thea made a little face. "And I dressed like this. Please deal with them, Keenan, until I change."

"Aye, ma'am. Come, Daffy, let's get you rubbed down."

Thea smiled briefly as he led the mare away and then turned, striding out of the stables toward the house. As she reached the door a figure stepped in front of her, blocking the way. Though the sun was at his back, she knew him instantly. "Jeremy!" she exclaimed, and all her hard-won peace fled in an instant of blinding knowledge. How could she go on with her life, without him?

Chapter 12

"Hello, Thea." Jeremy smiled, his eyes traveling over her leisurely. "That is an interesting outfit."

Thea flushed, confused by his presence and her memories. "I—to exercise the horses—it's more practical," she stammered.

"Of course." His eyes held amusement and something else, something she didn't want to identify.

Oh, lord! What was he doing here, when she'd just started to feel at peace again? Unbidden, the memories of the night they had shared came back, making her cheeks turn pinker, though she rarely blushed. "I—I'll go change."

"Don't bother on my account," he drawled.

Thea took one look at his face and fled. "I'll be with you presently," she said, looking back in time to catch a distinct look of appreciation on his face. Oh lord, she had never been so mortified in her life, she thought, but inside her a tiny spark of warmth glowed. No matter how she fought it, no matter how wrong it might be, she was glad to see Jeremy again, glad that he still cared about her. It could never be, she knew that. She also knew that seeing him like this, in short fragments of time with others present, would eventually destroy her. For now, however, with her newfound awareness of what she felt for him, she would take what she could get.

The warmth died abruptly as she ran into the garden to reach the house. There, strolling along the paths, was Evadne, fussily attired in a ruffle-trimmed spencer of deep pink over a white muslin dress. With her was her mother, and a small child. Thea stopped dead and turned, but too late. "Mrs. Jameson!" Agatha called. Thea turned, a sinking feeling in the pit of her stomach. Of all people for her to see. She wondered if her guilt and joy showed on her face.

"Mrs. Powell." She forced herself forward, smiling. "What a pleasant surprise. You've come from Moulton to visit?"

"Oh, no." Agatha frowned. "That is a most singular costume, Mrs. Jameson."

"Work clothes, ma'am." Thea kept her voice level with an effort. "I was just about to change."

"But you don't have to," Evadne said sweetly, and Thea briefly clenched her fists at the smirk on the girl's face. "We're here on business, you see."

"Oh?"

"Yes. Stanton has promised to buy me a team for my carriage and when I heard he was going to come here to select them, I just had to come along."

Thea let out her breath. "I see." Some of the pleasure from her encounter with Jeremy faded. He hadn't come to see her, then. For one crazy moment she had thought—but that was clearly a dream, only. "Who is that with you?" she asked, looking past Evadne to the child, who hung back, her eyes huge and her thumb stuck resolutely in her mouth.

Evadne waved a hand in dismissal. "Oh, that's Stanton's daughter. She wanted to come along."

"And why not?" Thea smiled at the little girl. "Why should adults have all the fun?"

"Make your curtsy to the lady, Gillian," Agatha said sharply. A rebellious look crossed the child's features, to be replaced by one less definable, but more disturbing. The child was terrified, Thea realized, watching her drop a quick, clumsy curtsy.

"It is a pleasure to meet you, Miss Vernon," she said gravely, holding out her hand. Gillian looked at it a moment, unsure what to do, and then put her small hand into Thea's, giving her a sweet, shy smile. Her father's smile, Thea thought. Gillian looked so like Jeremy, Thea's heart warmed to her instantly.

"Well." She stepped back. "I must change. Why don't you come inside? You must be thirsty after your drive."

"Don't mind if we do." They followed her inside, Agatha's small, sharp eyes darting everywhere. Thea wondered, as Lydia greeted them, if Agatha were doing sums in her head. It was a relief to leave her unwelcome guests and reach the privacy of her room, if only for a little while. She needed some time to recover from the shock of seeing Jeremy, which had again turned her world upside-down.

A few moments latter, attired in a gown of muslin sprigged with tiny blue flowers, with white frills at neck and cuffs, Thea came downstairs, patting a strand of hair back into place. It was not her ordinary working garb, but somehow she hadn't wanted to don the more sober, businesslike gown she usually wore when meeting with prospective customers. Hanson informed her that the ladies had returned outside, and so she went to the stables. Evadne was standing in the stableyard, smiling up at Francis, and the others were nowhere to be seen. Thea slipped into the stables, breathing in the familiar, comforting scents of leather, fresh hay, and horse. Within it was shadowy and dim, and it took a moment for her eyes to adjust. Then she saw him, and her heart leaped painfully.

Jeremy. He was standing with Keenan, examining the forelegs of a young colt. Thea watched his hands move expertly down the horse's flanks, and her heart contracted at the sight. No dandy's hands, soft and white and pampered, but working hands, a man's hands, hard and square and capable. Capable, too, of gentleness, as they caressed her. No, she mustn't think of that. He had made his choice.

Jeremy looked up admiringly. "Fine piece of horse flesh here."

Thea smiled and came forward. "We think so," she said, surprised her voice sounded so normal. "Fast, too. If he keeps up, we may enter him at Epsom."

"Hm." Jeremy looked at the horse with new respect. "I'd heard good things about these stables but I didn't realize you'd progressed so far, Thea."

"Mr. Keenan and I have worked very hard. Miss Powell said you are here to choose a pair of carriage horses?" It was a safe subject. Before, she'd been able to talk to Jeremy about anything. Now she felt stiff, uncomfortable, as if he were a stranger.

"Yes." Jeremy sounded stiff, too. Surely he couldn't be as uneasy as she was? Not when he'd got what he wanted. "I thought I'd ride over to see what you have.

Of course, once Evadne knew the reason for my trip, she insisted on coming along."

Thea forced a smile. "Well, of course! They're to be her team, are they not? Now, let's see." She frowned a bit. "I'm not sure I've anything suitable, not if you want a matched pair. I do have two young blacks, but they haven't been trained for a carriage."

"She has her heart set on a team of grays."

"Perhaps you can persuade her otherwise."

"If I'm lucky," he muttered.

Thea turned to him, a question in her eyes. He wasn't looking at her, but instead was rubbing the forehead of a rawboned chestnut in his stall, and Thea's heart turned over again. He looked so unhappy. No matter what had happened between them, no matter his reaction to it, she loved him. She would wipe that look from his face if she could, wrap her arms around him and cradle his head to her breast, comforting him, loving him. When had she started to love him? It seemed now that she had loved him forever. It didn't excuse her behavior at Rochester Castle, but it did explain it. She had been blind. It had taken only a brief moment of discovery for her to recognize it, too late. For he was taken, and the best she could hope for was to become his mistress. *Never!* she thought, revolted. She would not share him with anyone.

"Here's a beauty," Jeremy said.

Thea forced herself out of her daze. No matter how she felt, she must not let him see. "Yes, that's Daffodil," she said, smiling. "My mount."

"Sweet tempered, isn't she?"

"Yes, and a sweet goer. And she's not for sale. Now, here's one of the horses you might want to consider."

185

She stopped in front of a stall holding a handsome, fine-boned black mare, whose eyes rolled at their approach.

"Bit nervy," Jeremy said. "I'm not sure how she'd be in a team."

"Perhaps not. She's a fine jumper, though, and she does respond well to training, but you're right, she is high-strung. No matter, there's another over here," she said, conscious that she was chattering.

"Thea," Jeremy said, laying his hand on her arm, and she went very still. "I didn't ride all this way just to look at horses."

Thea didn't look at him. "We've discussed this, Jeremy."

"I know." He pulled away, running a hand distractedly through his hair. "But Moulton seems flat. Empty."

"Even with Evadne."

"Not fair, Thea." He put his hand on her shoulder, turning her to face him. "Thea—"

"Stanton? Oh, there you are." Evadne was briefly framed in the sun-lit doorway, and Jeremy and Thea both turned. Francis followed in her wake, an odd look on his face, Thea thought. She looked up at him questioningly as he came closer.

"I've told Miss Powell I didn't think we have anything she'd like," he said. "No grays, I fear."

"I want grays." Evadne's lower lip was thrust out as she stopped in front of Daffodil's stall.

"No, but I've seen one or two that might do, if we can find a match," Jeremy said. "There's a nice black over here—"

"I don't want blacks! Nasty dark things." She pointed at Daffodil. "I want this one."

"She's not for sale," Thea said quietly.

186

"Of course she is, this is a commercial establishment, is it not?" Evadne said, looking very like her mother as she glared at Thea. "Stanton, I want this one."

"I'm sorry, Evadne, but she's not for sale," Jeremy responded.

"I want her!"

Jeremy frowned, and Evadne quickly lowered her voice, smiling up at him and batting her eyelashes. "Pleath?"

Jeremy looked toward Thea. "It's out of the question," Thea said crisply.

"Please?" Evadne opened her eyes wider. "You can change her mind, Stanton."

"No, Evadne. You'll have to do without this time."

"Ooh!" Evadne stamped her foot. "You're heartless!" She whirled away, bits of hay swirling about her as she ran.

Francis looked uncertainly from her to the others and then turned. "I'd best go after her," he said.

Jeremy rolled his eyes and then turned, his hands shoved into his pockets. "I'm sorry, Thea. She's a bit spoiled, I'm afraid." He smiled. "You wouldn't consider selling?"

"No." Thea's tone was decisive. "You'll have trouble with her, Jeremy."

"She'll learn," he said grimly, turning away.

Thea gnawed at her lower lip. He was unhappy, and would be unhappier yet. She could ease his misery, a treacherous little voice said. She could give him the love he would miss. "I hope so," she said briskly, dismissing the sweet fantasies as she moved toward the door. "Was there anything else you wished, Jeremy?"

"Hm?" Jeremy glanced up, and his face cleared.

187

"Yes. I'll have to be thinking about a mount for my daughter. It's high time she learned to ride."

"Doesn't she know how?"

"No. She has an aversion to horses. I can't imagine where she comes by it. Her mother was a notable rider."

"But wasn't she thrown?"

"Yes, and it was her own fault." Thea gave him a questioning look. "I had a stallion I allowed no one else to ride. He was nervous and bad-tempered. Truth to tell, I couldn't always control him. One day when I was home on leave, I had him saddled for me. Iris mounted him instead, when the groom's back was turned. She'd always wanted to ride him." He was silent for a moment. "I had been detained at the house, and by the time I reached the stables, it was over. Apparently the stallion began bucking and rearing as soon as Iris mounted, and she was thrown to the ground. Her head struck a paving stone. She died a few hours later."

"Jeremy, I'm sorry," Thea said after a few moments, and Jeremy shook himself from the memory.

"It's past. But I want Gillian to ride and to learn her limitations, so she'll never be tempted to do something so stupid."

"Of course." Thea's smile was sympathetic. "You'll need something gentle, then. Have you a pony for her?" she asked as they emerged from the stables into sunlight. Francis and Evadne were standing a little distance away, she with her head bent while Francis talked, and Thea looked at them curiously.

"Yes, she has one. Never took to it, though."

"Hm? Oh, your daughter. Well, not everyone likes horses, Jeremy."

He frowned again. "I won't pamper her on this. If she

can do nothing else, she must learn to ride. Gillian!" he called. "Now, where the devil is she?"

"Here, Daddy!" Gillian ran around the corner of the stables and skidded to a stop.

"Where were you?"

"In the kitchen, Daddy."

"Did Cook give you some of her macaroons?" Thea said, smiling.

Gillian smiled shyly in return. "Yes."

"We're trying to decide on a horse for you," Jeremy said, and the child's smile faded, to be replaced by a wary look that puzzled Thea. "What do you think?"

"Do I have to?"

Jeremy frowned. "Yes. I saw one you might like when you're older."

"No!" Gillian broke free of Jeremy's grasp as he started toward the stables. "Don't make me go in there, Daddy!"

"Gillian! That is enough! Now we've talked about this," he said, his tone moderating. "Remember I told you there's nothing to fear about horses?"

"Yes, Daddy," she whispered.

"Jeremy, must it be today," Thea began, and he motioned her to remain silent.

"You said you'd be a big girl. Now, come. We'll go inside."

"I won't!" Gillian pulled back, her mouth set, reminding Thea of Evadne at her worst.

"Gillian—"

"I won't and you can't make me!" she cried, and turned, running.

"Gillian!" Jeremy started after her, and then stopped at the touch of Thea's hand on his arm.

"Let her go, Jeremy. She'll come to no harm," she said.

"She has got to get over this," Jeremy said through clenched teeth.

"Jeremy, she's a child. A little girl. Weren't you ever afraid of things when you were little?" She looked up at his set jaw, seeing a stranger. "She's terrified."

"Yes, well, she'll have to learn not to be."

"Was that Gillian I saw running away just now?" Agatha said, coming up to them.

"Yes."

"The child wants manners, Stanton. She needs a mother."

"Oh, honestly!" Thea exclaimed, and strode away, conscious that the others were staring at her in surprise. She would have expected such an attitude from Mrs. Powell, but to find it in Jeremy shocked, even enraged, her. The poor little girl, she thought, fuming. An uncaring father and a selfish, spoiled stepmother. How people could treat a child like that, when there were so many others who wanted children and would cherish them . . .

Thea stopped that train of thought, a lump in her throat. It did no good to think about that, her longing for a child. She'd do what she could, instead, to help Gillian.

She wasn't quite certain where the child had gone, but she went in the same direction, knowing where she would go if she were a frightened little girl. In the garden, against one of the old brick walls, was a trellis so overgrown with roses that it had created a bower of sorts. It was there that she found Gillian, huddled and shivering, and her heart went out to her. "Gillian?" Thea called softly, crouching down, and Gillian raised a tear-stained face to her.

"I don't want to look at horses," she said, and Thea thought that she sounded more mature than Evadne sometimes did.

"You don't have to," Thea said, sitting down with her back to the wall. "May I sit?"

Gillian stared. "You'll get your gown all dirty."

"It will wash."

"Miss Powell thought you looked funny wearing breeches." She sighed. "I wish I could dress like that all the time."

"So do I." Thea leaned back against the wall, her arms wrapped around her legs. "I've always thought this would be a good secret place. Do you have a secret place, Gillian?"

"Yes," Gillian said, looking down and plucking at her skirt, "but I don't want to tell you about it."

"Of course not, because then it wouldn't be secret. I remember, when I was about your age, I used to sit under an enormous azalea in our garden. I'd bring my dolls out and have wonderful tea parties with them. And sometimes my stuffed pony, and I would pretend I was riding, just like Mama."

Gillian's face went white. "No! No horses."

Odd. This was more than mere dislike. "Gillian?" she said, and Gillian raised her head. "I've something to show you that's much better than horses. Will you come with me?"

Gillian looked at Thea's outstretched hand with suspicion. "Will I have to go back in the stables?"

"Well, yes, but we can go in by the side door and you needn't see any horses. I promise."

Gillian gazed a moment longer at Thea's hand and then scrambled to her feet. "All right," she said and placed her hand in Thea's.

Thea was surprised to feel a lump in her throat at the trust implied in that gesture. "Very well. We'll go this way," she said, and led the way through the stableyard to another door, at the end of the stables. There was no one in sight, and so Gillian didn't hesitate, until they were inside and the sound of a horse whinnying made her freeze, whimpering a little bit. Thea laid her hand briefly on her head. "It's all right, Gillian. Nothing's going to hurt you."

Gillian looked up. "I don't like horses."

"I know. But I think you'll like this. Look."

"Kittens!" Gillian dropped to her knees in the straw lining the empty stall and reached out to touch a tiny ball of fur. "May I hold them?"

"No, they're too little yet, their eyes haven't even opened. See? Mother cat isn't happy we're here."

"She looks mad." Gillian tentatively held out her hand to the cat, who sniffed, and then turned away, apparently deciding her brood wasn't threatened. "I wish I could have a kitten, but Daddy says no. And Miss Powell has one."

"A kitten?" Thea said in surprise.

"No, a big, ugly cat. He scratched me. See?" She held out her hand, and Thea made the proper commiserative noises about the tiny scratch.

"Do you like Miss Powell?" she asked carefully.

Gillian shrugged. "She'll do, I suppose."

"I see." Thea knelt back on her heels, her hands on her thighs. She did see, a great deal. Beneath Gillian's apparent acceptance of her father's fiancée lay a world of resentment. *Dear lord,* she thought. *What is Jeremy doing to this child?*

"Thea?" a voice called from the other end of the corridor, and Thea rose, turning.

"Yes, Jeremy," she said. "We're here."

"I can't find Gillian—oh." He stopped as Gillian scrambled to her feet, her face shining.

"Daddy, kittens! May I have one?"

"I'm afraid not, poppet." He laid his hand briefly on her head. "They're not old enough."

"But when they are? Daddy, please?"

"No, Gillian. You know cats make me sneeze."

"But Miss Powell has one."

"Miss Powell is a guest."

"Daddy—"

"No, Gillian. That's enough." Gillian subsided, her lower lip thrust out much like Evadne's, and he turned to see Thea regarding him oddly. "We'd best be leaving. We have a long ride ahead."

"I'd like to speak with you, Jeremy," Thea said.

"Yes, well?"

"Not here. Gillian, I'm afraid we'd best leave mother cat alone."

Gillian took Thea's hand, swinging back and forth on it. "May I come back?"

"If your father agrees." Thea looked down at her, the lump in her throat threatening to choke her. "Come, kitten. Let's go back out and let these little ones sleep."

"All right." Gillian skipped beside her, now that the threat of horses was past, chattering about Moulton, and Jeremy followed behind.

Evadne came up to them as they emerged into the sunshine, Francis behind her. Gillian's step slowed, and

193

she backed away from them, going to stand with her father. Again Thea's anger rose, at the thought of that child with this foolish, selfish girl as her stepmother. "Mrs. Jameson?" Evadne said, her voice breathless. "I'd just like to say—"

"Go on," Francis prodded gently, smiling at her when she paused.

"I'd just like to say I'm sorry," she said in a rush. "For the way I acted, I mean. It was wrong of me, I know."

"No harm done," Thea said, startled not so much by Evadne's words as by the sincerity in her eyes. She glanced past Evadne to Francis, and then looked again, closer this time. *Heavens!* "I hope you're able to find a team you like."

"Oh, yes." Evadne turned to Francis, her face anxious, and smiled when she saw him nod in approval. Thea glanced over at Jeremy, who was watching the others with his brows slightly raised.

"Well," he said. "If we're to make Moulton by dinner we'd best be going."

"I'll have your team brought 'round," Thea murmured, turning.

"I'll come with you. I'm a bit concerned about the off-leader's hindquarter."

"You should have said something," Thea said, keeping up the fiction of polite conversation as they walked together back into the stable. "Mr. Keenan is a genius with horses."

"I did." He paused by the stall where the horse had been placed. "What did you think of that?"

"Hm? What?"

194

"Your brother made Evadne apologize. Amazing." He shook his head. "And what is more, she meant it!"

Thea took a deep breath. This time she was not going to rein herself in. "Jeremy, I swore I wouldn't meddle, but—"

"You're going to."

"Someone has to! Can't you see what a mistake you're making?"

"It's a mistake you could help me prevent, Thea."

"Ooh!" Thea pulled back from his outstretched hand. "I never thought you could be so selfish! You'll escape to London when you can, but what of Gillian?"

"We'll leave Gillian out of it, thank you. And speaking of Gillian, why did you encourage her dislike of horses?"

"Jeremy, the child is terrified! Can't you see that?"

"She'll have to grow out of it."

"She won't. It goes so much deeper than you think. But then, you're never with her enough to realize things like that, are you?"

"What do you know about it?" he retorted, stung. "I'm a damn sight better parent than my own father was. He never realized any of us were alive."

"But do you know anything else about her, Jeremy? Do you know why she fears horses, or that she doesn't like Evadne—"

"We won't discuss this," he said, biting off the words.

"Oh yes, we will, because if you marry Evadne, you'll have an unhappy little girl. And I seem to remember your telling me once about how your mother neglected you."

"I don't neglect Gillian! She has a governess, and there are servants—"

"But not you."

"Damn it, I can't be there all the time. I make sure she's cared for."

"Oh, certainly! By servants. She'll grow up just like you, selfish and lonely and not knowing why. And who will take care of Evadne? Oh, I know why you're marrying her. A child bride you can ignore, just like your own child."

Jeremy went very still. "I will pretend you didn't say that," he said, his voice very quiet and very cold. Without another word he turned and strode away. Thea stared after him for some moments and then whirled, fleeing out the side door toward the house. If she had to face any of them again that day, Evadne or Mrs. Powell or Jeremy, she would scream.

She was in the parlor, pacing angrily back and forth, when the sound of hoofbeats announced that her guests were leaving. She wanted to cry, she wanted to scream. Instead, she picked up a crewel pillow and flung it across the room.

Francis chose that moment to seek her out. "I thought that went well—hey!" he exclaimed as the pillow caught him on the chest. "What did I do?"

And Thea sank down upon the sofa and promptly burst into tears.

Three days he had been waiting for the wind to change, allowing the Dover packets to cross to France, and Roger DeVilliers was getting restless. Three days of imagining that his creditors would catch up with him and call him to account for all his debts, though he suspected they would have a hard time finding him. He was staying in a humble inn just outside of Dover, rather than the more well-known Ship Inn in town. It went against everything he had been brought up to hold dear, to abandon his estate and flee to the Continent, but he had little choice. His debts were too high ever for him to pay. He would have to go, if only he could find a ship in time.

He rode aimlessly, this afternoon, down some of the lanes near the inn, brooding on his damnable luck. He had hoped, this season, to mend his fortunes by marrying an heiress, but all the matchmaking mamas were too well aware of his reputation to let that happen. He had even thought, for a little time there at Rochester Castle, that he might have the heady experience of taking another girl away from Stanton, this time permanently, but that hadn't occurred. Miss Powell had apparently preferred Stanton's title to his own brooding, mysterious features. In her place, he would probably have done the same thing.

The scent of the sea, mixed with those of freshly mown grass and wild roses, came to him as he reached the top of the hill. Below him and to his right he could just see the roof and chimneys of a great house. Perhaps the home belonged to someone he knew and could visit, to pass the long hours, he thought, walking his mount toward the iron gates, which stood open. But the name on the plaque set into the pillar, Moulton Hall, meant nothing to him. Not at first. Then a memory came to him, of Stanton telling the Duke of Rochester that he would be returning to Moulton with Miss Powell.

Stanton's home! The horse danced beneath Roger as a surge of energy went through him. Of all the luck! Perhaps, he mused as he rode away, a devilish smile upon his face, matters weren't so bleak as they seemed. For if Stanton were there with his fiancée, then perhaps he would have another chance. DeVilliers let out a laugh. Damn, but he would have his heiress, after all!

Chapter 13

". . . and so, my lord, when you spoke of selling the Wales estate, I took the liberty of having an engineer look over it," Mr. Tuttle, Jeremy's solicitor and man of affairs, explained. He leaned back, placing his hands on his plump knees with an air of smug self-satisfaction. "It is well I did. You won't be wishing to sell now, my lord."

Jeremy lifted dazed eyes from the figures on the paper before him. "How much did you say it would bring in a year?" he asked, unable yet to believe what he had just heard.

"About fifty thousand pounds worth of coal, my lord, at market value. It's a rich vein, the engineer said. And with more and more factories demanding coal every day, why, it might even bring more than that. You'll be a wealthy man, my lord."

"Yes." Jeremy leaned back, his fingers drumming on the desktop. A wealthy man. A man who no longer needed to marry money. "Thank you, Mr. Tuttle," he said, rising and extending his hand. "I assume that is all?"

"Yes, my lord, but you'll be wanting to hire a surveyor, I'm sure, and another engineer—"

"Without a doubt. See to it, Tuttle, and notify me when you do." Jeremy opened his study door. "Good day, sir."

The solicitor bowed and left, clapping his hat on his head. Jeremy returned immediately to his desk, sinking down into the comfortable leather chair, staring ahead without seeing anything. A coal mine. Jeremy shuddered at the image that conjured up, of being trapped, confined. Smothered. Ironic, the tricks life played on one. Here he had considered selling the estate in Wales, one of the few pieces of property he owned that wasn't entailed and thus was his to dispose of as he wished. To save the estate, he had instead engaged himself to Evadne, something that was no longer necessary, something he no longer desired in the least. Now that he'd found what he really wanted, it was too late. He was trapped, indeed. "Good God, Stanton," he muttered. "You are a fool."

Loud noises in the hall distracted him from his thoughts. He flinched at the sound of an anguished howl. That damned cat. No matter what he said, Evadne refused to send the animal away. He listened to her shrill and angry voice, and someone else protesting. Gillian, he realized with surprise, and rose just as the door to his study burst open.

"Stanton!" Evadne cried, hurling herself inside so fast that he barely avoided colliding with her. Her curls were disordered, her cheeks were red, and in her arms she held the cat, which was struggling furiously. And that was the strangest sight of all, because the wretched animal was dressed in what he could swear was the

200

Stanton christening gown, with a baby's bonnet tied upon its head. Unholy glee rose within him, mixed with brief, reluctant sympathy for the creature. "You must do something! Look what that dreadful girl has done to my precious!"

"Daddy, I was only playing!" Gillian protested.

Jeremy looked at her, his lips twitching. "Did you, ah, attire the cat in those clothes?" he asked mildly enough.

"I was just playing, Daddy. I was pretending Fluffy was a baby. He likes it," she added.

"He does not!" Evadne exclaimed. "Look at him, Stanton! He's miserable, poor little kitty."

Jeremy's lips twitched again. Fluffy struggled in Evadne's death-grip, the bonnet tilted at a rakish angle that displayed his notched ears and made him look more disreputable than ever. "I admit it doesn't suit him," he said. "But has the creature actually suffered any harm, Evadne?"

"Fluffy is not a creature, sir!"

"Um, no, of course not. Is, um, Fluffy hurt?"

"Well, no," Evadne conceded reluctantly. "But think of the damage to his pride, sir!"

"Er, precisely." This time both sides of Jeremy's mouth twitched. "If he is unharmed—"

"It's no thanks to that daughter of yours that he isn't! Something must be done about her, sir, and—"

"And I will be the one to do it, Evadne," he said, his voice gentle, but so underlaid with steel that Evadne quieted. He glanced at Gillian, who had tried to wedge herself behind a chair near the door for protection, her eyes huge and one foot crossed over the other. Jeremy repressed the urge to wink at her. "I will speak to Gillian."

Evadne glanced up at him and then turned away hastily at the look in his eyes. "Yes, of course," she muttered. "But Stanton, I can't have this happening to Fluffy—"

"It won't happen again," Jeremy said soothingly, leading her toward the door. "Will it, Gillian?"

"No, Daddy," Gillian whispered.

This time Jeremy did wink at her. "Fluffy will be fine."

Evadne looked at him uncertainly. "Are you sure?"

"Yes. Don't you think you'd best get him out of those clothes before he's strangled?"

"What? Oh, yes, of course!" Evadne looked down at the struggling cat, who now had the bonnet strings between his teeth. "Come on, my pretty little kitty," she crooned. "Mommy will take care of you."

"Good God," Jeremy muttered, closing the door behind her. Already he could feel the onset of a sneeze. He devoutly hoped that his study would not now prove to be uninhabitable.

Gillian edged out from behind the chair. "Daddy, I'm late for lessons. May I go?"

"No, you may not. Come here." He sat in a chair facing his desk. "Now. What was that all about?"

"I'm sorry, Daddy," she whispered, standing before him on the carpet, her eyes down. "I was only playing. Honest."

Jeremy allowed the smile he had been holding back to spread across his face. "I know that, poppet. Come up here." He lifted her onto his lap and she threw her arms about his neck, holding on for dear life. "Hey." He loosened her clinging hands. "What is this, poppet?"

"Miss Powell said you'd beat me."

Jeremy winced at the look in her eyes, the same way he knew he had once looked at his father. "Gillian. Have I ever beat you?" he demanded.

"No, Daddy."

"All right, then. You know better than to think such a thing." But the truth was, he thought, as he curled his arm around her trusting little body, that she really didn't know him all that well, nor he her. "I suggest in the future, however, that you leave Miss Powell's cat alone."

"Yes, Daddy. He's really quite ugly," she said, and giggled. "He looked so funny with that bonnet on!"

Jeremy grinned. "Yes, poppet, he did."

"I thought he'd look like a baby, but he didn't."

Jeremy's smile faded. "Gillian, would you like a baby brother?"

"No." She swung her legs back and forth, kicking the chair. "Girls are better than boys."

Jeremy let out his breath. He hadn't explained the purpose of Evadne's visit to Gillian, though he expected she had heard the servants gossiping. "You'll think differently when you're grown."

"I'd rather have a kitten. When is Miss Powell leaving?"

"Not for a while yet, poppet. Why?"

"I don't like her. And she doesn't like me."

"Nonsense, of course she does."

Gillian responded with an oddly adult look of scorn. "She thinks I'm ugly," she said matter-of-factly. "I heard her say so."

"Oh, Gillian," he said, surprised at the anger that surged through him. "She didn't mean it."

Gillian shrugged. "When is she leaving?"

"Well, Gillian, it's not that easy. You see, I've asked her to marry me." His daughter went still in his arms. "So you see, poppet, she's going to live here with us."

"But Daddy!" Gillian wailed, scrambling down to the floor. "She doesn't like me! I don't like her!"

"Gillian, stop this." He took her shoulders in a gentle grip. "You'll learn to like her. Don't you want a new mama?"

"No!" Gillian broke free of his grasp. "I don't, and you can't make me!" she cried, and ran from the room.

"Gillian!" Jeremy crossed to the door, only to see her scrambling up the stairs toward the safety of her governess's arms. "Damn." He had bungled that, all right. What a disaster his engagement was turning out to be, he thought, stalking toward the front door.

Gregg, standing near the stairs, coughed discreetly. "May I ask where you're going, my lord, in case someone calls?"

"Out," Jeremy snapped, and strode toward the stables.

Lightning was quickly saddled for him, and soon he was astride, riding hard toward the sea, away from his formerly peaceful home and all the problems that beset him. At length, though, he came to a stop on the shingly beach far below the hall. Lightning was blowing hard, and Jeremy felt remorseful as he swung out of the saddle. "Sorry, boy," he said, leading the horse to a stream that emptied into the sea. "We'll take it slower going back." He slapped the horse's flanks lightly and then walked away, sitting on a boulder, throwing pebbles into the gray, treacherous-looking water and wondering about his life. God! What was he going to do?

Lighting was well trained and would come if called, and so Jeremy was free to think about other things. About Thea. Whenever his mind wasn't occupied, it automatically returned to her, remorselessly repeating all that had happened between them: their initial friendship; his growing awareness of her; his anger with her during his visit to her stables; and, most insistently, the interlude at Rochester Castle. Oh yes, that magical time he had spent with her. If he could only forget it—but how could he forget something that had been so precious, so important? He, who had had his choice of women and had sampled freely, now wanted only one, and she was the one he couldn't have. He would, instead, marry Evadne, who shied away when he kissed her and showed nothing but disdain for his daughter. Angry though he had been with Thea the previous week over what she had said about Gillian, what galled him the most was that she was right.

Jeremy muttered an oath and tossed the last pebble away. Life at Moulton was rapidly becoming insupportable. Instead of the peace he usually found there, there was Evadne, complaining about the food, the scenery, boredom; alternately flirting with him in the high-pitched voice he had come to dislike, or sulking. Try though he had, he had not been able to interest her in any of the things he enjoyed. The only pastime they had in common was riding, and even that was ruined for him by her incessant chatter. And there was that damned cat. The creature appeared everywhere, in spite of Jeremy's orders to the contrary, and the maids could not seem to rid the house of its hair. As a result, he was constantly sneezing and welcomed any chance to escape. Evadne was going to have to change her ways, he thought with little conviction, else life with her would be unbearable. *And if you can't bear to live with her now, what will it be like when you're married?* a voice in his head repeated. Thea's voice.

"Damn it, go away, Thea!" he said, and Lightning, brought his head up from the stream, looking almost enquiring. Feeling foolish, Jeremy rose and began to stride down the beach, too restless to sit still any longer, taking in deep breaths. Trapped, he was trapped, but, damn it, what could he do? He knew now that he had made a terrible mistake in becoming betrothed to Evadne, even if the time with Thea had never happened. A gentleman could not in honor cry off an engagement. What did his honor owe Thea, though? And Gillian? What, for that matter, did his honor owe himself? Surely not a shallow, empty marriage with no chance of happiness. Evadne was too concerned with herself to give much thought to the problems and concerns of a seven-year-old child, or, for that matter, those of a husband. He had indeed made a mistake, and he would have to find a way to live with it.

Of course you will. You'll escape to London and poor Gillian will be even more neglected than she is now, the voice spoke again. Not Thea's voice this time, but that of his conscience. "Damn it, I don't neglect her!" he yelled, and a gull standing on a nearby rock took to the air with a squawk. Abruptly he realized how foolish he must look, raving at the sky. And how foolish he had been. He had neglected Gillian. Oh, not to outward appearances. She had all she needed, and someone to look after her as well. So far as society was concerned, he had done his duty. None of that mattered, though, when he recognized deep down that he didn't really know his daughter. And that, he thought guiltily, was something he had sworn he would do, since his own father had made little attempt to know him.

So, he wondered as he turned and whistled for Lightning, what would he do now? He had hoped that remarrying would make them a family again, but now he knew better. Evadne would not make that possible. It was Thea he wanted, Thea he needed; Thea, who had shown some understanding of Gillian's needs. A gentleman could not in honor cry off, but . . .

For the first time since leaving the hall, Jeremy smiled, a mischievous, devilish smile. No, a gentleman could not break an engagement, but there were ways. There had to be. He had to do something, he thought as he mounted Lightning. And at last, he thought he knew the answer.

"I wish it would stop raining," Francis said from the window of the drawing room at Linwood. "Spring was the wettest I can remember, and this summer isn't turning out much better."

"God's will," Miss Proctor said as she sipped her tea.

Thea, engaged in disentangling her embroidery silk, frowned. She was as unhappy as Francis to be pent up inside, and having to listen to the pious maunderings of the vicar and his sister was almost too much to bear. "I do wish the sun would shine for more than a few hours at a time. There, that's untangled at last! More tea, Vicar?"

"No, no, my dear, I've had a sufficiency." Mr. Proctor

leaned back, patting his rounded stomach, which quite bulged the buttons of his waistcoat. "Excellent tea, and you must compliment your cook on the cakes."

"Thank you," Thea murmured. The vicar did like his food. Usually, that didn't bother her, but today it did. She'd felt queasy since awakening that morning. Perhaps Lydia was right. Perhaps she had been working too hard lately.

"I must say," he went on, "I do like to see a lady at her needlework."

"Oh thank you, Vicar!" Lydia, bent over yet another project, looked up, smiling with confused pleasure.

Thea hid her own smile. "I fear I do very little needlework," she said. "I much prefer to be out of doors."

"Yes, of course. The entire county has seen you riding. *Astride,*" Miss Proctor added, in case Thea had missed the note of censure in her voice.

" 'Tis the only way to exercise the horses properly."

Miss Proctor's nostrils pinched. "Of course, but it is such a mannish operation, Mrs. Jameson. Most unsuitable."

Thea carefully set a stitch before she replied. "I don't believe so. Particularly if I work only with mares."

Miss Proctor's face darkened, and the vicar brayed, far more heartily than the witticism deserved. "Got you there, Jane. But now you have your brother to help you. Of course, when you enter into matrimony again, ma'am, you'll no longer need to be concerned with it."

"I don't plan to marry again, sir," Thea murmured.

The vicar chuckled. "You say that now, but I expect you'll change your mind. When you meet the right man."

Thea looked at him and then quickly away, seeing the expression in his eyes. "Perhaps."

"Nonsense, Gerald!" Miss Proctor said sharply. "Mrs. Jameson surely knows her own mind."

"You think so, Jane?" The vicar chuckled again. "Well, could be you're right, of course, you usually are. But then, I've often found that ladies do change their minds. Particularly if they meet a persuasive man."

"Indubitably," Francis said, grinning.

Miss Proctor eyed her brother with undisguised alarm. "Come, Gerald," she said, rising abruptly. "We have visits to make. We've imposed on Mrs. Jameson's hospitality quite long enough."

"Oh, very well, very well." Mr. Proctor rose, grumbling, and waddled over to Thea, taking her hand in his damp one. "But I may call again, Mrs. Jameson?"

"Of course, sir."

"Mrs. Jameson." Hanson stood at the door. "There's another guest. Shall I show him in?"

Thea twisted in her chair. "Who is it, Hanson?"

"The Viscount Stanton, ma'am."

Jeremy! Lightning shot through her veins, dispelling the lassitude she'd felt all day. "Of course, Hanson." She was surprised her voice sounded so steady. "Do show him in."

Miss Proctor frowned. "I'm rather surprised at you, Mrs. Jameson. To receive a man like that in your house."

Thea looked up. "A man like what, ma'am?" she said mildly.

Miss Proctor colored. "Like—you know quite well what I mean!"

"Now, Jane." The vicar laid a hand on her shoulder.

"Doesn't the Bible teach us not to judge others? Though I must own, Althea," he said, frowning also, "that I cannot condone this acquaintance either."

Of all the nerve! Thea didn't think she'd ever felt such righteous indignation in her life. Who was this man, to speak of Jeremy in such a way? She was opening her mouth to speak when Hanson presented the caller. "Viscount Stanton, ma'am."

Silence fell in the room. Thea looked up and her eyes caught and held Jeremy's, whose own gaze was questioning. Jeremy. It pained her to see him again. It was wonderful to see him again. "Stanton," she said, rising as if nothing were amiss. "What brings you here today?"

"Hello, Thea." Jeremy bowed over her hand and nodded at Francis and Lydia. "I didn't realize you had guests."

"We were just leaving. Come, Gerald." Miss Proctor sailed past Jeremy, her nose in the air, and Jeremy turned to watch her go, a bemused look on his face.

"So you're Stanton. I am the Reverend Mr. Proctor." The vicar held out his hand. "An honor to have you in our humble village, sir."

Jeremy nodded in return. The two men looked at each other measuringly, as if sizing each other up. Thea hastened forward. "Would you like tea, Jeremy?"

The vicar started and cleared his throat. "Well, then, I'll be going, Mrs. Jameson. But I may come again?"

"Of course."

With a gallantry that was almost comical, the vicar bent and raised Thea's hand to his lips. "Thank you, dear lady. I shall be looking forward to that auspicious occasion."

"Yes," Thea said faintly as he left at last. "Oh dear."

"A most affecting scene, Thea," Jeremy drawled. "Am I to wish you happy, then?"

"No! And you didn't help matters, Jeremy."

Jeremy shrugged, the picture of innocence. "What did I do?"

"Looking at him as you did," she said accusingly.

"Poor Mr. Proctor," Francis said, laughter in his voice.

Thea sent him a look. "Oh, Fran, not you, too!"

Lydia took one last stitch before rising. "Do you know, dear, I think he has rather a *tendre* for you?"

"Oh lord," Thea groaned.

Francis laughed. "It would be an interesting match."

"Francis," Thea warned.

"I'm only funning, Thea, you needn't look at me like that." He grinned, holding out his arm to Lydia. "Come, Aunt. I don't believe we're wanted here."

"Oh, but—" Thea protested, but too late. Francis and Lydia were already out of the room. She and Jeremy were alone.

Silence descended on them. While there were others in the room, Thea hadn't realized the awkwardness of their meeting, but now she did. When last they had been alone together, she and Jeremy had quarreled. The time before that—well. It did her no good to think of that. What in the world would they say to each other? "Jeremy—"

"Am I to wish you happy, Thea?" he said again.

"Don't be silly." She sat down, crossing her arms over her chest and scowling at him. "You realize now I'll be the center of village gossip for days to come."

"Hardly my fault." Jeremy sat facing her. "But come,

Thea, could you not offer me some refreshment?" A smile spread across his face. "I grant you I'm not so appealing a suitor as your vicar, but do I really merit such shabby treatment?"

"No, of course not." Thea crossed the room to tug on the bellpull, then turned to face him. "Jeremy, why are you here?"

"To apologize, among other things." He glanced about the room. It was long and low, with beamed ceilings and whitewashed plaster walls. Plump chintz cushions and bright crewel pillows were strewn on the comfortable sofa and the Queen Anne chairs, and the diamond-paned casement windows were draped in matching fabric. The room smelled of beeswax, of cherishing, filling his soul with a peace he had thought lost. Moulton didn't have it, but then, Moulton didn't have Thea. "I like your house, Thea. It's restful."

"Thank you. You needn't apologize, Jeremy. I had no right to speak as I did."

"Even if you were right?"

"About Evadne?" she said, just as the door to the drawing room opened and Hanson appeared, bearing a tray with a decanter of Madeira and two glasses. Impatiently she stood while Hanson poured the wine and left, waiting, as if her entire life depended on the answer to her question. As perhaps it did.

"About Gillian." Jeremy raised his glass and Thea turned away, biting her lip. Foolish to think that he had come to tell her that it was she he loved, not Evadne. "Come, sit down, Thea. We can still talk, can we not? We've always been friends."

Friends, Thea thought, and she sank down in a chair facing him, her face again composed, serene. Her pride, her very life, depended on her hiding the painful emotions his visit had awakened. She didn't think he loved her, but knew he was fond of her. That could very well have been enough to start with. Such a wife as she would have made him! And such a mother for Gillian, the only child she'd likely have, she thought, her eyes stinging. Not for her Evadne's self-centered absorption and foolish ignorance of her fiancé. Thea would not have shared him with any woman, but then, he would not have needed another, she would have loved him so. At least, she didn't think so. She closed her eyes against the nagging doubts. She had not been enough for Hugh.

"What about Gillian?" she asked, and Jeremy rose, pacing to a window. Now they came to it. He'd thought over his strategy carefully before making his visit. If he told Thea that he'd had second thoughts about Evadne, there was no way of knowing how she would react. He'd expected her to be angry or bitter. What he hadn't planned on was seeing her being courted by another man, or the anger that awakened in him. Thea was his. Had she not given herself to him in the tower room at Rochester? It had to mean she cared. She had too much dignity, and too much self-possession, to do such a thing lightly. It could be enough. It should be enough, except that he had bungled it badly by not immediately renouncing his engagement to Evadne. To hell with his honor. He'd hurt her. He had no right to expect her to come to him for himself. If, however, he appealed to her on Gillian's behalf, he thought he had a chance. Thea had shown more true feelings for Gillian during their brief visit than Evadne had in all her time at Moulton.

"Evadne doesn't like her, I fear," he said finally. "And that's why I'm here."

Thea paused in the act of pouring out another glass of Madeira for him, the crystal decanter poised in her hand, her eyes wary. "Oh?"

He moved restlessly away from the window, picking up a crewel pillow and then replacing it, pacing across to the unlit fireplace. "I've been thinking about what you said, about Gillian, and I fear you're right. She *is* terrified of horses."

"I thought so." Thea set the decanter down and held the goblet out to him. "Come, drink your wine, Jeremy."

"Thank you."

"What have you decided to do about Gillian?" she asked him.

"Well, that's the thing, you see." He hunched forward, the crystal goblet held negligently between his hands. "I can't seem to talk to her anymore, Thea. Ever since we visited here she's changed. She used to be a lively, happy little girl. Now—" He waved his hand in frustration.

"Now?"

"Now she's do damned well-behaved!"

Thea smiled. "Most parents would appreciate that."

"Yes, well, I'm not like them. I don't particularly like being called 'sir' instead of 'daddy.' "

"As bad as that?"

"Yes." He leaned forward. "I need your help, Thea."

"Mine? What could I do?"

"You could, to start, teach her to ride."

"What, here?"

"No, of course not. I'd like you to come to Moulton.

"Jeremy, that's absurd!" She drew back. "I can't go to your home."

214

"She needs you, Thea." This was the crucial moment. He leaned forward, making his voice persuasive. "I don't like seeing her so frightened. My groom has tried to teach her, but he has no affinity with children. You do."

"I don't know anything about children, Jeremy."

"Gillian likes you. All she's talked about since we've got back, the little she's talked, is you. And the kittens."

"Well, yes, that's all very well, but—"

"She'd trust you, I'm certain of it. Thea, I don't know what else to do."

Thea leaned back, her eyes closed. It was tempting, so very tempting. Going to Moulton would mean seeing him every day, talking with him, being with him. Him and Evadne. "No."

"Why not?"

"I think you know quite well." She faced him levelly. "This isn't about Gillian at all, is it?"

Jeremy returned her look and then smiled. "No, not totally. Thea—"

"Get out." She rose and tugged on the bellpull again. "If you think you can bamboozle me like this, you're wrong."

"You've got it wrong, Thea. I care about you, and—"

"And I told you I won't be your mistress."

"That's not what I'm asking, Thea!"

"What else is there? Ah, Hanson, there you are," she said as the butler entered the room. "Lord Stanton was just leaving. Will you see him to the door?"

"Yes, ma'am. My lord?"

Jeremy stood still for a moment, gazing at her. "Very well, Thea, I'll go. But this isn't the end of it, you know."

"Goodbye, Jeremy," she said, standing with her hands clasped before her as he walked away. For of course this was the end of it. That he thought so little of her that he could make her such an offer cut her to her soul. She had been better off with Hugh. At least he had been honest in his cruelty.

"Ma'am?" Hanson stood in the doorway. "Is there anything I can get for you?"

"No, thank you, Hanson." She forced a smile to her lips, though the emotions evoked by Jeremy's visit were roiling inside her. She felt nauseated. "Please take the tray. I'm not at home to any more visitors today."

"Very good, ma'am," Hanson said, and left her to her thoughts.

With relief Thea sank down onto the sofa, closing her eyes and taking deep breaths, willing her stomach to settle. Lately it got upset at the oddest times, and though she had wondered if she were sickening for something, she knew now what was wrong with her. She was heartsick. Jeremy didn't love her and never would. She would have to make a life without him. Oh, she would manage. She'd done quite well since becoming a widow, and she knew she could continue. For now, though, the pain was almost more than she could bear. Jeremy was gone. She doubted she'd ever see him again.

"What did Stanton want?" Francis asked that afternoon, as Thea bent over the ledgers that held the accounts for the stud farm.

"Nothing. These look good, Fran. You're doing good work."

"Thank you. Whatever he said upset you, Thea. You didn't eat anything at luncheon."

"I ate," she protested.

"Not much. If he did anything to upset you, I'll—"

"What? Call him out? Don't be silly."

"Call him to account, anyway. He's a fool."

"Why do you say that?"

"Everyone can see he's not right for Evadne. Miss Powell, I mean."

Thea gave him a long look. Not for the first time, she wondered about Francis's feelings for Evadne. Not for the first time, she felt immensely sad for him. And for herself. "Well, there's not much one can do about it, is there? I think I'll have Daffodil saddled and—oh!" She grabbed at the edge off the desk as she straightened, her face very white.

"Thea!" Francis jumped up and grasped her arm, pulling her to a chair. She collapsed into it gracelessly, grateful just to be off her feet, her hand to her head. "My God, you're pale. Are you all right?"

"Yes, I think so." She took a deep breath. "I felt dizzy for a moment. It will pass."

"I don't think you should ride."

"Nonsense, Fran, I'm fine."

"No, you're not. I'll bring you back to the house."

Thea looked up and saw a look of resolution on his face. In spite of the sick, swirling feeling inside her, she felt a stab of satisfaction. Bringing Francis here, away from the temptations of London, had been a good idea. "All right," she said meekly.

A short while later she leaned her head back on the sofa in the drawing room. Francis had wanted to bring her to her room, but that she had steadfastly refused. Ordinarily in the stoutest of health, she wasn't about to give into such weakness. Not when it had been brought about by that dratted man, and the unpleasant emotions he awoke in her.

"You do look pale, Thea dear," Lydia said, glancing up from her crewel. "Wouldn't you be more comfortable in bed?"

"No, Aunt. I'll be fine in a little while." She gave Lydia a smile she hoped was reassuring. "I'm very rarely ill. You know that."

"Yes, dear. This isn't like you at all." Lydia returned to her crewel and then set it down, her expression resolved. "Thea, dear, could you be—" she began.

Thea looked up. "Could I be what, Aunt?"

"Oh no, no, never mind. It's silly."

"What is?"

"No, no, it's not important."

"Aunt." Thea kept her voice patient. "I can see that you're upset about something. Won't you please tell me?"

"Well, not exactly upset, dear. It just occurred to me."

"What?"

Lydia tilted her head. "Could you be with child?"

Chapter 14

Thea sat up straight, her head spinning with the shock of Lydia's question. "I can't—Aunt, what did you say?"

Lydia went placidly on with her crewel. "It seemed to be a possibility, dear."

"But—but I can't be. Stanton and I—" She stopped, coloring, at the look Lydia gave her. "How did you know?" she said weakly.

"Well, Thea dear, I do watch people, you know. Anyone with eyes can see how you feel about each other."

"But—don't you think—doesn't it bother you?"

"No, dear, why should it? I've thought all along you deserve some happiness." Lydia held her crewel at arm's length, studying it critically. "Though I must say you haven't looked happy lately."

"I can't be with child," Thea said, even as it dawned on her that her "illness" carried all the signs and symptoms of pregnancy.

"Perhaps not. I realize this must be a shock to you, dear." Lydia tilted her head to the side again. "There's a different look to you lately, though. I can't quite put my finger on it, but it is like the time I decided to add gold thread to a purse I was stitching. It made everything glow."

Thea bit back a hysterical desire to giggle. Oh, if only! She knew quite well, though, that what Lydia had suggested was impossible. "I'm not with child, Aunt," she said quietly. "I can't have children."

Lydia looked up, her eyes bright. "Oh? Who told you that, dear?"

"No one." She swallowed, embarrassed by the intimacy of the conversation. "When Hugh and I—well. I know Hugh was your nephew, but, well, he had children already. And I—we tried, but to no avail. It had to be my fault."

"Hugh told you that?"

Thea looked away, her cheeks pink. "Yes."

"I see. Hugh was many things, but I never realized before that he was a liar."

"Aunt!" Thea stared at her. "Whatever do you mean?"

"Hugh had no children, dear."

"But there were women. I saw them."

Lydia shook her head. "He was cruel, wasn't he? But I never realized the extent of it until now. Yes, Thea dear, there were women. After he died, I visited every one of them. Well, someone had to see that they were taken care of," she went on after Thea made an exclamation of surprise. "Hugh certainly didn't. And none of them, even with that, claimed that their children were his." She shook her head. "He lied to you, dear."

Thea stared at Lydia, stunned by the woman's cool practicality, so at odds with her woolly minded appearance. "He lied," she said, falling back against the sofa. "Then, all that time—good God, I might be!" Filled

220

with fierce wonder, she pressed her hand against her stomach. A child. After all this time, she was to have a child. And the child would have no father.

As abruptly as that, her joy faded. She was unmarried and would remain so, and her child would bear the burden. For all that, though, she wasn't sorry. She couldn't be. A child, the product of the love she felt for Jeremy, even if that love weren't returned. Against all the odds, in spite of all the difficulties ahead, she wanted this baby as she had never in her life wanted everything. "I'm going to have a baby," she said, her voice soft with wonder.

"Yes, dear. I'll have to be thinking about making a layette for it."

Mirth bubbled up inside her. "I think there's time for that, Aunt. I'm not even certain of it yet."

"Yes, you are." Lydia set down the crewel. "What are you going to tell Stanton?"

Thea's eyes were wary. "Nothing."

"For shame, Thea. Don't you think he deserves to know?"

"What could he do about it, Aunt? He's marrying someone else."

"This is not a time for foolish scruples, Thea," Lydia said in a stern tone Thea had never before heard her use. "You are not the only one involved in this. Stanton has a right to know, and what of the child?"

Thea looked away, gnawing at her lower lip. Lydia was right. Difficult though it would be, she would have to tell Jeremy. There was also the child to consider. She couldn't allow a child of hers to be branded with the cruel names that were given the fatherless. "You're right," she said finally. "I will have to tell him."

221

"I knew you would do the right thing. Oh dear." Lydia laid down her needlework. "I shall have to get in some wool for knitting, but what color do I choose?"

"I wouldn't worry about it yet." Thea rose and crossed the room, bending to kiss Lydia on the forehead. "Thank you, Aunt. I don't know what I'd do without you," she said. She then went into her study, to pen a note accepting Jeremy's invitation to Moulton.

The barouche jounced as it rounded the turn and carefully edged its way down the hill, making Thea reach for the strap to steady herself. She took a deep, calming breath. Ahead of her, seen through the windows of the carriage, was the sea, blue-gray on this day of scudding clouds, with the chimneys of Moulton Hall just visible behind the trees. She had arrived. After arguing the wisdom of the trip with herself, she was here, and she knew at last it was the right thing to do. Jeremy had to know about his child.

The doctor in the village near Linwood had confirmed her pregnancy, hiding his shock behind a mask of concern, both of which Thea ignored. A child. She would be a mother at last. She exulted in the changes in her body, however slight: the slight thickening of her waist, the new fullness of her breasts; even the nausea that assailed her at unexpected times. For so long she had wanted this, and had resigned herself to not having it. Now she indulged herself. She was in love, and she was to have a child. She also was not married. Instead of being worried, she felt a vast contentment that went bone deep. For the first time in many years, she felt complete.

The carriage drew up to the hall and a footman opened the door for her. "Welcome to Moulton," she heard, and turned to see Jeremy descending the broad, shallow stairs toward her, smiling.

Thea's heart jumped. "I didn't realize you were so near the sea," she said quickly, to cover her reaction at seeing him.

Jeremy looked down at her. "Do you like the sea, Thea?"

"I don't know, I've never really been so close before," she said, returning his smile and hoping her feelings didn't show in her eyes. The constraint that had been between them during their last two encounters was suddenly gone.

"You've the chance now. Come, you must be tired after your trip." He took her arm. "Gillian and I like to sail. Do you think you'd like to try it?"

The very thought made her stomach turn, but she forced herself to smile. "Yes, that sounds enjoyable. Where is Gillian?" she asked as they walked into the entrance hall. His daughter, after all, was her excuse for visiting. "I've a present for her in the carriage."

"You didn't have to do that, Thea. But thank you."

"Don't thank me until you know what it is." Mischief sparked in her eyes. "I brought her a kitten."

Jeremy's face twisted. "A kitten! Dash it, Thea, you know animals make me sneeze."

"And horses frighten Gillian." She faced him directly. "We all have our fears, Jeremy."

"I suppose we do." He turned to look at her. "And what do you fear, Thea?"

Thea, about to answer, stopped. Jeremy was holding open the door of the drawing room for her, and there, sitting on the sofa, was Evadne. Pouring out tea, she looked as if she belonged here. There was what Thea feared. That Jeremy didn't love her. That he had, instead, fallen in love with his fiancée, unsuited for him though she was. If that had happened, neither she nor her child would have a chance. "Miss Powell. How nice to see you again," she said, forcing a smile to her lips.

"Mrs. Jameson." Evadne's smile was equally insincere. "So kind of you to visit us." Her eyes narrowed slightly as Thea sat facing her, drawing off her gloves. "Do you plan to stay with us long?"

Thea's fingers tightened briefly on her gloves at the proprietary tone of Evadne's voice. "Until I know whether or not I can make any progress with Gillian."

"Miss Gardner is not with you?" Agatha Powell, seated beside her daughter on the sofa, made no attempt to conceal the note of censure in her voice.

Thea smiled. "I asked Lydia to come with me, of course, but she's been invited back to Rochester Castle. Apparently the duke's brother is quite taken with her." She smiled. "She's embroidering a pair of carpet slippers for him."

"And what of Mr. Thorne?" Evadne asked, keeping her eyes on the teapot as she poured.

"Francis? He stayed behind to manage the stables." She looked at Evadne for a moment, and then turned to Jeremy, who was standing by the fireplace, an elbow propped on the mantel. "Does Gillian know why I'm here?"

He shook his head. "No. I haven't said anything to her. Do you have any idea what you'll do?"

"Yes. But, mind you, Jeremy, I won't see her threatened to go on a horse."

"Stanton must be considered to know how best to raise his daughter," Agatha said.

"Of course," Thea murmured, and Jeremy sent her a look, his lips quirked.

"I'll send for her, shall I?" he said, tugging on the bellpull. For the next several moments the conversation centered on such trivial subjects as the weather and Thea's journey, until Gregg opened the door from the hall. Gillian entered the room, her eyes properly lowered, until she saw Thea.

Her face brightened. "Mrs. Jameson!" she exclaimed. "Father told me you were coming."

Thea, glancing up at Jeremy, saw him wince at the word "father." Things were indeed bad between them. "Hello, Gillian," she said, rising and smiling at the child. "If I may, Jeremy, I'd like to take Gillian outside to show her something."

"Of course." Jeremy smiled. "I think you'll like it, poppet."

"Yes, Father," Gillian said, and Jeremy winced again. He crossed to the window to see them emerge from the house and walk to Thea's barouche. Gillian was holding trustingly to Thea's hand, her face puzzled, until Thea withdrew a box from the carriage. He couldn't keep from smiling when he saw Gillian suddenly begin to jump up and down with excitement.

"Good Lord," he muttered amusedly.

"What is it, Stanton?" Agatha demanded.

Jeremy didn't turn. "Thea's brought Gillian a kitten."

"Thea? Oh, Mrs. Jameson. She'll spoil the child, Stanton."

"Perhaps." He turned and smiled at Agatha's disapproving face. "But then, I must be considered to know what is best for my daughter. Excuse me." He bowed and left the room.

"Well!" Two spots of color appeared high on Agatha's cheeks. "I'm not sure I like this, Evadne."

"No, Mama," Evadne murmured. For once, she was in perfect agreement with her mother. No matter what relations were like between her and Stanton, it went beyond all bounds of propriety for him to bring his mistress here. She didn't like it at all. Something, she decided, would have to be done.

". . . and Daddy keeps his boat in the boathouse down there," Gillian said, swinging Thea's hand as they walked along. It was morning, just after breakfast, and Thea had secured a postponement of Gillian's lessons to begin the task of gaining her trust. "Do you want to see it?"

Thea smiled down at her. "Not just now, kitten. I'd like to see the stables."

Gillian's smile faded, and her steps slowed. "Why?"

"Why, because I'd like to see how my team is doing in a strange stable. And because I like horses."

Gillian's brow furrowed. "Why?" she said again.

"Why?" Thea stopped, her head tilted to the side. "I don't know, really. Why do you like kittens?"

"Because they're small and soft and cuddly and they don't hurt you."

"Did your pony throw you, Gillian?" Thea asked gently, and to her dismay saw Gillian's frown turn into a mutinous pout.

"I don't want to go see the horses," she declared.

"All right, you don't have to."

Gillian gazed up at her, amazed. "I don't?"

"No. But I do want to visit my team for a moment. I've brought sugar for them." Reaching into the pocket of her skirt, she brought out several lumps of sugar. "I think they deserve a treat, don't you?"

"I suppose." Gillian's steps slowed as they passed under the archway leading to the stableyard. "May I stay here?"

"Of course." Smiling, Thea left Gillian in the care of a groom, and went inside. It would not be easy to break through the girl's fear, she conceded reluctantly as she stopped at her horses' stalls, petting each one and feeding them the sugar. Whatever it was that caused it ran deep and strong. Thea only hoped she could deal with it, more for Gillian's sake than for any desire to see her mounted on horseback. She was, she found with just a little surprise, as concerned about this little girl as she would be about her own child.

Gillian brightened once they left the stables, and by the time they reached the shore was laughing and chattering as if she'd never known fear in her life. Thea dutifully admired Jeremy's boat, and then steered the girl back toward the house. "Time for your lessons, kitten," she said as they walked toward the door, gravel crunching beneath their feet.

"Couldn't you ask Daddy to take us sailing and let me miss lessons just for today? Please?"

"Not today, poppet," Jeremy said, coming out and standing on the top step. "Been showing Mrs. Jameson around?"

"Yes." She threw herself at him. "Oh, Daddy, I went to see Snowball this morning. Couldn't I keep him in the house? Please? He's such a pretty kitten. I'll keep him in my room, I promise."

"I'm afraid not, poppet." He smiled down at her to soften the refusal, his hand resting briefly on her head. "Now run along and find Miss Moffett. You're late for your lessons."

"Yes, Daddy." Gillian took a few steps, and then suddenly ran back to Thea, hurtling herself into her arms. "I'm glad you're here. Will you stay for a long, long time?"

Thea's eyes misted over, but not before she saw Jeremy give her a startled look. "As long as I can, kitten," she said. Forever, if she could. She wanted, with sudden ferocity, to be this little girl's mother. "Go along, now. Miss Moffett is waiting." She patted Gillian on the back and the little girl turned, skipping into the house.

Jeremy watched her musingly for a moment, and then turned. "You've done wonders for her already, Thea," he commented, descending the remaining stairs.

"Yes, but it won't be easy." Thea fell into step beside him. The constraint was back. It was there in his eyes, in her awareness of him. She wished he'd touch her. But she was glad he hadn't, for she didn't know how she would react. Gillian, thank heavens, was common ground for them. "She's so frightened she wouldn't even come into the stables with me. Jeremy, was she ever thrown from a horse?"

"No, not so far as I know. She's hardly been on the back of one long enough."

"So I thought. But something's frightening her."

"Can't you ask her?"

"I don't believe she'd tell me." She stopped, taking a

228

deep breath of the salt-scented air. "I do like your home, Jeremy."

"I'm glad. Evadne doesn't."

"No? Why not?"

"She thinks it's small and poky. She much prefers my Berkshire estate."

"But it's not poky at all! It's cozy and homey."

"Yes, well, Evadne's already talking about changing things."

Thea opened her mouth to speak and then closed it again. No. Now was not the time to say anything to him. She would have to, soon enough. Wasn't that why she had come here. "I'd like to ride, Jeremy," she said lightly.

Jeremy smiled. "Then you shall," he said, and they set off, companionable and comfortable, toward the stables.

Evadne was not happy with recent events. Riding her horse up the hill, away from the sea she hated so much, she brooded and puzzled over what had gone wrong with all her fine plans. She had envisioned life with her betrothed so differently. She had seen herself as mistress of Stanton's estate in Berkshire, with an adoring husband bowing to her every whim and her mother acknowledging her as the leading lady of the neighborhood. The reality was far different. Stanton actually seemed to prefer this poky old house, small and unpretentious though it was, and nothing she had said had swayed him. At first, he had laughed when she had pouted and cajoled; now he merely dismissed her. Not at all the ardent lover she had imagined. Lately she had found herself daydreaming about another type of man altogether, a tall, lean man with fair hair and patrician features, though that did her little good. She was betrothed to Stanton, and she could see no way to free herself.

It would be so much better if he just paid some attention to her. He cared more about his daughter, plain though she was. And pert! Evadne would not countenance such behavior from any child, though she had learned not to criticize Gillian to Stanton. How anyone could be so fond of children, she didn't know. She would have to have at least one child, to provide her husband with an heir, but she intended to have as little as possible to do with that child's upbringing.

The worst that had happened, though, the unforgivable insult, was Stanton's bringing his mistress to Moulton. Everything had changed since Thea's arrival. Stanton no longer even pretended to care about what Evadne wanted, or to change his schedule to suit her. Instead, he spent a good deal of time with Thea, discussing Gillian, riding, or sailing on that miserable boat of his. Thea had no right, coming in and taking over as she had. She was not to be mistress of this house. Evadne was. And it was high time she did something about that.

At the top of the hill that rose from the sea she stopped, leaning over to pat her mount on the neck. "Good girl," she crooned, contrite that her fast riding had winded the mare. Stanton kept a good stable, she'd say that for him. She didn't think as much of his groom, who had not wanted to saddle this horse for her if she were riding alone. Evadne had had to be very firm with him, and at last he had given in. She'd have to do something about him, too. "We didn't need that nasty groom with us after all, did we?"

The horse nickered in reply, and an answering nicker came from ahead. Startled, Evadne looked up as a man, his thick, dark hair blowing in the wind, emerged from the trees, riding a chestnut hack that to her trained eyes had seen better days. Even in her winded state her mount could outrun such poor competition, she was thinking, when the man raised his hand in greeting and she realized it was Roger DeVilliers.

Surprise held her still for a moment, and then a kind of elation filled her. Here was a man who had always appreciated her. Here was someone who could possibly be helpful. "Mr. DeVilliers!" she exclaimed, urging her mount forward. "Why, what a surprise. Are you come to visit Stanton?"

"Is this Stanton land?" he asked in apparent surprise, belied by the way he looked at her.

She batted her eyelashes at him. "Why, yeth, it ith."

"So it is. And Stanton lets you ride alone?"

"He's not my keeper, sir!" she said, tossing her head.

"More fool he." He reached for her hand and brought it to his lips, pressing a lingering kiss on her wrist. It took all of Evadne's willpower not to snatch her hand away. "Are things not going well between you?"

She tossed her head. "We're managing." She batted her lashes again. "But what brings you here, sir?"

Roger smiled, elated. It was obvious that all was not well with Stanton and his fiancée. Excellent. "Managing? I thought you were happy with him. After all, has he not a title?"

Evadne shrugged as she turned her horse to walk with his, her discontent evident. What harm could it do to confide in him? "He is not what I expected, sir. He scolds me! And he has brought his mistress here."

DeVilliers looked at her in surprise. "Surely not!"

"Oh, yes. Mrs. Jameson." Her voice was bitter. "He claims she is here to teach his daughter to ride, but I cannot believe it. I am not a child."

"I can see that," he said, letting his eyes linger on her, and spots of pink appeared on her cheeks. "It sounds most uncomfortable, Evadne. I may call you that?"

Her blush deepened. "Of course."

"I must go. Stanton would not be pleased were he to learn I'd trespassed on his land. But my dear Evadne, you must allow me to help you in some way."

Evadne's eyes widened. "How, sir?"

"However you desire. Shall we meet here again? Tomorrow at about the same time, perhaps?"

"I'm not sure that is wise, sir."

"Let me help you, Evadne. It pains me to see you so unhappy."

"Oh, sir, if only you know how good it feels to hear someone talk like that!" She held out her hand to him. "I would be motht glad of your help, thir."

"Then you shall have it." He pressed another kiss to her wrist and then wheeled away.

Evadne watched him for a moment and then turned her mount, returning to the stables in vastly better spirits. Stanton would see, she thought. She'd show him, him and Francis Thorne. They'd learn not to cross her.

Chapter 15

"Jeremy," Thea called as she came down the stairs the next morning. "Have you a moment?"

Jeremy, standing by the door, turned. "Not just now, Thea. I have to see one of my tenants about something."

"Oh." Thea crossed to him, ignoring the impatient way he shifted from one foot to another. What she had to say to him was important and could not be put off much longer. Already she had been at Moulton Hall several days, and she hadn't told him her news. "I need to talk to you about something."

"About Gillian?"

"No, something else. But it can wait." She wasn't about to detain him now, while he was so obviously eager to be off. "When you come back?"

"This afternoon, after luncheon. Is that acceptable?"

"Fine." Thea followed him out onto the drive where a groom stood holding Lightning. "I had a letter from my brother, by the way. He has some questions about the stud and he's doing to come here for a few days. If that's all right with you."

"Of course." Jeremy leaped into the saddle, and

Lightning, sensing his impatience, danced a few steps. "I like your brother. I'll see you at luncheon, Thea."

"Yes, Jeremy." Thea stepped back and watched him gallop down the drive. That was Jeremy, taking everything at full speed. She wondered how he would react when she told him her news.

"Thea," a voice pulled her from her thoughts. She turned to see Gillian. "Is he gone?"

"Yes, quite." Thea held her hand out to the little girl. "Didn't you want to see your father?"

"I don't like his horse." Gillian smiled trustingly up at her. "I went to the kitchen to see Snowball," she went on, linking her hand with Thea's. "May we walk down to the beach?"

"Of course." Their daily walks had become a ritual each enjoyed. "I'd like to stop at the stables first."

"All right," Gillian said, if reluctantly, and Thea reflected that she'd made some progress. Gillian's fear of horses hadn't abated, but in the last few days Thea had managed to coax her into going into the stables. That the child still kept her distance wasn't as important as the trust growing between them, which was why Thea allowed Gillian to use her name, much to Mrs. Powell's disapproval. "Are you going to check on your horses?"

"No, I want to see old Polly. I've an apple for her. Follett thinks she won't be with us much longer, poor old thing."

"My mother used to ride Polly," Gillian volunteered, and Thea took a quick look at her. Gillian rarely talked about her mother. "But she didn't like her."

"No?"

"She said Polly was too slow. She liked fast horses."

234

Gillian fell quiet, her eyes blinking rapidly, and Thea thought it better not to comment.

"Well. Here we are. I'll just give Polly her apple, and we may go to the beach. Hello, old girl." Thea stopped in front of Polly's stall and the horse, an old piebald, loped over, snuffling at Thea's hand. "How are you today, girl?"

"Her teeth are awfully big," Gillian commented, watching as Thea fed the horse the apple.

"Well, horses are big animals. Yes, you're a good girl," Thea said, stroking the horse's nose. "Your nose feels like velvet."

"May I feel?"

Thea turned in surprise. "Of course," she said, managing to keep her voice normal. "Here, bring that stool over and you may stand on it. There. What do you think?"

Gillian hesitantly reached out a hand to touch the horse, drawing back when Polly snuffled inquiringly in her direction. "Why does she do that?"

"It's her way of saying hello."

"Oh." Gillian reached out again, and this time her hand stayed where it was, carefully stroking the horse's nose, even when Polly turned toward her.

"I've a bit of apple left," Thea said softly after a few minutes. "Would you like to feed it to her?"

"All right." Gillian took the apple and held it out, snatching it back when Polly's teeth got a bit too close. "That tickles!" she exclaimed as the horse took the apple.

"See? Polly likes you."

"Do you think so?" Gillian turned back to the horse,

who was watching her through liquid brown eyes. "She's a nice old horse, aren't you, girl?"

"So she is," Thea said briskly, hiding the tangle of emotions she felt, triumph, joy, compassion, and just a little anxiety. She had succeeded in breaking through some of Gillian's fear, and that meant that soon her task would be accomplished. She would have no reason to stay, unless she told Jeremy about the baby. Putting her hand on her stomach, she steeled herself against the swift upsurge of nervousness. Of course she was going to tell Jeremy. It was simply turning out to be harder than she'd expected. But suppose he didn't want to break his engagement to Evadne? What would she do then?

"Thea? May we go to the beach now?"

Thea took a deep breath. "Of course. Say goodbye to Polly."

"All right." Gillian looked back at Polly, and then, with a surprising show of reluctance, climbed down from the stool. "Goodbye, old girl."

"We'll come to see Polly tomorrow," Thea promised, taking Gillian's hand as they went out.

"And may we take her another apple? She likes apples, doesn't she, Thea?"

"So she does. Now, I wonder who that is," she said, as a post chaise came down the drive.

"Are we having visitors?" Evadne, dressed for riding, walked toward them. "Stanton might have told me."

"I think it might be—yes, it is. My brother, Miss Powell."

"Your brother!"

"Yes. He's been managing the stud farm for me while I'm here, but he has some questions. Francis." Thea went forward, smiling, aware that Evadne was trailing behind her. "How good to see you. Are things really that bad at Linwood?"

Francis bent to kiss her cheek. "No, nothing serious," he said, looking past her. "Good morning, Miss Powell."

"Mr. Thorne," Evadne replied with none of her usual flirtatiousness.

Thea looked at her speculatively.

"Will you be with us long?" Evadne asked.

"A few days. I've some matters about which I need to consult with my sister."

"Well, we are happy to have you. Would you like to see our stables?"

"If you will allow me to wash off the dirt of the road first, I'd be happy to."

"I'll see if Gregg has a room prepared for you. It's a small house, really," Evadne said, her voice floating back to Thea as she took Francis's arm and led him inside. "I shall have to make some changes once we are married."

Francis's reply was lost to Thea, who stared after them, her eyebrows slightly raised. Why was Francis here? The stud surely could get by without her for a few days; it had in the past. She suspected that Evadne had more to do with his appearance at Moulton Hall than any problems at Linwood, and the thought raised her spirits immeasurably.

"Come, kitten," she said, taking Gillian's hand and swinging it back and forth. "Let's go down to the beach."

* * *

"Evadne?" Francis called, peering into the dimness of the stables. He had expected to find her waiting for him at the house, but Gregg had informed him that she had come ahead. Francis grinned to himself. He was the first to admit that he didn't understand women, but he thought he understood Evadne very well, indeed. Flirtatious she might be, but he knew it was all a game. When things grew more serious, as he suspected they were between them, she changed. She became frightened. He might very well have to do his fair share of pursuing during this visit. "Are you here?"

"Ooh!" Evadne brushed past him so quickly that he pulled back in scant time to prevent a collision, and went running out into the stableyard. "I hate him, I hate him!"

"Evadne." Following her, Francis laid a hand on her shoulder and swung her around to face him. In contrast to her usual sweet demeanor, her face was contorted with anger and chagrin. Oddly enough, Francis preferred this look. At least it was honest. "What has happened to overset you so?"

"It's Stanton! I hate him! He doesn't want me to have any fun at all."

"I see." The gravity of his tone was belied by the twitching of his lips. "What has he done now?"

"He's forbidden me to go riding."

"Has he?"

"Well." Evadne looked down, straightening the lace at her cuffs, and then raised defiant eyes to him. "He won't let me go riding by myself."

"Without a groom? Ah, I see. So you're angry."

"Yes! And all I asked was to have mounts saddled for us."

"And that made you feel as if you can't make your own decisions."

"Yes! Oh, you do understand! Why can't he?"

"I daresay he would, if you explained it to him."

Evadne gazed up at him. He hadn't needed to have it explained; he had understood, without words. A hard little knot of loneliness that Evadne hadn't known was inside her began to dissolve. For the first time in her life, someone saw her as herself. "Most likely he would," she agreed, "but I suppose he is right. I really shouldn't ride by myself. Suppose my horse threw me?"

"That is a thought," Francis said, his eyes twinkling at her in such a way that she felt warm all over. "Come, let's go riding together, and you can show me the countryside."

Evadne smiled up at him, for once without any artifice or flirtatiousness. Never mind about Stanton; she would even forget about Mr. DeVilliers and the meeting they had planned for that evening. Being with Mr. Thorne was much better. "I'd like that," she said, and took his arm. Life suddenly looked far more pleasant than it had just that morning.

Luncheon over, the guests rose from the table, to Jeremy's immense relief. With the arrival of Francis Thorne to Moulton Hall, things were getting very interesting indeed. Francis did not appear to pay any special attention to Evadne, but when their eyes happened to meet, both looked at each other for a moment and then quickly away. This was not mere flirting. This looked like something more serious. At another time, Jeremy might have been annoyed. Not now, though. Not with Thea here.

He turned to her, smiling. "Thea, you wished to speak with me about something?"

Thea, talking with Francis, turned to look at him, her eyes startled and wary. "Yes, Stanton. If you don't mind?"

"No, of course not. We'll go into my study."

"Very well." Thea smiled at him, but her eyes remained wary. Now what, he wondered, was she so nervous about?

"You seem to be making progress with Gillian," he commented, as they crossed the hall toward his study.

"Yes, I hope so. She fed Polly a piece of apple this morning."

"Did she, indeed." Jeremy stopped at the door of his study, smiling down at her. "That is progress. Now, what, I wonder, could we do to convince you to stay for a while?"

Thea looked up at him with startled eyes as he opened the door. "Jeremy—"

"What the devil?" he said, stopping dead on the threshold, and both looked into the room. Curled up on the desk, on top of Jeremy's correspondence, was Fluffy, looking coolly at them through slitted eyes, as if they were the intruders. It was too much. A man could handle just so much, and he had had enough. "Evadne!" he roared, and then sneezed. "Damn! Gregg!"

"Jeremy," Thea said, putting her hand out to him.

"That damn cat. Gregg!"

"Yes, my lord, what is it?" Gregg said at his elbow.

"Where is Miss Powell?"

"In the drawing room, I believe. Shall I see, sir?"

Jeremy sneezed again. "Yes. Go and tell her to get her damned cat out of my study. Damn!" Jeremy glared at the cat. The study would have to be thoroughly cleaned and aired before he could use it again. "And I'm to put up with this, while I can't even allow Gillian to have her kitten?"

Thea looked up at him, her eyes filled with amusement and understanding. "He really is an ugly cat, is he not?"

"Ugly is not the word for it. Evadne."

"Yes, Stanton?" Evadne said as she came into the hall.

"You will go into my study and get that hell-born animal out of there."

Evadne stared at him and then looked into the room. "Oh! Fluffy! You naughty cat, there you are!" She flew over to the desk, where the cat was unconcernedly grooming itself. "What a thing to do to mummy, to run off and hide like that!"

Gregg, coming back into the hall, snickered, and Jeremy's lips tightened. "Evadne," he said with admirable restraint, "get that cat out of here."

"Of course, Stanton. This won't happen again."

Jeremy sneezed and stepped back from her. "On that we agree. I want that cat out of my house. Now."

Evadne stared at him. "But, Stanton—"

"You may as well resign yourself to it. I won't have that cat in this house, now or when we are married."

"No!" Evadne stamped her foot and clutched the cat tighter. "I won't give Fluffy up! I won't! Oh, you're cruel and heartless!"

"Evadne." Francis, who had come into the hall, put a

hand on her shoulder. "Let's take Fluffy away from here."

"You can't take Fluffy away from me," Evadne said, staring at Jeremy. "You can't."

"I'm sorry." Jeremy's tone was firm. "He must go."

Evadne stared at him, her pansy eyes filling with tears, and then spun. "Ooh! You're a beast and you're cruel! I hate you, Stanton, I hate you!"

Francis took a step forward. "Evadne!" he called, and then stopped, turning to look at Jeremy, his eyes cool and challenging. "She's upset. I'd best go after her."

"Do what you wish," Jeremy said, raking his hand through his hair. "Damn. She's done nothing but turn my life upside down and now this."

"Then why marry her, Jeremy?" Thea asked, and he looked down at her in surprise, as if he'd forgotten her presence.

"I have no choice." His voice was clipped. "What was it you wished to speak to me about?"

Under that hard, harried gaze, Thea lost her nerve. "It can wait," she said, and fled, leaving Jeremy to stare after her in surprise. Now what had that been all about?

Francis found Evadne in the rose garden, sitting on one of the stone benches and squeezing Fluffy to her, though the cat yowled and squirmed. "Evadne."

"Go away," she said without looking up.

He sat beside her. "Are you all right?"

"No, I am not all right! He said I have to give Fluffy up! And I won't, I tell you! I won't."

"Evadne, Stanton's allergic to cats," Francis said reasonably. "Surely you knew you wouldn't be able to keep it."

"I don't care. He's a beast."

Francis leaned back, not understanding her misery at all, and yet completely in sympathy with her. "When I heard the uproar, I thought perhaps Stanton had broken your engagement."

"No such luck," she muttered.

"Excuse me?"

"I said, of course not. But what am I going to do? I can't live without Fluffy."

The corners of Francis's mouth twitched. "I don't see why not. Why do you have such an ugly cat, anyway?"

"He's not ugly!" Evadne squeezed the cat, and he meowed in protest. "He's my own little kitty, my only friend, and he loves me."

Francis managed to turn his involuntary laugh into a snort. It really wasn't very funny, he thought, his eyes softening as he saw, with some surprise, that the cat was rubbing its head against Evadne's jaw. There was a wealth of loneliness behind her words. "Evadne, once you're married you won't be lonely," he said, choosing his words carefully and wondering why he was pleading Stanton's case for him.

"What do you know about it?" Evadne stared ahead, dry-eyed. "I won't give Fluffy up."

Francis took her arm as she rose. "You'll have to do something, Evadne."

"Yes." Her eyes were fixed on something in the distance, something only she could see, as she bent and let the cat jump from her arms. "There, Fluffy, go and play. Oh, yes." She turned and faced Francis, looking suddenly much more mature. "I'll do something."

* * *

"I thought I might find you here," Jeremy said, and Thea, sitting on a rock on the beach, turned with some surprise.

"How did you know?" she asked as he sat next to her.

"Gillian told me that sometimes you and she come here and talk." He hesitated, shifting his position. "I can't thank you enough for what you've done with her, Thea. She's a different child."

"I like her." Idly Thea reached down and let sand sift through her fingers. Beyond the shingly beach, the sea was dark as wine, reflecting the clouds gathering above. "I wish I could convince her to try riding, but so far she's too frightened."

"If anyone can win her trust, you can." He shifted again. "Thea—"

"Something's scared her. I think she'd like to try, though. She so wants to please you."

"Me?" He looked at her in surprise. "I don't want her to learn to ride for me. I want her to learn for herself."

"Yes, I know that, Jeremy. But she's a child. She wants to please you." She paused. "So you'll love her."

"Of course I love her, Thea. She knows that."

"Then, Jeremy, why are you marrying Evadne?"

"We've discussed this, Thea," he said sharply. "A gentleman cannot cry off an engagement."

"That's nonsense. We hear about broken engagements all the time. Are you telling me it's fair that the woman should be branded a jilt?"

"No, of course not, Thea." He ran his hand through his hair. "But I gave my word. Devil take it, I know it's not going to be easy, but I cannot break it off now."

"For any reason?"

"For any reason."

"I see."

Something in her tone made Jeremy look down at her. "What did you want to speak to me about?"

Thea sifted more sand, not looking at him. "It's not important." Not now, when she knew it would have no effect on him. She'd realized that this afternoon, after the scene in his study; she had to face the fact now. He was going to marry Evadne, and nothing would change his mind. Knowing that, how could she tell him of her own predicament?

"Was it about Gillian?"

"No, not at all. I like the sea. It's wild and yet comforting at the same time."

Jeremy cast an experienced sailor's eye up at the sky. "Storm's coming. We'd better not stay here much longer." He rose and held a hand out to her. She took it with reluctance, releasing it as soon as they had left the beach and were on firmer ground. She couldn't bear touching him, not now, not when she knew how she had been used. For that was all it had been, that night in the tower room. What had been a transcendant experience for her had been only another encounter for him; she had been only another woman. He didn't love her. If she told him about the child, he would probably do right by her. Or as right as he could. He was committed to another. Thea and her child would come second, and that, she couldn't bear.

The storm broke when they were still a distance from the house. Catching at her hand, Jeremy pulled Thea along, and she allowed him. For a moment she let herself pretend that things were different, that he did love her and that she would stay with him forever. Only for a moment, though. That kind of fantasy was dangerous.

Gillian and her governess reached the house at the same time they did. Miss Moffett would have bundled her charge upstairs to get her into dry clothes, but Gillian threw herself at Jeremy. "Daddy! Thea gave an apple to Polly, and I helped!"

Jeremy smiled at her. "Did you, poppet? That's nice."

"Polly's lips tickled. I was afraid she was going to bite, but Thea told me she wouldn't." She nestled confidingly against her father. "I like Thea, Daddy. Don't you wish she could stay here forever and ever?"

Startled, Jeremy looked up and caught Thea's stricken eyes. Thea, here in his house, with him forever. Damn, but he had been blind. "Yes, Gillian," he said, his eyes never leaving Thea's. "Yes, I think I'd like that."

Chapter 16

Thea's startled eyes met Jeremy's and then dropped, unable to face the warmth there. "I can't stay, Gillian," she said, smiling, though the smile didn't reach her eyes. "I've the stables to manage."

"Couldn't you hire someone to do that for you? Daddy does," Gillian said. "Please? Make her say yes, Daddy."

"What do you think, Thea?" Jeremy said, his gaze never leaving her face. "Does it sound like a good idea to you?"

"What of Evadne?" Thea's voice was tart.

"I don't like her," Gillian said.

Jeremy's mouth quirked. "Out of the mouth of babes. Will you at least think about it, Thea?"

"There's nothing to think about," Thea snapped. Oh, how could he? When he had made it clear that he would marry Evadne, that she herself was nothing to him? "As I believe I told you once before when you made such a suggestion."

"Thea, I didn't mean—"

"I think we'd best forget this topic. If you'll excuse me, I'd like to get into some dry clothes."

Gillian huddled next to Jeremy as Thea strode away. "Is she going to leave, Daddy?"

"I don't know, poppet." Absently Jeremy fondled her silky curls, looking up the stairs after Thea. She couldn't leave. Not now, when he finally knew what he wanted. *God, Stanton, you are a fool.* "You'd better get into some dry clothes too, poppet. Go on with you, now." He gave Gillian a little push, and then turned toward his study.

The front door opened then, letting in gusts of wind and rain and bringing with them Evadne and Francis. Both were laughing, but they stopped when they saw Jeremy. "You got caught in the storm, too, I see," he said mildly, and noticed how they both visibly relaxed at this calm tone.

"Yes. We were in the rose garden. You have a fine estate, Stanton," Francis said.

"Thank you." He looked at Evadne, whose eyes were downcast. "Is all well?"

"Yes. Stanton," Evadne said, putting her hand on Jeremy's arm as he brushed past her. "I wish to apologize. I promise I'll keep Fluffy away from you in the future."

"Thank you, Evadne," he said, a little surprised. "I'd appreciate that." He went into his study, brow furrowed. What hold did Thea's brother have on Evadne, to make her behave so well? If he could figure that out and use it himself, if Evadne were like that all the time, he almost wouldn't mind marrying her. Almost. For the fact remained that something fundamental within him had changed. His world had shifted on its axis and only now

248

was beginning to revolve again. There was no use denying the truth: he was in love with Thea.

He leaned back in his chair, his legs stretched out and crossed at the ankle. This was something he had never expected to happen to him, not since losing Iris. He had thought he'd learned a lesson then, that love wasn't real, was not to be trusted. Thea, however, was not Iris. Good lord, what would he do with a wife like Thea? She was independent and sharp-tongued, and would demand far more of him than Evadne ever would. She was also far more loving, with both himself and Gillian. For all her independence and strength, there was a vulnerability to Thea that Evadne, armored by her selfishness, lacked. Thea cared, and that meant that he would have to care back. The easy, uncommitted life he had planned for himself lay in pieces at his feet.

"Damn," he muttered, but he was smiling. The smile faded, however, as reality began to penetrate his fog of happiness. He had a serious problem. He was engaged to the wrong woman, and somehow he must break it off.

"All right, girl," Thea murmured softly to the bay mare that was hers to use during her visit. "We'll go home." Clucking softly, she set the horse into motion along the path that led through the wood. Thank heavens her doctor had told her she could still ride, as long as she was careful. She thought better on horseback, and she had much to think about. Coming to Moulton had been the biggest mistake of her life.

It hadn't seemed so at first, of course, and even now she felt that Jeremy should know about his child. For her own sake, though, she couldn't tell him. For herself, she had to get away. Jeremy didn't love Evadne; that she knew. However, he would marry her. He made that clear. He was lost to her.

Buck up, my girl, she told herself. *You didn't want to marry again, anyway.* But that had been before she had known it was possible to feel as she did, as if without Jeremy she was only half alive. It had been before she had known she was going to be a mother. That had changed everything. She couldn't think only about herself anymore. But what could she do, when the man she loved didn't love her? It was exquisite torture, living in his house, talking with him, and never, never showing what she felt by either word or action. She couldn't seem to stop looking at him, as if to memorize his face, to store it within her for the lonely days ahead. For lonely they would be. She hadn't known it was possible to be so aware of a man physically, to hunger for his touch. She hadn't realized that knowing Jeremy would never be hers would devastate her so much.

And so she would go. She would have to. Not back to Linwood, however. It was bad enough that her child would not have a father without its having to carry the stigma of illegitimacy. She would leave England, for Italy perhaps, now that the Continent was open for travel again. There she would have her child, and when she returned she would tell everyone that she had decided to adopt an orphan. She wouldn't quite be believed, she knew, but it was the best she could do. She had no intention of leaving England forever. Linwood would someday belong to her child. She wanted to raise him there.

Thea emerged from the trees onto the lawn leading up to the house, under a sky as low as her spirits. She had only ridden a few paces when she saw Gillian running toward her from the house. Instantly her spirits picked up. If nothing else came of the visit, she had come to care for Gillian. Leaving her would be as hard as leaving Jeremy.

She raised her hand in greeting. As she did, a rabbit bolted out from the undergrowth to her right. Her horse, startled, reared, and it took all of Thea's considerable skill to stay in the saddle. Her hands competent and firm, she brought the horse, trembling and snorting, back down. "There, Maggie, girl, you're all right," she murmured to the horse, bending over to pat her neck and controlling her own shudders of reaction. A fall now would be disastrous.

From ahead of her there was a cry, a small, inarticulate sound of distress. Thea looked up just in time to see Gillian, her face white, turn and begin to run away. "Gillian!" Thea called, but the girl didn't stop. With an exclamation of surprise, Thea slid down off her horse, stopping only to loop the reins over a branch before she set off after Gillian, raising her skirts and running in a way that ladies weren't supposed to. The child was much more important than any sense of propriety could ever be. "Gillian!"

Gillian stumbled and fell, and Thea reached her side, dropping to the ground and gathering her into her arms. "Gillian! Honey, are you hurt?"

"I—saw you," Gillian gasped, her small hands, balled into fists, beating at Thea's shoulders. "I saw you."

"Yes, honey. You saw me do what?"

"I saw what the horse did. You almost fell!"

"Shh. Shh." Thea tightened her embrace, rocking

back and forth as Gillian's voice rose. "But I didn't, honey, and I'm not hurt. I'm all right."

"But—I saw you. The horse—the horse reared and you went back—just like Mother, just—"

"Gillian." Thea pulled away, putting her hand on the girl's shoulders, "look at me. Look at me. There, that's better." With gentle fingers, she reached out and brushed a tangled strand of hair away from Gillian's eyes. "I'm not hurt. I promise."

"You do?" Gillian's eyes searched hers. "But when my mother's horse did that, she fell and she died—"

"Merciful heavens!" Thea exclaimed. "Gillian, were you there when your mother died?"

"Yes! And it's my fault, my fault." She threw herself onto Thea's chest, sobbing in an agony of remorse and long-suppressed pain. "I made it happen."

"No, darling, surely not!" Dear lord, no wonder the poor child feared horses. "How do you think you caused it? Did you startle the horse?"

"No, no! Mother wouldn't let me near it!"

"Then how, dearest?"

"Because I wanted it to happen! Because she called me ugly and said I should have been a boy and I hated her, I hated her. And I wanted something bad to happen to her, but not that. Not ever that." Gillian stared up at her, the tears streaming down her face. "I didn't mean it. I really didn't."

"Of course you didn't Gillian. I know it. I know." Thea pulled her close and rocked her back and forth while she cried. Merciful heavens. The child had carried the guilt of her mother's death for three years. It was a wonder she could function at all, with such a burden. "Gillian, Gillian, hush now," Thea said after a few minutes, when Gillian's sobs had turned to hiccups. "Hush and listen to me." Gillian pulled back, wiping at her cheeks with the back of her hand. "Are you listening?" Gillian nodded. "This is very important, honey, and I want you to believe I'm telling you the truth. What happened wasn't your fault."

"But I wished it! I did!"

"Yes, I'm sure you did. Your mother hurt you, lovey, and when someone hurts you, the first thing you want to do is hurt back. But if every time someone wished another person harm, that wish came true, there wouldn't be many people left." She smoothed Gillian's hair back from her face. "Everyone does it, sweetheart. That doesn't mean it's right, and it certainly doesn't mean someone actually gets hurt that way." Thea sat back, her eyes holding Gillian's. "What happened to your mother was an accident. You didn't cause it."

"But I did—"

"No. You didn't. Sweetheart, would I lie to you?"

Gillian considered that for a moment, and then shook her head. "No."

"Of course I wouldn't. And your father would tell you the same thing."

"You won't tell him!"

"No, not if you don't want me to. Gillian, just because you wish for something doesn't mean it will come true. Surely you know that?"

"I wished for a kitten," she said in a low voice, her head bent, and Thea smiled. "And I wish you could marry Daddy, instead of Miss Powell."

"Oh, Gillian—"

"She's like my mother. She doesn't like me, either."

Thea sat back on her heels, feeling helpless. The poor

253

child, suffering for years under a burden of guilt she didn't deserve, and now saddled with a selfish woman as stepmother. She couldn't deny Gillian's words; she'd promised not to lie. "I'd like to be your mother, too, dearheart," she said, and Gillian raised her head sharply, her eyes filling with hope. "But it can't be that way."

"But I want you to! It's not fair."

"I know. But I promise that I will always be your friend. All right?"

"All right," Gillian said after a moment.

"Good." Thea got briskly to her feet before she had a chance to burst into tears like a child herself. "Wait here, I'll get Maggie and we can go home together."

"Aren't you scared?" Gillian's eyes were huge as she scrambled to her feet.

"Of Maggie? Of course not. It's not the first time I've had that happen. And it wouldn't have been the first time I fell." Thea unlooped the reins and led the horse toward Gillian. "In fact, if you weren't here, I'd ride home."

"You would?" Gillian's face was thoughtful as she fell into step beside Thea, their hands linked. "Thea? Would you teach me to ride?"

Thea stopped and looked down at her in amazement. "Of course I will, kitten," she said, striving to sound calm. "Come, let's go home."

Jeremy met them in the hall as they came in, laughing and breathless from having raced up the drive. A slow smile lighted his face as he watched Thea struggle to regain her composure. "Running, Mrs. Jameson? How very unsuitable for a lady."

"If I weren't a lady I'd stick my tongue out at you,"

she retorted, forgetting, in the stress of what had just happened, her own misery.

"That might be interesting," he said, and gave her such a long, considering look that she blushed.

"Daddy, Thea almost fell off Maggie," Gillian said.

Jeremy's eyes went swiftly to Thea, and he took an impulsive step forward. "You're not hurt?"

"Of course not, Jeremy. I'm fine," Thea said, surprised. Was he actually concerned? But then, it was perfectly proper to be concerned about a friend.

"It was awful, Daddy," Gillian said, her eyes large and round.

"I'm all right, and so is Maggie." Thea smiled down at Gillian and ruffled her hair. "I must go change. I'll see you at dinner, Jeremy."

"Yes. Thea?"

She turned from the stairs. "Yes?"

He shook his head, an odd smile upon his face. "Nothing," he said, and Thea continued on her way. She loved him. Oh, how she loved him, and he would never be hers.

"Miss Powell! Hold up, there!"

Evadne, strolling through the garden, turned and saw Francis on the other side of the hedge. She started to smile, to raise her hand in welcome, but then a little imp of mischief caught her and she began to run instead. This was fun! Much better than staying in that stuffy old house and listening to Mama prose on about her responsibilities once she married. As to her fiancé, she rarely saw him, which didn't bother her. He treated her as a child, not the woman she knew she was.

"Evadne!" Francis called. Evadne let out a giggle and lifted her skirts, giving him an entrancing sight of a neatly turned ankle as she ran. She could hear him pounding along behind her, and almost imperceptibly she slowed her steps. It was quite thrilling when he suddenly caught at her arm, bringing her to a halt.

"I say!" He stared down at her. "Whatever made you run like that?"

"Oh, it's you, sir!" she exclaimed, opening her eyes very wide.

"Yes, who did you think?"

"I didn't know." She pressed her hand to her heart. "La, sir, you gave me such a start!"

Francis made a sudden move toward her, as if to comfort her, and then the corners of his lips twitched. They twitched again, and suddenly he was laughing. Evadne stared at him a moment in chagrin, but his laugh was infectious. She joined in, her eyes sparkling up at him. "You, miss, are a minx," Francis said with mock severity as he took her arm firmly in his. "I see through you, you know."

"I know," she said as they strolled along, wondering why she wasn't displeased. No one had ever seen through her before. It should have been disconcerting. "You are ever so much nicer than Stanton about it. He just frowns at me or ignores me."

"And which is worse, I wonder?"

"Oh, ignoring me, by all means. Something I am persuaded you would never do, sir."

"No. Evadne." He stopped, grasping her shoulders and turning her to face him. "What do you see in him?"

"In Stanton?" Evadne tilted her head to the side, pretending to consider. "Why, he is wonderfully handsome, sir, do you not think so? And, of course, he is a viscount," she went on, ignoring his gathering frown. "I know he's not wealthy, precisely, else he wouldn't be marrying me, but he does have all those lovely estates—"

"Stop it." Francis gave her a little shake, and she stared up at him, her eyes genuinely wide now. "He doesn't love you. What does all that matter, against that?"

Evadne tossed her head. "As I don't love him, I expect we shall suit very well."

"Stop it," he said again, and pulled her ruthlessly against him, smothering her words with his lips. Evadne made a little sound, of protest, of compliance, but she didn't struggle.

"Why, Mr. Thorne!" She stared up at him when he at last released her. "Such a thing to do!" And she threw her arms enthusiastically around his neck. Francis was not about to refuse such an ardent invitation, and they stood, entwined, for what felt like eternity.

"You'll marry me," he said, when at last they separated and she was standing with her head resting on his shoulder.

"I will?" She pulled back, the light of mischief dancing in her eyes again. "Have I any say in the matter?"

"No." Francis tightened his grip, so that she could barely breath. "None."

"You have no money and no prospects," she pointed out.

"Damn, don't you think I realize that? But if I could find someone to sponsor me I'd gladly stand for Parliament, and make something of my life.

Evadne's eyes brightened. "Oh, do you enjoy politics,

sir? I've tried to talk to Stanton about it once or twice, but he ignores me."

"You would like to be a political wife, Evadne?"

"Perhaps." Her smile was tantalizing, filled with the headiness of the moment. He was hers, and she couldn't resist teasing him just a little, goading him to say the one thing he had yet to say. "Perhaps I prefer Stanton."

Francis's face darkened. "You don't."

"I don't know. Perhaps I do."

"Damn it, Evadne!" He released her so fast that she stumbled backward. "What game is this you play with me?"

"Oh, Francis!" She held out her hand, but his back was to her and he didn't see. "No game. I merely want you to—"

"Have a title and a great deal of money," he said bitterly.

"Well, they would be nice," she said candidly, and he turned and gave her such a hard look she hurried on. "But they don't matter to me anymore, Francis, really they don't! I have piles of money, and as for a title—"

"You want to be a lady. By God, I thought I knew you." He stared at her, breathing heavily. "I thought there was more to you than you let anyone see, and now I'm beginning to wonder. Was I wrong?"

"No! Francis, there is more to me, but you don't understand. I'm betrothed to Stanton, and—"

"And is that the way you want it?"

Joy shot through Evadne; she knew what he was saying. He was hers! Giddy with happiness, again she couldn't resist the urge to tease him. "Well, I don't know," she said, and Francis drew himself up.

"That won't do," he said sternly. "I want an answer from you, Evadne."

"Well, he is a viscount—"

"That tears it," he said, and turned on his heel.

"Francis!" She picked up her skirts and ran after him, alarmed now. Too late she realized she'd gone too far. "I didn't mean it—"

"Go marry your viscount, Evadne," he said, not breaking his stride. "I see I was wrong about you, after all."

"No! Francis!" she cried. Of course she would marry him. She loved him. He paused for a moment but then continued on, walking away from her, walking out of her life.

Evadne sank down to the ground on knees no longer strong enough to support her, watching him until he had disappeared around the corner of the house. "But you never said you loved me," she said, and burst into tears.

Jeremy was just coming down the stairs into the hallway the next morning when the front door opened, and Thea appeared. "I'll just see if your father's busy" she said over her shoulder, then halted. "Oh. Jeremy. There you are."

"Yes." He crossed to her, smiling. Something had happened in his house in the last few days. Evadne, pleading a headache, was keeping to her room in a perpetual sulk; Francis went around with a dark look on his face, hardly speaking to anyone; and, worst of all, Thea avoided him completely. Evadne and Francis weren't his concern, but Thea was. If he could not get her to stay with him for more than a few moments, how could he tell her how he felt? And how could he possibly do it in such a way so that she realized that he was not again trying to entice her into an *affaire?* He would have to break it off with Evadne, he thought suddenly, raising his chin. No matter the scandal, no matter the stain on his honor. Better that than to marry her and make so many people unhappy.

"I haven't seen much of you the last few days," he said, stopping in front of her and smiling.

"Yes, well, I've been busy." Thea's tone was unconvincing as she looked down, her fingers pleating the skirt of her gown. "I've something to show you, though, outside. Have you a moment?"

"For you, Thea, I have more than a moment." She gave him a startled look as he took her arm, escorting her out the door. "In fact, if you would come inside afterward I think we need to have a little talk—"

"Perhaps," Thea broke in, pulling away from him. "This is important. Pay attention, mind."

"Yes, Thea. What am I supposed to be looking at?"

"Stand right there." She moved away, stopping on the bottom stair, and Jeremy looked around, seeing only the lawn and a milky-white sky. "All right, Gillian! We're ready."

Chapter 17

"Gillian?" Jeremy frowned as he heard hoofbeats. He looked in their direction, and there, around the corner of the house, came Gillian, riding her pony at a sedate trot. Follett was beside her on his own mount, watching her with a sharp eye, but she apparently needed no such supervision. Gillian sat straight and tall, and her every movement bespoke confidence. She was riding. "My God," he murmured. "My God, I didn't think you'd do it."

"Gillian did most of it," Thea said softly, so as not to distract her. "She's a very brave little girl."

"My God," he said again, not taking his eyes from his daughter. "She was so scared. Did you ever find out why?"

Thea stole a quick look at him. "Yes. She saw the accident that killed her mother."

Jeremy drew in his breath sharply. "Good God." At that, he at last looked at Thea. She had done it. Thea, her face glowing with love and pride as she watched his daughter. Thea, who was made to be a mother but who, by a cruel irony of fate, never would be. He hadn't forgotten the look on her face at Rochester when she had told him she couldn't have a child. It didn't matter. More than anything, he wanted her as his wife. "Good God, you did it."

"Yes," Thea said, and her voice sounded flat, now that Gillian had rounded a curve in the drive and disappeared from sight. She could let her guard down and admit to some of the other feelings Gillian's accomplishment had brought her. She had ostensibly come to Moulton to teach Gillian to ride. Now she had, and she no longer had an excuse for staying. It was time to go. It was time to leave Jeremy.

"I did it, Daddy, did you see?" Gillian cried, running toward them, and Jeremy stepped onto the drive, swinging her up into his arms. Thea, watching, swallowed past a lump in her throat. Father and daughter. For a time she had pretended that Gillian was hers, and that she would stay at Moulton forever, with Jeremy. Now that pretense was over. Jeremy would marry someone else, and she would be out of his life.

It hurt. Oh, how it hurt, more than it had when his engagement first had been announced. Now her last hopes had been shattered. She was nothing to Jeremy, nothing, not even his mistress. He'd made that clear. The irony was that, should he suggest it again, she would gladly compromise herself, in spite of her ideals, in spite of her child. Such was what she was reduced to. She loved him so much that she would take him on any terms whatsoever. It was not right, it would not even be particularly satisfying, but it was all she would have of him, and all she could ever expect.

Jeremy, his eyes sparkling with happiness, turned toward her as he set Gillian down. "Thea. I don't know how to thank you." He took her hand, and though she tried to pull free, he would not release her. "You've given me my daughter back."

Thea smiled, acutely aware of the warmth of his hand on hers. Even this brief contact was welcome, sweet torture though it was. "She's a lovely girl, Jeremy. You should be proud of her."

"I am. And of you."

"Daddy," Gillian called, and Jeremy turned, at last releasing Thea's hand. "Will you ride with me?"

"Yes, poppet." He turned back to Thea. "We'll talk more later."

"Yes," Thea said, and through a haze of tears watched father and daughter walk away. Her job was done. Tomorrow she would leave, and when she next saw Jeremy, he would be married. The thought was too painful to bear.

Francis came out to stand next to her on the step. "Stanton must be pleased with you. Even Evadne is impressed."

Thea blinked several times before turning to face him. "Evadne?"

"Excuse me. Miss Powell."

"Mm-hm." Thea turned to go back into the house. "I shall be leaving tomorrow, Fran. Will you escort me?" She would tell Francis the truth when they were away from Moulton. If she were to carry her charade off, she would need his help.

He followed her into the hall. "I say, that's too bad of you, Thea! I'm not ready to leave just yet."

"Oh? I thought you were concerned about Linwood."

"Dash it, Thea, you know that's not why I came here! What does she see in him?"

"I don't know, Fran." She pushed her hair wearily away from her face. "What, for that matter, does he see in her?"

Francis looked at her sharply. "Like that, is it? I thought you had your chance already."

"I did. More fool I." She laid her hand on his arm. "We Thornes seem to be prodigious unlucky."

"I haven't given up, Thea. Not yet."

"I fear I have." She turned toward the stairs. "I'll tell Stanton we'll be leaving tomorrow."

"Damn," Francis muttered, turning toward the drawing room. Dashed poor-spirited of Thea, he thought. Well, he hadn't given up. Perhaps he would have to leave tomorrow, but he would be back.

"Leaving!" Jeremy exclaimed, looking up sharply as Gregg handed him a cup. Dinner was over and they had gathered in the drawing room for coffee and conversation.

"You're leaving?" Evadne said at the same time, sounding startled.

"Yes." Thea nodded, her head down. "I came here to teach Gillian to ride, and that's been accomplished."

"You needn't rush away, you know," Jeremy said, his eyes never leaving her face. "Gillian is by no means an expert."

"No, but she is more comfortable with Follett now." Thea kept her eyes on her cup. "She'll do well with him. And I've been away from Linwood long enough. I must return."

"You'll be staying, won't you, Mr. Thorne?" Evadne asked, her tone casual.

"Afraid not, Miss Powell." Francis threw her a smile meant to be both apologetic and reassuring. "I'll be escorting my sister home."

"Oh." Evadne's eyes dropped, too, at that bit of news. "I wish you a pleasant journey, sir," she said, and rose, crossing the room to the pianoforte and listlessly turning the pages of music on the stand. Jeremy watched her for a moment, and then turned his attention to his other guests.

"Are there problems at Linwood?" he asked quietly, his eyes holding Thea's.

Thea's eyes dropped again before his steady, almost accusing gaze. She had to tell him. She had to. "No, nothing serious, I believe. Francis has done well managing for me, but there are some matters I must see to myself."

"And then?" Jeremy's eyes shifted to Francis, who rose.

"It's Thea's stable, after all. Excuse me," he said, and left them to join Evadne. "Miss Powell."

Evadne glanced up quickly, and then returned to the music, picking out a tune with one finger. "Sir?"

"You are looking uncommonly well tonight."

"Thank you," Evadne murmured, and turned a page of the music, seemingly so absorbed that Francis frowned. This was deucedly uncomfortable. Never before had Evadne been so discouraging. Was she glad he was going?

"Evadne," he said, his voice low and urgent, "you do realize leaving tomorrow is not my choice?"

Evadne glanced swiftly up at him, and then away. "No, sir, I'm not certain of that at all."

"Aren't you?" There was an odd smile playing

around his lips, and it did strange things to her, making her heart pound faster. "Do you care?"

"Why, sir, why should I?" she said, tossing her curls.

Francis grinned. "Why, Evadne, because I—"

"Evadne," Agatha called. "Play something for us."

Evadne glanced toward her mother, and then back at Francis. "Will you stay?"

"I can't," he said regretfully. "I've no choice. But I'll—"

"Evadne! Play the Bach sonata you do so well," Agatha commanded. "I'm sure we'd all enjoy hearing it."

Evadne looked up at Francis again, searching his face, but his eyes were impenetrable. Oh, why had her mother had to interrupt just now? And why wouldn't Francis defy them all? "I'm sorry, Mama," she said abruptly, turning away from the pianoforte. "I have the headache."

"Nonsense, girl, you never have headaches!"

"But I do tonight. Will you excuse me, sir?" she said, turning to Jeremy, who had risen. "I'd like to go to my room."

"Of course, Evadne. The rest will probably help you."

"Of course, sir," Evadne murmured. Dropping a curtsy, she fled the room. In the hall, however, she turned, not to the stairs, but to the door, running lightly out onto the graveled drive. She had no intention of going to her room. Moulton Hall was too oppressive for her just now.

At first she had thought that Francis might follow her out, but after a few moments, it became obvious that he wouldn't. What was wrong with him, she wondered, stamping her foot, and then wincing as a stone cut into the sole of her thin satin evening slipper. Of course she couldn't encourage him, not when she was engaged to someone else, but surely he had given him enough clues as to her feelings? Even if she had teased him when he was trying to be serious, surely he realized how she felt? And yet, he was leaving tomorrow. It was hopeless! If she wanted to change her life, she would have to take matters into her own hands.

Walking with more purpose now, she climbed the drive on its winding path upward until she had reached the top of the hill. Dusk was beginning to fall, and so she would have just enough light to leave a message for Mr. DeVilliers. Since the first afternoon she had met him, she had managed to slip out to meet him many more times. Oh, there was nothing romantic about it; mysterious and dashing though he was with that scar, he was not at all anyone she would consider marrying. Why, he was quite old, and almost as dark as Stanton! Nor did he seem interested in her in that way. Rather, he listened to her when she poured out her misery and frustration over all that had happened. Stanton treated her as a child, and Francis was leaving, but Mr. DeVilliers gave her respect. She needed that now. Her heart was set on someone who would not come up to scratch.

Unwinding the silver ribbon that was threaded through her curls, she walked toward the oak tree. There she would tie the ribbon around the branch, a signal to Mr. DeVilliers that she wished to see him. As she neared the tree, however, a figure stepped out of the shadows. Startled, she turned to run, then heard her name.

She turned. "Oh! Mr. DeVilliers!" she exclaimed, her hand flying to her heart. "Such a turn as you gave me!"

"My apologies, Miss Powell." He bowed. "But what are you about, coming here at this time?"

"I could ask you the same thing, sir."

"Spying on Stanton," he said, his voice light, and went on as her eyes widened. "No, I was merely out for a ride before retiring for the night." He gestured toward his horse, tethered nearby. "But come, Miss Powell, you look pale. Sit." He lead her to a fallen tree trunk, and sat beside her. "What has happened to overset you?"

"Nothing, sir."

"No?"

"No, I—oh, sir it's all so awful!" she exclaimed. The entire story tumbled out, her desire to free herself from Stanton, her feelings for Francis, the botched proposal and his subsequent reluctance to do anything. "I thought, when he came here that it would all work out," she finished, "but he's leaving tomorrow."

Something flickered in DeVilliers's eyes at the mention of Francis Thorne, and then was gone. "The man is a fool, Evadne," he said, patting her shoulder.

"Oh, sir, I knew you'd understand!"

"Yes, of course I do, child. Now, come, you must let me help you."

"Oh, would you? I was hoping you would."

"You may trust in me. What you must do, Miss Powell, is something that will make Mr. Thorne notice you."

"Oh, yes!" Evadne leaned forward, her lips parted eagerly. "That is exactly what I want to do! But, how?"

Roger's teeth flashed in a smile that looked devilish,

a fancy Evadne immediately dismissed. "Well, child, there is something I've been thinking of."

Jeremy sat down again after Evadne had left the room, and smiled at his guests, proposing a few hands of whist to pass the time. Sitting back with his cards, he mulled over the situation. Evadne clearly did not wish to marry him, and yet she was being pushed into it by her mother. Lord knew he didn't wish to marry her, but if she didn't break the engagement, he would have little choice. A gentleman could not in honor cry off, but what would happen if he didn't care about honor? What if he decided to put happiness first, his own and others'? For he knew Evadne would not be happy with him, and he was certain he would not be with her. And Thea was not meant to be alone. Oh, he would not come out of the affair well, he knew. He would be looked on as a cad, but he cared little for the opinions of others, not when his future was at stake. Tomorrow he would talk to Evadne.

Thea glanced around the room through the haze that had clouded her vision all day, looking at everything and avoiding Jeremy. She had not suspected that even the thought of leaving would be so hard, though she knew she was doing the right thing. If he would say something, give her some sign—but he wouldn't. He was betrothed. It was a bitter lesson, one she had finally to learn. He was a man of honor, and he would put his commitments first.

Thea remained in the drawing room until she could stand it no longer. Then, claiming an early rising the next morning as an excuse, she retired to her room, where at last she could be alone with her unhappiness. Tears only left her feeling drained, however, and she was lying in bed, wretched and unhappy, when there was a light tap on the door.

She rose up on her elbow. "Come in?" she called. The door opened, and Jeremy, carrying a candle, stepped in. "Jeremy!"

"Shh." He put his finger to his lips. "I need to talk to you, Thea."

"But you shouldn't be here!" she hissed, clutching the coverlet around her.

"You hardly gave me a chance to say anything downstairs." He set his candle on the bedstand and sat on the side of the bed as she edged away. "Why are you leaving?"

"Jeremy, this isn't right—"

"I don't want you to go."

"I have to, Jeremy. There's Linwood, and—"

"That's not why you're going."

"There's nothing for me here."

"There's me."

"No, there isn't! What can you offer me, Jeremy? You're engaged." Her fingers combed through her hair, and he watched their motion. "And I will not be your mistress."

Jeremy opened his mouth to speak, and then closed it again. "No, of course not, Thea. I'm not asking it of you. Just—don't go."

"I have to, Jeremy," she said, her voice little above a whisper. For the sake of her child, she had to.

"Will you at least allow me a goodbye kiss?"

"Jeremy—"

He leaned toward her. "I think you owe me that, Thea."

She shrank back against the headboard. "I don't think—Jeremy—"

"Shh." He brushed his thumb lightly over her lips, and they parted. "One kiss, Thea," he said and bent his head.

She had expected a long, passionate kiss. Instead it was very brief, and very gentle, a true kiss of farewell. When he drew back she gazed up at him, her eyes clear and yet unreadable, and suddenly she hooked her arm about his neck, bringing him back down to her. This time the kiss was neither gentle nor brief. His arms went around her, pulling her hard against him, only her nightgown and his shirt acting as barriers to their closeness. Their lips met and clashed, almost desperately, in kisses that were both illicit and sweet. She wanted this, oh, how she wanted it, she thought, and when Jeremy at last released her she could read his own desire in his eyes, in his uneven breathing, in his flushed cheeks.

"Thea." His voice was ragged. "Stay with me tonight."

"Jeremy, not here—"

"My room, then."

Thea looked up at him for a moment, her eyes wide and vulnerable. One night. What would it matter? One night, to hold and to treasure against all the lonely days ahead.

She scrambled out of bed, affording him a glimpse of shapely calves. "You have beautiful legs, love," Jeremy commented, his hand slipping caressingly down her arm. Thea flushed and snatched up her dressing gown, her arms tangling in it in her haste. "Slowly, love."

Jeremy reached out to knot the sash of the wrapper and then dropped a quick kiss on her lips. "We have all night."

"Yes." She allowed him to lead her out into the hall, after he had first checked to see that it was deserted, and then to his suite of rooms, not thinking, only feeling. She would not allow herself to think about what she was doing. She wanted tonight, wanted one last time with him. She wanted one last time of joy.

Jeremy's bedroom was empty, his valet having been sent away, for which she was grateful. She stood in the middle of the floor, gazing about her appreciatively. It was a very masculine room, done in shades of brown, rust, and cream, with touches of green in the carpet and the bed curtains. The bed itself was massive, of carved mahogany, and it was on this that her eyes fastened, her mouth growing dry. At Rochester Castle she could have pleaded the madness of the moment, but this was something else. This was deliberate. "Jeremy—"

"Come here," he said at the same time, in a voice which brooked no disobedience. Swallowing hard, Thea crossed the room and stood unmoving before him, her head bent. Jeremy tilted her chin upward with his thumb, and they surveyed each other, very seriously, before his head lowered to hers. His arms went around her, his hands slipping down to curve about her hips and pull her close to him. She gasped, but before she could make any protest his lips were on hers, and all desire to pull away died. She wrapped her arms around his neck, opening her lips under the relentless pressure of his, returning the kiss with a passion she had never before known she was capable of. When his hands went to the sash of her wrapper she let him untie it and then brush

272

the robe from her shoulder, and when his fingers began to fumble with the buttons of her nightgown, she shifted to make it easier for him. Then he was lifting her in his arms and carrying her to the bed.

They were together again, and it was as sweet as she had remembered, it was better. No impetuous coupling, done thoughtlessly and in haste; this was slow and deliberate, the first time, the last time. All of it, she must remember all of it, the caress of his hands on her, the strength of his arms, the feeling of his skin against hers. And then he was a part of her, and she was his, moving with him, rejoicing at the closeness, the wonderful, incredible sensations, until, at the end, there was pleasure unimagined and yet remembered, and a joy that bound her to him forever.

She lay, drowsy and somehow complete, in his arms, feeling his fingers lazily stroke her hair and her arm, completely at peace. "I never knew," she said, more to herself than to him, and felt him stir.

"Sweetheart." He pressed a kiss to her forehead. "What was he like, your husband?"

"Hugh?" She thought about that a moment, startled that he would ask such a thing at such a time. "Selfish," she said finally. "He cared only for his own pleasures and pursuits. And an heir."

Jeremy's arms tightened about her protectively. "Did you ever feel this way with him, did he ever make you feel like this?"

"No, I—no."

Jeremy smiled a little at the embarrassment he heard in her voice, but his eyes remained grim. Foolish to be so jealous of a dead man, and so angry, but if Hugh Jameson were to appear, Jeremy thought he could kill the man with his bare hands because of what he had done to Thea. The man had been a fool, not to avail himself of her warmth and her passion. And she was his! Only he had kindled the fire inside her. If he could only tell her how much she meant to him, speak of his love—but he couldn't, not yet. Tomorrow, after he had spoken to Evadne, he would be free to tell her. "You won't leave now," he said, and Thea rose up on her elbow.

"How can I stay?" she asked, and realized that he was not listening, but was looking at her where the sheet had fallen away. Oh dear. But she had to tell him. She had to try one last time. She owed him, and herself, that. "Jeremy."

"What?" He traced her breast with his fingertips. "You are very beautiful, Thea. Did I tell you that?"

"N-no. Jeremy." She gasped as he pressed her back into the bed, his lips stroking over one soft mound until they reached the peak. "Jeremy, no, we have to talk—"

Jeremy raised his head, stroking her with his fingers until her nipple tautened. "Not now, love," he murmured, and bent his head to kiss her. Thea sighed, and gave in, hopelessly lost. No words of love, no talk of the future. He couldn't promise her tomorrow, she realized that, and the thought, as his hands stroked lovingly, knowingly, over her, was bittersweet. It didn't matter what happened next. She would not have foregone this night for the world.

The second time was, if anything, more beautiful than the first. Afterward Jeremy curled up on his side, holding her close against him, his breathing slipping into the easy rhythm of sleep. Thea lay still, treasuring their brief moment of joy. She must not be here when morning came.

When she was convinced that he was so deeply asleep that she wouldn't wake him, she slipped from the bed. He murmured something, his arm moving as if seeking her, and she nearly faltered, nearly climbed back in with him. But she couldn't. Before she could stop herself, before she let her emotions overrule her good sense, she picked up her nightgown and wrapper from the floor, slipped them on, and walked to the door.

There she stopped, turning to look back at the room where so much had been revealed to her, so much love, so much joy. Jeremy still slept; as she looked at him her eyes burned with unshed tears. After this, she must never see him again. He would belong to someone else, and it would only cause her pain. She must make this one night, this time of happiness, last forever, a shining memory to treasure, to sustain her. Tomorrow, she would leave.

Thea opened the door noiselessly, turned back for one last look, and then was gone.

Chapter 18

Evadne opened the door a crack and peeked out. Good, no one was about. Carrying a satchel in one hand, a box in the other, she ran lightly down the hall on stockinged feet, hoping no one would hear her. It was early yet; the only people stirring would be servants. With luck, her disappearance would not be noticed until late morning, and by then it would be too late. She would be well on her way home.

The front door was standing open, which meant that Gregg was somewhere about, but Evadne didn't see him as she slipped out, stopping only to put on her shoes. Following the drive as it curved around the house and rose to meet the Dover road, she nearly broke into a run. She had an appointment to keep. She was going to meet Mr. DeVilliers and let him take her away from this poky old place. And, she thought with a little thrill of excitement, teach Mr. Thorne a thing or two!

A howl issued from the box, and Evadne glanced hastily around. "Be quite, Fluffy!" she hissed, and the cat howled again. "Hush! We're going home, Fluffy. We're finally leaving." The cat meowed again, piteously this time, and she set the box down, crooning to it, until the cat had quieted. Then she rose, continuing on her way. Mr. DeVilliers had indeed offered her a solution to her problems the previous evening: leaving Moulton. She would see if Francis would determine to see her again. She would go home to Berkshire, escorted by Mr. DeVilliers, and there wait to see what developed as a result of her flight.

At last she reached the top of the hill. Looking down toward the road, she saw a traveling carriage of antique design waiting. It looked decidedly uncomfortable, but Evadne didn't care. She would show them, she thought. Stanton surely wouldn't want to marry her now. She would finally be free of him. If Francis chose to come after her, so much the better.

"Hello!" she called, and ran down the hill toward the carriage and the man who stepped out from behind it. At last, she was taking her life into her own hands.

Thea, too, rose early. She hadn't slept at all the night before; her mind was too full of memories and thoughts of the bleak future ahead, without Jeremy. She wanted nothing so much as to run back to his arms and tell him that she would take him on any terms whatsoever, but she couldn't. Hard as leaving him would be, sharing him would be worse. This was, she told herself yet again as she finished packing, the best way.

A sunbeam through her window shone into her eyes, dazzling her and making her blink back the moisture that had collected in her eyes. As if drawn by the sun, she went to the window and looked out. In the distance the Straits of Dover sparkled golden, and the lawn below glowed emerald. Thea's heart contracted. How could she bear to leave? She had come to love this house almost as much as she loved the people within. Once she left, she would never see it again, and oh, how lonely her life would be. One more ride, she thought, turning toward her wardrobe and pulling out her riding habit. She would ride once more about the estate, and then she would be able to bid it goodbye.

"Thea!" A voice called to her as she strode toward the stables, the heels of her boots crunching on the gravel.

She turned. "Gillian!" she exclaimed, and went down on one knee just as the little girl reached her, throwing herself into Thea's arms. Thea held the trembling little body close. "Gillian, honey, what is it? Whatever are you doing out so early?"

Gillian's chubby arms tightened around Thea's neck. "I don't want you to go."

"Oh, honey." Thea rocked her back and forth. "I don't want to, either, but I have to."

"But I don't want you to!" she wailed. "Why can't you stay and marry Daddy?"

Thea closed her eyes in pain. "Darling, I can't. Your father's going to marry Miss Powell and then you'll have a new mother."

"I don't like her." Gillian pulled back, her lips set in a straight line. "She doesn't like me, either."

"Oh, sweetheart." Thea rested her hand on the child's dark curls. "Your father loves you, Gillian. It will work out."

"I wish you could be my mother." Gillian's clear blue eyes, so like Jeremy's, gazed at Thea with complete honestly and trust, and Thea again closed her eyes.

"Gillian, sometimes we can't get what we want," she said softly. "You know that. We have to do the best we can with what we have."

"But it's not fair!"

"No." A child's cry, but true nonetheless. It wasn't fair. More people than herself would be made unhappy by Jeremy's marriage. "I'm going for a ride, kitten. Would you like to come?"

Gillian's struggle with herself was mirrored in her face. In spite of her newfound accomplishment, she still feared horses. Thea was proud of her when she nodded. "Yes."

"Good." Thea took her hand and they walked toward the stables.

That morning would always have a dreamlike, bittersweet quality in Thea's memory, as she rode over lands she had come to know and love, almost as much as she loved their master. There was the paddock where she and Gillian had spent so much time, the fields she'd ridden over with Jeremy, the beach where, with both of them, she had felt part of a family. It was all precious to her, and it was all lost.

The horses were growing winded as Thea and Gillian topped the rise from which they could see the entire estate spread out. Thea turned to look at it, and her eyes blurred. This was goodbye. She would never return.

Gillian tugged on her sleeve. "Thea. Thea, look. Isn't that Miss Powell?"

"What? Where?" Thea turned in the saddle to look in the direction in which Gillian pointed, where the Dover road was just visible through the trees.

"Down there. Isn't it?"

"Good lord! Yes." Thea stared transfixed, as Evadne,

a bag in either hand, ran toward a carriage at the side of the road. A man came forward to help her, a tall thin man, and Thea recognized him with a shock. "Good lord!" she said again. "Mr. DeVilliers!"

"Who is he?"

"Oh, that little fool," Thea said softly, ignoring Gillian's question. If the child hadn't guessed what was happening, Thea had quite a good idea. Even at this distance, the smile on Evadne's face was obvious. The silly little ninny was eloping with Roger DeVilliers.

Well, let her! she thought, turning away. If Evadne left with someone else, then Jeremy would be free. Free to marry her? Of course, after last night! But, Thea reluctantly admitted, he had not said he loved her. He had never said that. He had asked her once to be his mistress, and never, by word or deed, had he shown he thought of her as anything more. What guarantee would she have that he would marry her if Evadne left? Oh, if she told him about the child, he would, of course, but she didn't want him to marry her out of obligation. And what would he say if he knew that she had sat here while Evadne went blithely to her ruin, and did nothing about it? "The idiot!" Thea exclaimed.

Gillian glanced up curiously. "Is she leaving?"

"Yes."

"Oh good, then you can stay!"

Thea frowned. "No. Gillian." Thea turned to her. "You must be very brave. Do you think you can be?"

"Yes. What do you want me to do, Thea?"

"I want you to ride back to the house and tell your father about this."

"No! He'll only bring her back, and I don't want her!"

"Gillian," Thea said firmly. "You must be a big girl. Your father must be told. Will you go?"

Gillian swallowed hard. "You mean, ride back all by myself?" she said in a small voice.

"Yes, darling. Do you think you can?"

Gillian looked toward the road, where the carriage was moving toward Dover, and swallowed again. "I think so."

"Good girl! Now go, fast as you can, but be careful!"

"Will you come back—"

"Yes! Go, Gillian!" Thea's heart was in her throat as she turned to watch Gillian ride away, but to her relief, the child seemed steady in the saddle. Oh lord, of all things to happen, she thought, slapping the reins and setting her mount into a trot, toward the road. Who would ever have thought that she'd be doing so much to keep Stanton with another woman?

The carriage had a good start on her, and her mount was not fresh, but Thea was a very good, and a very determined, rider. Within a few minutes she had reached the road. Speaking words of encouragement to her mount, she increased their pace, until at last they had closed the distance and were riding in the carriage's dust. If they were lucky, no one would hear of this ridiculous escapade and Evadne's reputation would be safe, though why that should matter escaped her.

She judged, at last, that she was close enough to the carriage to be heard. "Hallo!" she yelled over the noise of carriage wheels and pounding hooves. "Stop! Stop, I say!" There was no apparent reaction, and then, suddenly the carriage speeded up.

Thea muttered an oath and bent over Maggie's neck, urging her on, until at last they were close. "Stop," she

281

cried again, half expecting the carriage to speed up again. Instead, it slowed, forcing her to drop back to avoid a collision. She congratulated herself on having won the day when the carriage came to a lurching, jolting stop, slewed halfway across the road.

"Mr. DeVilliers!" Thea called, walking her horse toward the front of the carriage and ignoring the sounds that came from within, Evadne's shrieks and the banshee wail of a cat. "Come forward, sir!"

From the box of the carriage came a distinct "Damn!" and Roger DeVilliers jumped down, his driving coat swirling about him, its capes flapping. He glared at her. "What in hell do you want?" he demanded.

"What do you think you are doing?" Thea replied.

"Leaving with Miss Powell." He leaned back against the carriage, his arms crossed and a wicked smile on his face. "I should think you'd be glad."

"For God's sake, have you no care for her reputation?"

"Go away," a muttered voice came from inside the carriage, and Thea sent it an exasperated look.

"I cannot let you do this, sir."

"You can't stop me," he pointed out.

"No, but Stanton can."

DeVilliers grinned. "But he won't know, will he, Althea?"

"Yes, he will. I sent back word."

"Damn! Why did you have to meddle?" DeVilliers put his hand to his hair in frustration and then snatched it away. "You'll have to come along."

"What? Of course I won't, sir," she began, but her voice faltered as he withdrew his hand from his pocket.

In it, gleaming in the sun, was a serviceable-looking pistol, pointed directly at her.

Thea froze. Beneath her Maggie danced restlessly, but she hardly noticed. Her entire being was focused on the gun. "Please, sir," she said, her voice shaky, "put that away. You won't need it."

"I'm afraid not, Althea. Come." He stepped over to her, holding out his free hand. "Down with you, now. And don't think to try anything."

"N-no, I—"

"What, does this little thing scare you?" He gestured with the pistol and she shrank back. "Good." His smile was devilish. "Perhaps you'll learn a lesson. I had no intention of compromising you as well," he went on, taking her arm in a rough grip and dragging her toward the carriage, "but it can't be helped."

"Is that what you're planning on doing with Miss Powell? Compromising her?" Thea said, finding her voice.

"Of course. How else am I to secure her father's permission to marry me? Tell him I need her money? In with you now." He opened the carriage door and thrust her in, roughly. "And don't forget, my dear. I have this." He held up the pistol, and Thea shrank back. Smiling, he backed away, slamming the door closed.

Thea somehow found her courage. She sprang forward, reaching for the door, but at that moment the carriage started with a lurch, and she was thrown back against the seat. Her chance for escape was gone. As the carriage gathered speed, she was left, sprawled on the seat, staring at an obviously disgruntled Evadne.

* * *

"You'll be leaving today, then," Jeremy said as he walked toward the stables after breakfast for his customary ride about the estate.

"Yes. I thought Thea wanted to make an early start, but she's not in her room," Francis said, frowning.

"Gregg says she went out riding with Gillian. I expect they'll be back soon." And then, he thought, he'd straighten out this nonsense about her leaving.

"Of course, but we probably won't set off till noon, at any rate."

"Yes." Jeremy glanced quickly at the other man. There had been a time when he could have sworn that Francis and Evadne—but Francis was leaving, and Jeremy was still engaged. For now. After last night, his betrothal was an annoyance he wished only to put behind him. He would speak to Evadne today. What would Francis do then, he wondered, and was considering telling him of his plans, when the sound of hoofbeats made him turn with a start.

"Daddy!" Gillian road around the corner of the house, her eyes huge in her pale face. "Oh, Daddy!"

"Gillian! Are you hurt?" Jeremy ran forward to catch the pony's bridle, and Gillian tumbled off into his arms. "Where is Thea?"

"I was brave, Daddy," Gillian said, her arms about his neck, her voice muffled. "I was."

"I know, poppet, I know." Jeremy spoke soothingly, but his eyes, meeting Francis's, were alarmed. "Where is Mrs. Jameson?"

Gillian pulled back, telling in a breathless voice what had happened, starting with her first sight of the carriage and ending with Thea's request that she fetch her father. Several times during the tale Jeremy and Francis looked at each other in astonishment, but by the time she was finished, they each looked grim.

Jeremy set Gillian down. "Go on back into the house, poppet," he said, patting her back. "And next time, let Miss Moffett know where you are going."

"Yes, Daddy. I bet Miss Powell's just gone for a ride."

"Yes. Now, go on with you," he commanded, turning back to Francis, whose mouth was set in a thin line. "Damn it, who the hell is it?"

"She's eloping," Francis asked flatly. "We have to stop her."

"Yes," Jeremy said, but he remained still as Francis strode toward the stable.

"Aren't you coming?" Francis turned, tapping his foot impatiently. "We've got to stop them."

"I imagine Thea already has." And why she couldn't have let well enough alone, he didn't know. In any event, he would not marry Evadne now. Her flight had given him the excuse he needed to end the engagement.

"In that case, they could both be in danger," Francis said crisply.

Alarm flared in Jeremy's eyes as the possibility that Thea was in harm's way assaulted him, and he began to run toward the stables. "Damn. We'd best hurry."

"Toward Dover?" Francis asked as they mounted and rode out of the stableyard.

"Yes. I can't think where else they'd go, unless—" Their eyes met. "Damn! He might be taking them out of the country!"

"Then we must hurry."

Jeremy's mouth set in a grim line. "You go on. I'll catch up with you."

"What?"

"My pistol. I need my pistol. Go! I'll catch up with you."

"I'll wait." Francis's expression was hard. "Have an extra gun for me?"

Thea breathed deeply in an attempt to still the erratic beating of her heart. Events had moved so quickly that she was stunned, off balance, not quite certain what to do next. She only knew she somehow had to get herself, and Evadne, out of this predicament.

She looked across to the other seat, where Evadne was sitting, gazing out the window, her lips set in a stubborn pout. "Are you all right, Miss Powell?" she asked, and Evadne turned to look at her for the first time.

"You've ruined it all!" she burst out. "Oh, why did you have to come around meddling, anyway?"

"But—" Thea stared at her. "Surely you didn't want this?"

"Of course I wanted it! Did you think I wanted to spend the rest of my life in that poky old house with—with—*Stanton?* He's so old! And he's mean. He wouldn't even let me keep Fluffy!"

As if in agreement, the cat, trapped in its box, let out another howl. In spite of the gravity of the situation, Thea felt a smile tugging at her lips. "I do wonder if Mr. DeVilliers knows what he's getting into."

Evadne tossed her curls. "He's been very kind. A perfect gentleman. Not like some I can name. And he likes Fluffy."

"Really." Thea bent her head to hide her smile. "But are you really sure he's the husband for you?"

"Husband!" Evadne stared at her, and then started to laugh. "Oh, really, Mrs. Jameson, you are just too absurd! Why would I marry him? Why, he's almost as old as Stanton!"

"But, that's what he said—"

"He's taking me home," she said simply. "I told him what life has been like with Stanton and that I couldn't bear it anymore and he offered to take me home."

"But why couldn't you just tell Jeremy and break the engagement?"

"Don't be a goose! Do you suppose my mother would let me? Besides, Stanton wants to marry me."

Thea, remembering the events of the previous evening, wasn't so certain. But there had been no words of love, she thought again, and her spirits dropped. "Nevertheless, I'm sure he'd release you if you asked."

"Well, now he has no choice, has he?" Evadne said coolly. "I imagine this will cause no end of a fuss."

"I imagine it will." Thea looked at her consideringly. In her own way, Evadne was quite as formidable as her mother. Jeremy was well out of that match.

"And then you had to come along and ruin everything," Evadne went on. "I don't know what Mr. DeVilliers will do with you. We can't take you along, but if we leave you—"

"The alarm's been given already, Evadne. I sent Gillian back to Moulton."

"What? Oh no! Then you *have* ruined everything!" Evadne cried. "I hate you! I do!"

"I don't doubt it," Thea said wryly. "But it appears we are stuck with each other, at least until Dover."

"Dover!" Evadne stared at her over her handkerchief. "We're not going to Dover."

"But we are. At least we're headed in that direction."

"But—" For the first time, Evadne looked uncertain. "Can we get to Berkshire by way of Dover?"

"Berkshire? Why Berkshire?"

"That's where I live."

"What?" Thea stared at her. "But, then—"

"Why are we going to Dover? Mr. DeVilliers!" Evadne reached up and pounded on the roof. "Mr. DeVilliers! I demand you stop! There has to be some mistake," she said to Thea as the carriage rolled to a halt. "There must be."

The carriage door swung open and DeVilliers, the pistol held negligently in his hand, faced them. Thea couldn't help it; she shrank back against the seat, remembering how blithely she had told Gillian to be brave in facing a fear. Hard words to live up to. "Ladies?" he said impatiently. "Is there some problem?"

"We're going the wrong way, sir."

"Are we?" DeVilliers grinned. "I assure you, we're going exactly where I want to go."

"But you promised you'd take me home!" Evadne wailed. "Oh, why are you doing this?"

"Because I need money as much as Stanton does. I apologize for any discomfort you may suffer, Althea," he said, bowing toward her, and his eyes raked over her in such a way that she wanted to shield herself, "but having you along might be interesting."

"I want to go home!" Evadne wailed, and the cat, hearing her voice, responded with a long, mournful howl.

"We will. Eventually. Enjoy the trip, ladies." He slammed the door and walked away.

"But no!" Evadne sprang for the door and then fell back, just as Thea had, when the carriage started up again. "He can't do this! He can't!"

Thea sat up straighter, recovering some of her spirits now that the gun was no longer in sight. "But he is. And unless Jeremy catches up with us, he'll get away with it."

"No, he won't." Evadne's eyes suddenly began to dance. "We're two against one."

Thea stared at her. "But he has a gun."

"Oh pooh! That little toy? I've shot better guns than that," Evadne said, making Thea look at her with new respect. "We'll have to distract him somehow. He's only a man. Surely we can outwit him."

Thea laughed. This was a side of Evadne she had never seen before, and she rather liked it. "You aren't at all what I expected, Miss Powell."

"Neither are you." Evadne studied her. "When I first met you, I couldn't think at all what Stanton saw in you. You looked so old!"

"Why, thank you," Thea murmured.

"And I couldn't imagine why he might prefer you to me, and I didn't like that at all."

"If I had thought he were truly happy with you, I would have left him alone. I never was his mistress, you know," Thea said quietly, and for the first time Evadne's eyes met hers without pretense. "You don't love him, do you?"

"No." Evadne glanced away. "I never did, and that's partly why I said what I did to you, accusing you of being his mistress. But I suppose I'll have to marry him, if he'll still have me after this. I don't know what else I can do."

"You could refuse."

"My mother wouldn't let me." Her voice was dull. "But you can have him, Mrs. Jameson. I might have to marry him, but you can have him. I don't care, anymore."

Thea impulsively reached over and covered Evadne's hands with her own. No longer did Evadne's extraordinary offer repulse her, now that she knew what lay behind it. "I thought you were in love with my brother."

Evadne started, and withdrew her hands. "I've ruined that, too. I don't think he'd have me now, either."

"He came to Moulton," Thea pointed out.

"Oh! Is that why he did? For me?" Evadne brightened and then as quickly drooped. "But he's leaving today."

"Perhaps." Thea leaned back, studying her. "Things may yet work out."

"I don't think so." Evadne laid a hand on Fluffy's traveling case. "No, I'll have to marry Stanton, and the only one who will love me is my cat."

At another time, Thea might have laughed at such a statement, but not now. Evadne looked too woebegone. "Excuse me for saying this, but he is a most unusual pet for you to have."

"Because he's ugly, you mean. I don't mind. Your brother said the same. But you aren't ugly, are you, my little kitty cat?" she crooned to the box. "Fluffy loves me."

"Why do you have him?"

"Because he was the smallest of the litter, and the ugliest, and he would have been drowned if I hadn't taken him."

Thea stared at her. *Heavens!* The things one learned about people when one was being held captive at gunpoint. "Well, he certainly isn't the smallest now."

"No, but he's still the ugliest," Evadne said, and they both laughed.

"Yes, he looks like he's been through the war."

"Oh, he's a fighter," Evadne said, and went very still. "Mrs. Jameson!" she said momentarily. "I've had an idea!"

Chapter 19

The sun hid behind thickening clouds as the two riders pounded along the Dover road. "This had best not be one of Evadne's tricks," Jeremy growled, "else I'll wring her neck."

"I say!" Francis stared at him. "A beautiful girl like that?"

"Try living with her," he tossed over his shoulder as he urged his horse forward. In the mood he was in, he had no desire to hear anyone sing Evadne's praises. Becoming engaged to her was one of the worst mistakes he had ever made. Now it seemed there might be a way out. "If your sister hadn't gotten involved I think I would have just let her go."

Francis's mouth set in a straight line. "Just like that? You don't know who she's with."

"It would be one way of getting rid of her," Jeremy muttered, raising an eyebrow at the glare Francis gave him. "Don't worry about Evadne. She's stronger than you think."

"But not as strong as you think, Stanton. How do you think she feels, being married only for her money?"

"She's getting what she wants."

"No, she isn't. I don't think she's ever gotten what she wants. My God, man, can't you see? She acts the way she does just so someone will pay attention to her."

Jeremy, who had never put this construction on Evadne's actions, was quiet a moment, thinking. It was possible. With a mother like Mrs. Powell, and a distant father, Evadne could very well have grown up feeling neglected and unloved. As he had. With some chagrin, he wondered why he hadn't realized it earlier. "Thorne," he said, his voice carefully casual, "you wouldn't by chance have a *tendre* for her, would you?"

"And if I did?" Francis retorted.

"How could you support her?"

Francis stared at him. "My God! You sound like a father."

"Never mind that. What kind of life could you give her, if she didn't have any money?"

"Not a good one," Francis said bitterly. "You must know we Thornes are always under the hatches. Except for Thea, of course, but I wouldn't take money from her." *Not anymore,* he added to himself.

"What would you do with your life, if you could? I seem to remember you're interested in politics."

"A lot of good that does me. You need money for that, too. And someone to sponsor you."

"Mm." Jeremy fell silent, thinking.

"I say," Francis said after a few moments, "are you sure we're going the right way?"

"Gillian said they were heading toward Dover."

"If he's taking them to the Continent—"

"Wind's in the wrong direction. There won't be any ships leaving the harbor. We'll get them," he said.

What Francis heard in Jeremy's voice must have reassured him, for he fell silent, leaving Jeremy to his thoughts.

What a damned nuisance, Jeremy mused. Had Evadne not gone off on this mad start he might have managed to work things out with her by now; he might even have become engaged to Thea. Instead, here he was, haring after them, trying to save Evadne from herself and putting his concern about Thea aside. Until he could find her and talk with her about last night, he would not rest easy.

Letting his riding instinct and skill take over, he lost himself in memories of the previous night. It had been special, like nothing he had ever known before. It was the first time he'd truly made love. Oh, he'd had women before, of course, but never had he felt toward one of them as he did toward Thea. Never had an encounter been so special, not even their first time together, so far did it go beyond mere pleasure. It had been an act of love, and he had lost himself in her, seeking and finding something he hadn't even realized was missing from his life, a total acceptance, a total involvement that was new. It had left him dazed, disoriented, unable to tell where she left off and he began, and only this morning, waking to find himself alone, had he been able to separate himself from her. It was exhilarating, but it was also frightening. Perhaps she felt frightened too; perhaps it was why she still wanted to leave.

Jeremy frowned. But had not their lovemaking been as shattering, as overwhelming an experience for her as it had been for him? Had it not been as special? But of course it had been! There had been no mistaking her response to him, her little gasps and sighs of pleasure. No,

294

it had been good for her, and a revelation as well. Jameson had been a fool not to avail himself of her warmth and passion, not to show her how special she was. But he would make it up to her, once he was free of Evadne.

And if she wasn't hurt. He was not as easy in his mind about the situation as he had pretended to be with Francis. Who knew who the women were with, and what the fiend might be capable of? He wasn't worried about Evadne; she had, after all, got herself into this, and, in any event, like her cat she would always land on her feet. Thea, however, for all her appearance of strength was far more vulnerable, and also likely to try to protect Evadne to her own cost. It was a good thing he had thought to bring his pistols. Thea had been through enough.

"What was Jameson like?" he asked abruptly.

Francis looked over at him. "A bounder. You wouldn't know it, looking at him. He was very pleasant, very bluff. But Thea had a hard time with him."

"Did he beat her?"

"I don't know." Francis's gaze was troubled. "I do know it hurt her deeply when he flaunted his mistresses. I was there once when he did it. He rather took pleasure in humiliating her."

"Good God! Why the devil did she marry him?"

"Don't you know? Our father was under the hatches, as usual. Jameson offered to pay his debts, in return for Thea."

"God!" Jeremy exclaimed, and at that moment Francis pointed with his riding crop.

"Look! Someone's coming this way." They stopped as a farmer, jogging along in his cart, pulled up, and asked him if he had passed a carriage carrying two ladies. Yes, he'd seen such a carriage, the man said, being driven at a mad pace by a man with a scar. Jeremy and Francis looked at each other blankly. "Who the devil?" Francis began, and Jeremy shook his head.

"Thank you," he called to the farmer, and urged his horse onward. "No need to let anyone else know about this."

"No, there'll be enough scandal as it is if this gets out," Francis agreed, drawing up level with him. He glanced at Jeremy, opened his mouth to speak, and then closed it again. "Sounds like he's not too far ahead, whoever he is."

"Yes, we should catch up with him soon," Jeremy agreed. And when they did, he would finally straighten out the mess he was in, and Thea would be his.

"We're stopping," Evadne said.

Thea raised her head and blinked at her. "I fell asleep," she said in surprise.

"Didn't you sleep well last night?"

Thea blushed. "No," she said, her eyes not meeting Evadne's. She didn't mind being so sleepy, not when she thought of the reason. It had been a wonderful night, though now, away from Jeremy, she felt doubts creeping in. Had it been as wonderful for him? Because it had been a revelation to her. She hadn't known she could feel like that, that love could be like that between a man and a woman. She hadn't known it was possible to feel so close to someone. She was irrevocably changed. After last night, her heart would forever be his.

Evadne craned her neck to see out the window. "It looks like some kind of inn. Do you know it?"

Thea leaned over. "No, I've not ridden this far afield. We've been on the road awhile."

"Nearly an hour." Evadne absently stroked Fluffy; the cat was curled up on her lap. "I wonder why we're stopping."

The carriage door opened suddenly, startling them both.

"Ladies," Roger DeVilliers drawled. "We'll be stopping here for a time."

"I'm surprised, sir," Thea said coolly, hoping her voice was steady and betrayed the fear DeVilliers's pistol inspired in her. "Aren't you afraid of Stanton catching up with us?"

Roger laughed. "History won't repeat itself this time. We'll change carriages here. The innkeeper has been well-paid not to betray us." He gestured with the pistol. "Come now, we haven't all day. Evadne, my dear?"

"I'm not coming," she said, her lower lip thrust out.

"Come, come, my dear, losing heart so soon? You'll soon be eager enough. Though, perhaps I'll take this opportunity to become better acquainted with Mrs. Jameson." His gaze raked over her; in spite of herself, Thea shrank back against the squabs, making him chuckle. "Come, ladies."

"Oh, very well." Evadne sounded sulky as she rose. "But you take Fluffy," she said, and thrust the cat at him.

DeVilliers recoiled; the cat, snarling with surprise as Evadne suddenly released it, clawed at empty air, and then at DeVilliers. He threw his arms up to protect his face, but not before the cat raked him with his claws.

"Get this hellcat off me!" he shouted. Fluffy, having landed on his shoulders, now was clawing frantically at his head, where he perched howling. DeVilliers staggered, and the cat, dislodged from its precarious perch, slid off, taking with him a mat of hair that left DeVilliers's bald head shining in the sudden sunlight. Thea forgot to be frightened of the pistol, which flew from DeVilliers's wildly flailing hand, and giggled at the sight. The cat clawed at his face again and slipped, clutching first at his coat and then at his pantaloons, to the ground. DeVilliers aimed a kick at him, but Fluffy was faster, disappearing into a hedge, dragging the hairpiece with him. DeVillers staggered again and then regained his balance, righting himself and turning to face them—only to see Evadne standing very cool and calm, the pistol held steadily in her hands.

It was too much. His carefully conceived plans had turned into a farce, first with the cat and now with this mindless debutante actually pointing a gun at him. "Give that to me," he said peremptorily, holding out his hand.

"I think not." Evadne took a step forward and he retreated. "You tried to kick my cat."

"My God!" He lowered the handkerchief he had pressed against the worst of the scratches to stare at her. "Is that all you care about? A damned cat?"

"Yes, Mr. DeVilliers. That, and returning to Moulton."

"Damn. All right, Evadne, you win. I'll bring you back if you'll give me the gun—"

"Do you think I'm stupid?" Evadne advanced another pace. "I warn you, sir, I do know how to use this. And at this range I'd hardly miss, would I?"

Thea climbed carefully down from the carriage and stood next to Evadne, her eyes avoiding the pistol. "Good lord, Evadne, it worked!"

"Of course it did. I only wish Fluffy had not run off."

"We'll look for him afterward. My, Mr. DeVilliers, those are nasty scratches." Thea grinned at him and received a sour look in return. "Perhaps you should go inside and have them attended to."

"And don't think to try anything, sir," Evadne said, gesturing with the pistol. "After you."

"There it is!" Francis shouted, pointing with his riding crop; he set his horse to the gallop. Jeremy was close behind him, and they drew up next to the ramshackle carriage, standing before the long, low, rambling inn. Except for the carriage and the horses hitched to it, blowing and stamping, the inn yard was deserted.

Jeremy frowned as Francis swung down from his horse and sprang for the open door of the carriage. Something was not right here. Why would the man they were chasing, whoever he was, stop so close to Moulton, and with the carriage in plain sight? "Careful!" he called sharply as Francis disappeared into the carriage. "We know not who we're dealing with!"

"They're not there, but they were." Francis jumped lightly to the ground, a satchel in one hand and in the other a box that Jeremy recognized as Fluffy's traveling case. He let out an oath as he dismounted.

"Damn! We'll have to find someone to take the horses. Travers!" he bellowed.

"You know this place?"

"Of course. I've stopped here several times."

"Stanton. Look."

At the odd note in Francis's voice, Jeremy turned. What he saw made him blink in disbelief. Sitting under a hedge by the side of the road, unconcernedly grooming its face with a forepaw, was a huge, brindled cat. Beside him lay what appeared to be the remains of some field animal, though Jeremy couldn't identify it. "Good God!"

"Fluffy." Francis dropped the bags and strode over to the cat, lifting it in his hands. "Where are they, you mangy ball of fur?" he demanded.

"My lord!" The innkeeper bustled out, wiping his hands on the towel tied at his waist. "Forgive me, Lord Stanton, but we're at sixes and sevens today. Some travelers arrived before you, and the ladies—"

"What ladies?" Jeremy demanded swiftly.

"Why, the young ladies, sir, and the gentleman. I've put them in my best parlor. They're seeing to his injuries, and—"

"The devil!" Jeremy exchanged a swift, startled look with Francis and then turned. "See to the horses, Travers," he snapped over his shoulder, and strode into the inn, Francis running behind him.

And so it was that after a hard, tense ride, believing their loved ones to be in danger, Jeremy and Francis entered the inn's private parlor to see a most unusual tableau. Roger DeVilliers was seated on a stool, having some nasty scratches attended to by Thea, while Evadne, of all people, was leaning against a table, a pistol held almost carelessly in her hand. After the unremitting tension of their ride, the scene was almost farcical, and both men stopped short, at a loss for what to do next.

300

Evadne looked up and her face brightened. "You found Fluffy!" she exclaimed. "Oh, thank you!"

Jeremy nearly choked. "Good God, Evadne, what are you doing with that gun?"

"Making sure he doesn't escape. Will you hold onto him, Mr. Thorne? Good kitty, you took care of that nasty man, didn't you?"

Francis exchanged a startled glance with Jeremy and then let out a bark of laughter. "I say, Stanton, look at him! Done in by two females and a cat."

"Appropriate, I'd say." Jeremy smiled, but his eyes were cold and hard. "I might have known it was you."

"You can have her—ouch." DeVilliers jerked his head back as the damp cloth Thea held touched one of the deeper scratches. "Though God knows what you see in her. Mrs. Jameson is much more interesting."

Jeremy's eyes flickered. "Thea, you're all right?"

"Yes, of course I am. Hold still, sir," Thea said to DeVilliers. "The cat got frightened and tried to run away. Mr. DeVilliers very kindly tried to stop him, and got scratched for his pains. At least, that's what we told the innkeeper."

Francis was grinning. "And how do you explain the gun?"

"Oh, we don't. He didn't notice it, thank heavens. There, sir, that's the worst of it. I don't think they'll leave a scar."

"And if they do, the hairpiece will cover 'em." Francis held up Fluffy's trophy. "Didn't know you were bald, sir."

"A pity. You won't have another scar to boast to the ladies about," Jeremy said, and held out his hand. "Evadne, come here."

301

Thea glanced up, her eyes unreadable, as Evadne crossed the room to Jeremy. "I'll take that." He took the pistol from her unresisting fingers, and then looked down at her, shaking his head. "What in the world did you think you were about?"

"I'm sorry, Stanton," Evadne said meekly, her head bent. Jeremy's eyes were chips of blue ice. It occurred to Thea that she'd rarely seen Jeremy angry, and she wondered what he would do. Would this be the goad he needed to break with Evadne once and for all?

Jeremy let out his breath. "We won't discuss it here," he said crisply, "but when we return to Moulton I wish a word with you."

"Yes, Stanton," Evadne said in the same meek voice. "I am sorry, sir. And Mr. Thorne."

"Don't apologize on my account." Francis was grinning broadly, obviously enjoying himself. "Do you want your cat?"

"Yes. Oh, good kitty," she crooned to the cat, struggling in her arms. "Didn't he do well, Thea?"

"Indeed, he did," Thea said, stealing a quick glance at Jeremy. Aside from those few words when he'd entered, he'd said nothing to her. He seemed to be far more concerned with Evadne. Her heart sank. Had their night together meant nothing to him?

"God," DeVilliers muttered, and they looked at him. He was sitting with his head down, his arms dangling between his knees. All in all, he presented a pathetic sight, without the luxuriant dark hair that had been his best feature.

Francis let out another laugh. "Better leave the country, DeVilliers. You'll never live this down."

"Oh yes, he'll leave," Jeremy said, his voice so soft

and so cold that Roger raised his head to look at him, "and no one will hear of this. Is that clear?"

"Of course, Jeremy," Thea said, picking up her hat from the table and putting it on. "I told the innkeeper that Evadne is my sister. I'm not sure he believes it, but—"

"He will. I'll see to it. Thorne. Will you see the ladies home? I'll follow shortly."

"I say, you're not going to let him get away with it, are you?" Francis exclaimed.

"Oh no. This is twice he's tried this on me, and last time I had no satisfaction. By God, sir, this time you'll fight."

Evadne gasped. "Another duel? Oh, how romantic!"

"No!" Thea said sharply. "You can't—"

"Thorne, will you take them out of here?" Jeremy snapped.

"But you have no second," Francis protested.

"Just think, Mr. DeVilliers, perhaps you'll have another scar, after all! To think of the two of you dueling again, and over me," Evadne exclaimed.

"I won't need a second," Jeremy said, and then looked sharply at Evadne. "What do you mean, 'again'?"

"He told me you dueled before, and that is when he got the scar."

"Really." Jeremy smiled maliciously. "Is that what you've told everyone? I wonder what they'll think when they know the truth?"

"God," DeVilliers said again, drawing his hands down his face and wincing.

"You see, it is true that I once challenged him to a duel," Jeremy explained. "He had tried to elope with my wife before we were married—he has a habit of doing that—and I couldn't allow it. But rather than face me, he ran away." Jeremy's grin was mocking. "He fled in such haste that he didn't watch where he was going and rode into a tree limb. It split his cheek open. And that, my dear Evadne, is how he came by the scar. History does seem to be repeating itself, doesn't it, sir?"

"Jeremy." Thea caught at his sleeve. "You won't duel, you can't—"

"Thorne," Jeremy snapped. "Get them out of here."

"Jeremy, please—"

"Come, Thea," Francis said, taking her arm, though she tried to pull away. "Stanton does not want us here."

"But he can't," she said frantically as Francis pulled her into the inn yard. "Francis, you must stop it."

Evadne followed them out of the inn. "Stanton just slapped Mr. DeVilliers in the face with his glove! And the innkeeper is making them go out in the field in back."

"Can't stop it, then," Francis said. "In with you, Thea."

Thea reluctantly climbed into the carriage. "Francis, can't you at least stay and make sure he's all right?"

"He will be, Thea, don't worry. I think he just wants to teach DeVilliers a lesson."

"But Mr. DeVilliers has a choice of weapons, hasn't he?" Evadne said, her eyes shining. "Oh, I wish I could stay to see it! What will he choose, do you think?"

"Can't see there's much choice." Francis closed the door and spoke through the window. "Looks like it will be pistols."

"No!" Thea jumped to her feet, swaying as the carriage started off. "No, I can't let that happen again!"

"Thea!" Evadne exclaimed, but Thea had already opened the door and jumped out, stumbling to the ground. "Thea, wait!"

Thea didn't answer. Already she was running into the inn, dashing down the hall past the startled innkeeper, to find the way to the field where Jeremy was to fight. She couldn't let it happen, not again. It had been bad enough to lose Hugh, and over another woman's honor; how much worse would it be to lose Jeremy. And not even because of her, she thought bitterly. It was Evadne he fought to protect, Evadne he loved, Evadne he would marry. Their night in each other's arms had been only a moment's pleasure to him, and she was a fool to have hoped he loved her. But she could not stand idly by and let him be killed, even if it meant saving him for Evadne.

The sun broke out just as she dashed from the inn. In the distance the sky was black with clouds, and the golden light lent an unreal brilliance to the scene: Jeremy and Roger, their coats removed, their shirtsleeves dazzlingly white against their dark waistcoats, pacing away from each other, pistols ready in their hands. "No!" Thea said, but her voice caught in her throat, as in a nightmare when she tried to scream but couldn't, tried to run but couldn't. Time had slowed down, and each step she took seemed excruciatingly, agonizingly slow. She would never reach them in time.

They had stopped, now, they were turning, standing almost in profile, so as to present a smaller target, raising their hands. "No!" Thea screamed; this time her voice exploded in her ears. Time returned to normal, and she was running, running, her lungs burning so she thought they would burst, pushing aside the fear of

305

guns, that threatened to choke her. Someone called her name, but she didn't stop, she veered instead toward Roger DeVilliers in a desperate attempt to protect Jeremy. She was almost there, almost there—

And the guns went off, so closely together they sounded like one loud report. Something hit Thea hard, in the shoulder, and she rocked back. Through a red mist, she saw Jeremy, whose pistol had been hastily pointed into the air, drop his gun and start to run, saw DeVilliers standing very still, a look of horror on his face. Then the red mist swirled and swirled and darkened into black, and she knew no more.

Chapter 20

She was being carried. A voice was calling her name, over and over and over. "Thea. Thea, my darling, my love, I'm sorry, don't die, don't—"

Another voice, Francis's voice. "God, I tried to stop her. Is she—"

"I don't know. Get the innkeeper to send for a doctor. Thea, Thea, hold on, my love, don't die, don't leave me—careful, don't touch her!"

Pain lancing through her. She heard someone whimper, and then the blessed darkness descended again until, a long time later, she opened her eyes. She could make no sense of her surroundings, other than that she was lying on a bed in a room with plain plaster walls, a casement window and a beamed ceiling. A strange woman, plump and motherly, was leaning over her, and an elderly, bearded man, and someone was gripping her hand so hard it hurt. Again someone whimpered as she tried to pull her hand away, and the grip tightened.

"Thea. Thea, darling. Hold on."

"Jeremy?"

"Yes, darling. Hold on."

"I can't," she gasped, as the strange man suddenly probed at her shoulder with something that sent fire through her. The darkness swirled around her again, and this time she went with it gladly.

The doctor stepped away from the bed. "She'll do," he said briefly to the worried-looking young man who sat on the other side of the bed, holding the woman's hand. "Ball went clean through her shoulder."

"She'll be all right?" Jeremy asked anxiously. It had been one of the worst moments in his life, seeing Thea fall, shot by DeVilliers's gun. When he got his hands on him—

"Yes, she and the baby. Lost some blood, but that's to be expected. Keep her quiet for a few days and she'll be all right." The doctor had snapped his bag shut and was headed for the door before his words penetrated Jeremy's mind.

"The what?" he exclaimed, shooting up from the chair. He ran after the doctor, catching him in the hall. "What baby?"

The doctor gave him a shrewd, measuring look. "Didn't you know? She's pregnant. Shouldn't let your lady jaunter about in her condition, sir," he said sternly.

"She's not—I mean, I won't." He followed the doctor down the stairs. "You're sure?"

"Of course I'm sure. She's about two months along, I'd say." He stopped at the door. "What are you standing about here for, man? Go on back to your wife."

"She's not—" Jeremy began, and closed his mouth. No, she wasn't his wife, but she would be. And she had some explaining to do.

He walked into the little bedroom and stood, staring down at her. Thea, the mother of his child—because it had to be his—and the love of his life. What had she been thinking, to leave him without a word? And then to run between him and DeVilliers. The thought made him shudder. He had nearly lost her. How very lucky he was, to have another chance.

Mrs. Travers, the innkeeper's wife, looked at him sympathetically as she continued cleaning up after the doctor, bundling together several bloody cloths. "Poor lady," she said. "And such a pretty riding habit as it was."

"I'll take her back to Moulton," Jeremy said as if he hadn't heard. Take her back, and never let her go. Never. "Stay with her."

"Yes, of course, my lord." Mrs. Travers curtsied as Jeremy strode by her and shook her head. The quality surely did get up to some strange goings-on.

"Stanton!" Francis jumped up from his seat in the private parlor as Jeremy entered. "Is she—"

"She'll be all right. I could use some of that brandy." He sprawled into a chair and tossed back the liquor, ignoring the blood that stained his shirtfront and sleeve. Thea's blood. His baby. *Good God.* "She's asleep."

"I tried to stop her," Francis said, "but she got too far ahead of me."

Jeremy waved his hand in dismissal. "I should have known better," he said regretfully, "but nothing would do but that I had to fight that bastard. Where is he, by the way?"

Francis looked confused, realizing for the first time that DeVilliers wasn't there. "I don't know."

"He's gone," Evadne said in a very small voice. "I saw him take the carriage and leave."

"Good. Maybe he's leaving the country," Francis said.

"He had better," Jeremy said grimly. "Next time I won't miss." He reached for the brandy. "Damn. Now how will we get Thea back to Moulton."

"I'm sorry," Evadne said.

Jeremy looked at her. "Why?"

"Because it's my fault!" she burst out. "If you hadn't been fighting over me—"

"Don't be ridiculous," Jeremy said, and took a gulp of his second glass of brandy. "You had nothing to do with it."

"But—"

"You were fighting for Thea," Francis said, staring at him.

"Yes, of course. I'm sorry, Evadne, but you're simply not important enough for me to fight over."

Francis jumped to his feet, his hands balled into fists. "I say! You can't say something like that to her!"

Jeremy's eyes glinted. "And why not?"

"Because she's the woman I'm going to marry."

"Mr. Thorne!" Evadne gasped.

"Are you?" Jeremy said, and drained his glass.

"Yes. And no one's going to stop me, not her parents and not you."

"Oh, I wouldn't dream of it." Jeremy was grinning. "In fact, I happen to have an estate in a borough that needs someone to stand for Parliament. I'll support you, if you're interested."

Francis abruptly sat down, staring at him. "You mean it."

"Of course I do. Take her with my blessings. Though she'll lead you a merry dance," he added, but Francis was no longer listening. He had jumped up and caught Evadne in his arms, cat and all.

Jeremy looked at them a moment, and then, smiling, left the room. He was free. He didn't think Mrs. Powell would approve of this new match for her daughter, to a penniless, untitled man, but that didn't bother him. Evadne, he suspected, would win the fight to get, for the first time in her life, what she truly wanted. And the best part of that, he thought as he climbed the stairs to Thea's room, was that he could at last tell Thea he loved her. The future was theirs.

She felt very odd, lying still with her eyes closed. Light and heavy at the same time, as if she were being pressed into bed by a giant, invisible hand. Her shoulder hurt. She had no idea why, or where she was, and when she at last opened her eyes her confusion increased. She didn't know this room, though something about it caught at her memory. For a moment she almost thought herself back at Linwood, and then someone spoke. "Well, hello. Welcome back."

Thea turned her head on the pillow, startled by the amount of effort it took, and saw Jeremy. In the state she was in, half-dreaming, half-awake, she didn't question his presence, but only smiled, lifting a lazy hand to touch his face. He looked wonderful, and at the same time terrible, as if he had been through a great strain. As if—

Her memory flooded back all at once, and she saw again the two men pacing off, the sun glinting off their pistols. "No!" she gasped, and sat up in the bed. Pain like fire shot through her, and she was gasping with it when Jeremy, his hands gentle, helped her to lie down again.

"Thea," he said, and she opened her eyes to see his face, very near, very concerned.

"You're all right," she said, studying him as if she had never seen him before, as if she would never see him again. Because now she remembered. He had survived the duel with Mr. DeVilliers, and now he would marry his little bride. Thea couldn't even find it in her heart to resent Evadne any longer. There was so much more to her than anyone had known.

"Yes, of course I am." He lifted her limp hand from the bed and pressed a kiss on it. "I suspect I would have been in any event. DeVilliers's shot went wide, you see," he explained. "If you had really got between us, you wouldn't have been hurt." His face darkened. "Why did you do it, Thea? It was mad of you."

"I couldn't bear the thought of losing you that way. Not again."

"Again?"

"The way I lost Hugh."

"Oh, my dear." He lowered his face to her hand again, his eyes briefly squeezed shut. "Because of my stupid honor, you have to suffer."

"No, it's all right," she said, and disproved her words by grimacing as she shifted her position.

"No, it isn't. God, Thea, I'll never forget it, seeing you run between us."

"I had to." She lifted her hand to feather it through his hair. "Even if it meant saving you for another woman."

Jeremy raised his head at that. "Saving me for—oh, Thea." And to her chagrin, he burst out laughing.

"I don't see what's so funny," she said testily.

"No, of course you don't," he said, his eyes brimming with mirth. "You don't know. Your brother has taken Evadne away from me."

This time, Thea's eyes grew wide. "He has? But—oh, Jeremy, I'm sorry! How terrible for you."

"Don't be ridiculous."

"But you love her."

"My dear, sweet, silly Thea." He took her face in his hands and bent to give her a brief, gentle kiss. "After last night, you can say such a thing?"

"But—" she stared at him in confusion. "This afternoon, before the duel, you wouldn't even look at me."

"Because I was afraid I'd start kissing you and never stop. Darling, haven't you realized I haven't wanted Evadne for a very long time? Now I'm free." He bent to kiss her again. "To marry you."

"M-marry!" She pulled back, wincing. "Jeremy, there's something I must tell you."

"About the baby? I already know."

She pulled her head back and stared at him. "But how—?"

"The doctor told me. Scolded me for not taking better care of you. Which I intend to do. Someday you'll have to explain why you weren't going to give me the chance."

She shifted again, not meeting his eyes. "I wanted to tell you. 'Tis why I came to Moulton. But then I thought you really wanted to marry Evadne, and I couldn't."

"So you were just going to leave?"

"Yes." She kept her eyes closed. "I thought I'd go to the Continent, where no one knew me."

Jeremy didn't speak for a moment. "I should be angry with you for that, though it's not a bad idea."

She opened her eyes. "It isn't?"

"No. By the time we come home, no one will realize when the child was born."

"We?"

"Yes. You'll marry me, of course." He stroked her fingers. "You thought you couldn't have children."

A smile curved her lips. "I was wrong, apparently. Are you very angry?"

"About the baby? Good God, no. I've always wanted another child."

Thea's eyes flew open. "Are you marrying me for the baby?"

"No."

"For my money, then."

Jeremy laughed again. "Dear, silly girl. Never. I want you for myself."

Thea's eyes widened. "You do?"

"Is that so hard to believe?" Jeremy's face grew tender and grave as he shifted from the chair to the bed, bracing himself with his hands on either side of her. "Darling, I know you had a hard time of it with Jameson, and I know you never wanted to marry again. But do you think you might want to try it with me? Our child should have a father. And I promise you, I'll treat you well, I'll take care of you. I promise I won't be like Jameson."

"Of course not, you could never be." She searched his face. "You're certain about this?"

"Of course I am. I want you at Moulton, with Gillian and me."

"Oh, Gillian! Is she all right? She was so scared."

314

"She's fine. Well, Thea?" He leaned closer. "What do you think?"

Thea's glance shifted away. To hear him say these things now was unutterably sweet, but he had yet to say the one thing that mattered. "I—don't know."

"Thea, don't turn away from me." His fingers under her chin turned her to face him. "Don't shut me out. My God, Thea, when I saw you go down, I thought you were dead, I thought I'd lost you. And I couldn't bear the thought of living without you. Don't leave me now."

Thea gazed at him in wonder, and her fingers reached up to touch his hair. "Jeremy. I love you."

Jeremy raised his head and looked deeply into her eyes, his own eyes glowing with joy. "And I love you. Will you marry me?"

"Do you know, I think I will?" She tilted her face to look at him. "But, mind you, only because of the baby."

"Gammon," Jeremy said, but he was grinning. Quite without warning he leaned toward her and caught her up in his arms, cradling her gently against him. "My love," he said, his voice husky, "I should have known. It was you, all along."

"Well of course." She smiled up at him. "Now, are you ever going to kiss me?"

Jeremy's eyes gleamed. "Well of course." And bending down, he did just that.

A Memorable Collection of Regency Romances

BY ANTHEA MALCOLM AND VALERIE KING

THE COUNTERFEIT HEART   (3425, $3.95/$4.95)
by Anthea Malcolm
Nicola Crawford was hardly surprised when her cousin's betrothed
disappeared on some mysterious quest. Anyone engaged to such an
unromantic, but handsome man was bound to run off sooner or later.
Nicola could never entrust her heart to such a conventional, but so
deucedly handsome man. . . .

THE COURTING OF PHILIPPA   (2714, $3.95/$4.95)
by Anthea Malcolm
Miss Philippa was a very successful author of romantic novels. Thus
she was chagrined to be snubbed by the handsome writer Henry
Ashton whose own books she admired. And when she learned he considered love stories completely beneath his notice, she vowed to teach
him a thing or two about the subject of love. . . .

THE WIDOW'S GAMBIT   (2357, $3.50/$4.50)
by Anthea Malcolm
The eldest of the orphaned Neville sisters needed a chaperone for a
London season. So the ever-resourceful Livia added several years to
her age, invented a deceased husband, and became the respectable
Widow Royce. She was certain she'd never regret abandoning her girlhood until she met dashing Nicholas Warwick. . . .

A DARING WAGER   (2558, $3.95/$4.95)
by Valerie King
Ellie Dearborne's penchant for gaming had finally led her to ruin. It
seemed like such a lark, wagering her devious cousin George that she
would obtain the snuffboxes of three of society's most dashing peers
in one month's time. She could easily succeed, too, were it not for
that exasperating Lord Ravenworth. . . .

THE WILLFUL WIDOW   (3323, $3.95/$4.95)
by Valerie King
The lovely young widow, Mrs. Henrietta Harte, was not all inclined to
pursue the sort of romantic folly the persistent King Brandish had in
mind. She had to concentrate on marrying off her penniless sisters
and managing her spendthrift mama. Surely Mr. Brandish could fit in
with her plans somehow . . .

*Available wherever paperbacks are sold, or order direct from the
Publisher. Send cover price plus 50¢ per copy for mailing and
handling to Zebra Books, Dept. 4271, 475 Park Avenue South,
New York, N.Y. 10016. Residents of New York and Tennessee
must include sales tax. DO NOT SEND CASH. For a free Zebra/
Pinnacle catalog please write to the above address.*

PASSIONATE NIGHTS FROM
PENELOPE NERI

DESERT CAPTIVE
(2447, $3.95/$4.95)

Kidnapped from her French Foreign Legion escort, indignant Alexandria had every reason to despise her nomad prince captor. But as they traveled to his isolated mountain kingdom, she found her hate melting into desire . . .

FOREVER AND BEYOND
(3115, $4.95/$5.95)

Haunted by dreams of an Indian warrior, Kelly found his touch more than intimate—it was oddly familiar. He seemed to be calling her back to another time, to a place where they would find love again . . .

FOREVER IN HIS ARMS
(3385, $4.95/$5.95)

Whispers of war between the North and South were riding the wind the summer Jenny Delaney fell in love with Tyler Mackenzie. Time was fast running out for secret trysts and lovers' dreams, and she would have to choose between the life she held so dear and the man whose passion made her burn as brightly as the evening star . . .

MIDNIGHT CAPTIVE
(2593, $3.95/$4.95)

After a poor, ragged girlhood with her gypsy kinfolk, Krissoula knew that all she wanted from life was her share of riches. There was only one way for the penniless temptress to earn a cent: fake interest in a man, drug him, and pocket everything he had! Then the seductress met dashing Esteban and unquenchable passion seared her soul . . .

SEA JEWEL
(3013, $4.50/$5.50)

Hot-tempered Alaric had long planned the humiliation of Freya, the daughter of the most hated foe. He'd make the wench from across the ocean his lowly bedchamber slave—but he never suspected she would become the mistress of his heart, his treasured sea jewel . . .

DISCOVER DEANA JAMES!

CAPTIVE ANGEL   (2524, $4.50/$5.50)
Abandoned, penniless, and suddenly responsible for the biggest tobacco plantation in Colleton County, distraught Caroline Gillard had no time to dissolve into tears. By day the willowy redhead labored to exhaustion beside her slaves . . . but each night left her restless with longing for her wayward husband. She'd make the sea captain regret his betrayal until he begged her to take him back!

MASQUE OF SAPPHIRE   (2885, $4.50/$5.50)
Judith Talbot-Harrow left England with a heavy heart. She was going to America to join a father she despised and a sister she distrusted. She was certainly in no mood to put up with the insulting actions of the arrogant Yankee privateer who boarded her ship, ransacked her things, then "apologized" with an indecent, brazen kiss! She vowed that someday he'd pay dearly for the liberties he had taken and the desires he had awakened.

SPEAK ONLY LOVE   (3439, $4.95/$5.95)
Long ago, the shock of her mother's death had robbed Vivian Marleigh of the power of speech. Now she was being forced to marry a bitter man with brandy on his breath. But she could not say what was in her heart. It was up to the viscount to spark the fires that would melt her icy reserve.

WILD TEXAS HEART   (3205, $4.95/$5.95)
Fan Breckenridge was terrified when the stranger found her near-naked and shivering beneath the Texas stars. Unable to remember who she was or what had happened, all she had in the world was the deed to a patch of land that might yield oil . . . and the fierce loving of this wildcatter who called himself Irons.

Available wherever paperbacks are sold, or order direct from the Publisher. Send cover price plus 50¢ per copy for mailing and handling to Zebra Books, Dept. 4271, 475 Park Avenue South, New York, N.Y. 10016. Residents of New York and Tennessee must include sales tax. DO NOT SEND CASH. For a free Zebra/ Pinnacle catalog please write to the above address.

THE ROMANCES OF LORDS AND LADIES
IN JANIS LADEN'S REGENCIES

BEWITCHING MINX (2532, $3.95)

From her first encounter with the Marquis of Penderleigh when he had mistaken her for a common trollop, Penelope had been incensed with the darkly handsome lord. Miss Penelope Larchmont was undoubtedly the most outspoken young lady Penderleigh had ever known, and the most tempting.

A NOBLE MISTRESS (2169, $3.95)

Moriah Landon had always been a singularly practical young lady. So when her father lost the family estate over a game of picquet, she paid the winner, the notorious Viscount Roane, a visit. And when he suggested the means of payment—that she become Roane's mistress—she agreed without a blink of her eyes.

SAPPHIRE TEMPTATION (3054, $3.95)

Lady Serena was commonly held to be an unusual young girl—outspoken when she should have been reticent, lively when she should have been demure. But there was one tradition she had not been allowed to break: a Wexley must marry a Gower. Richard Gower intended to teach his wife her duties—in every way.

SCOTTISH ROSE (2750, $3.95)

The Duke of Milburne returned to Milburne Hall trusting that the new governess, Miss Rose Beacham, had instilled the fear of God into his harum-scarum brood of siblings. But she romped with the children, refused to be cowed by his stern admonitions, and was so pretty that he had the devil of a time keeping his hands off her.